The

Winds Of Astor

Book one of the "Tales of Phoria"

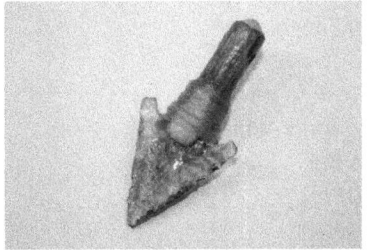

By

Jackie W Fitzgerald

THE WINDS OF ASTOR

Copyright © 2011 by Jackie W Fitzgerald

Cover art by Taylor Louis
Maps by Jackie W Fitzgerald

Published by Fitzgerald Publishing
10293 W Wapato Rd.
Wapato, WA. 98951
www.fitzgeraldpublishing.com

ISBN-10: 0615555381

ISBN-13: 978-0-615-55538-6

First edition: print edition 2011

Dedicated to my father

Jackie C. Fitzgerald

(1946-2005)

Thank you for sharing with me the love of reading and your passion for Science Fiction. Your stories ended way too soon.

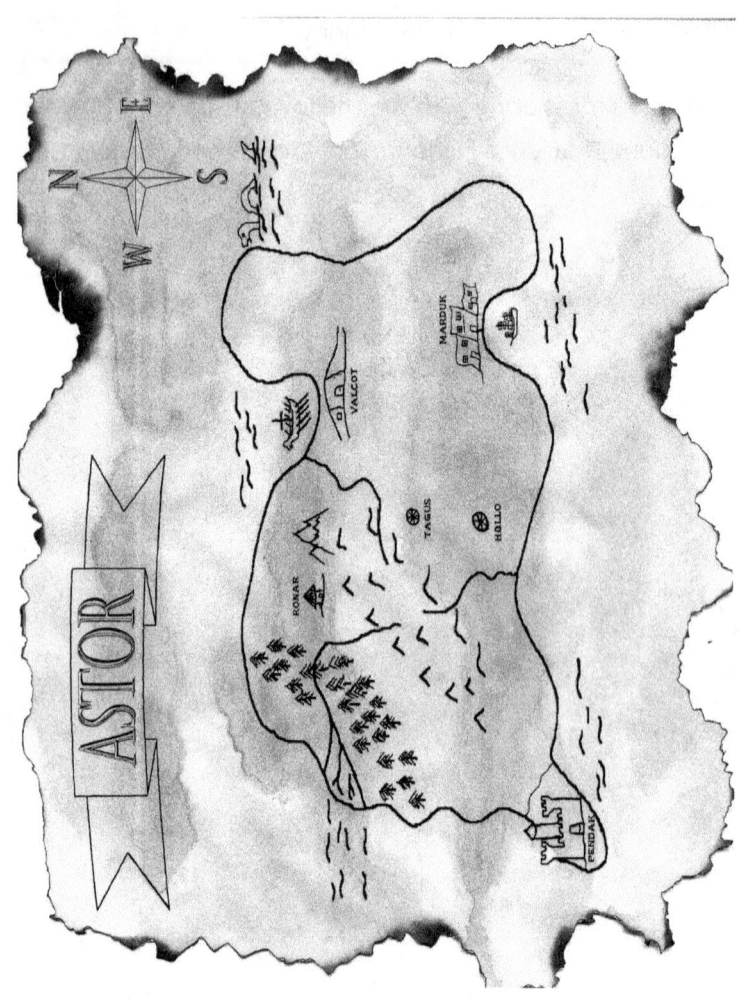

Table of Contents

Chapter One

The Flight

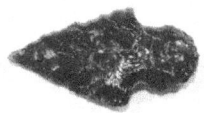

I awoke to a screeching wail. Listening intently I tried to determine the location from which it had come.

My name is Jack Wilde. This morning I was Commander Jack Wilde, a U.S. Navy test pilot. I had only one job in the world and that was to fly and fly fast. Now my one job was survival.

My last mission was the cause of my current situation. The day started like any other. I was working for a laboratory that experimented in nuclear propulsion systems for space craft. Their goal was to develop the next generation propulsion engines that would allow aircraft the ability for interstellar travel. With distances in space being measured in light years it would take generations for humans to travel to anywhere with the existing propulsion systems.

The aircraft that I was test flying today was equipped with an engine constructed using the latest in nuclear propulsion technology. I knew very little about nuclear propulsion and honestly didn't care. For 18 years I had been test flying experimental aircraft and had quit trying to learn the details of what propelled them long ago. It was for the scientists to worry about that. My job was to put the craft through its paces and determine its capabilities.

During the morning flight brief the mission commander clarified my job for the day. Upon lift off I was to assume a steep angle of climb to gain elevation as quickly as possible using the conventional aircraft engines. At 70,000 feet I would level off the aircraft and verify stability. If all systems checked green I would engage the nuclear propulsion engine and accelerate to near light speed, 186,282 feet per second. Once the desired speed had been reached I would decelerate, bring the conventional engines back on line, disengage the nuclear engine, return to the landing field and be drinking a cold beer at the local pub by late afternoon. I had repeated this routine numerous times over the last year, each time getting closer and closer to the target goal of traveling near the speed of light. The speed objective of this flight was to accelerate to 180,000 feet per second and evaluate the stability of the aircraft platform. It was just another day at the office.

The flight had gone exactly as planned. I had achieved the desired elevation, transitioned to the nuclear propulsion engine and had accelerated. The aircraft passed through 170,000 feet per second without any problems. The platform was stable and I was racing through the lower atmosphere faster than anyone had ever travelled before. The craft continued to accelerate and at 180,000 feet per second I pulled back on the acceleration lever to stabilize the speed. Something was wrong, the craft continued to accelerate. Passing through 182,000 feet per second, I pulled the throttle lever further back, still the speed increased.

I needed to slow the acceleration. The one thing that I did learn from the scientists that had constructed this craft was that nobody knew what would happen if the speed of light were achieved. Theoretical science believed that anything traveling at the speed of light would become light and cease to exist in its natural form. Not being a scientist my mind translated this to becoming a flash of light similar to the flashbulb of a camera. Being light would definitely make it hard for me to enjoy my beer after this thrill ride.

At 185,000 feet per second, the craft continued to run away with me. Trying everything to disengage the nuclear engine I repeatedly cycled the control switches and popped all the circuit breakers on the engine control panel. Nothing I tried had any effect on the engine and it continued to gain speed. Bailing out was impossible. This aircraft was equipped with a crew ejection module designed to protect the pilot by ejecting the entire cockpit and not just the pilot's seat. At this speed the module would come apart as soon as the aerodynamic structure of the craft was compromised. I would be torn to shreds the instant that the module ejected. I had no choice but to see this ride through.

The craft was approaching 186,000 feet per second. I found myself wishing that I had paid closer attention to my science professors in college and a lot less time playing sports and drinking beer. Here I was seconds away from proving a theory that had been contemplated by scientists for years. Could my day get any worse?

Punching through the speed of light a blinding flash engulfed the cockpit as the aircraft began to shake violently. Buffeted around in my seat I was thankful for the five point harness that kept me strapped in tight. Fighting to retain control I was disappointed to find that no matter what I tried it had no effect on the attitude of the aircraft. Spiraling through the air like a rocket the gravitational forces being generated by the speed became too much and my head began to swim as I lost consciousness.

I do not know how long I had remained unconscious but when I came back to my senses I was still hurtling through the air and the craft was decelerating. The nuclear engine had shut down and the craft was flying on inertia alone. I tried in vain to engage the conventional engines but they would not fire. I had no control of the movement of the aircraft either. All of the control surfaces had been fused. As the craft lost speed it began to descend and I was losing elevation rapidly.

The friction of the atmosphere was slowing the craft considerably. Descending through 30,000 feet my only hope now lay in the aircraft slowing enough that I could bail out before it hit the ground. At 10,000 feet the craft was still traveling faster than the recommended ejection speed but I was rapidly running out of options as the craft neared the ground.

It was now or never, I had to trust to the strength and integrity of the ejection module to keep me safe. Reaching behind my head I grabbed the ejection loops and pulled sharply.

The explosive detonation sequence that would separate the module from the craft began immediately. Bracing myself, the module rocketed away from the aircraft and began to spin in the air. Another explosion was heard as the arresting parachute deployed and the module was jerked violently upright. The module swung like a pendulum from the parachute and drifted slowly to the ground. Taking stock of myself, I seemed to be okay. Nothing was broken and aside from nausea induced by the violent separation of the module from the craft I was physically in one piece. This wasn't the first time that I had had to bail out of an aircraft but every time is just as shocking to the body as the first.

My attention was now directed outside the canopy. Having no idea where I was in relation to the airfield when I bailed out I needed to get my bearings. Looking out through the tinted glass of the canopy I could clearly see land below. Okay, so I could scratch preparing for a water landing from my checklist. The ground was coming up rapidly and I could now see that my angle of descent was going to put me down right in the middle of an arboreal forest. It was definitely going to be a bumpy landing.

There barely was enough time to brace myself as the ejection module ripped through the upper levels of the trees. Jerking violently from side to side my protective cocoon bounced from branch to branch on the way to the ground. With a sudden jolt the arresting parachute tangled in the tree branches and the module flipped upside down and impacted the ground. Inverted and still strapped into my seat, I sat there for a few moments. The impact with the ground had knocked the wind out of me and I struggled for a few minutes to catch my breath. Reaching down to my waist I twisted the release mechanism of my harness and rolled out onto what had been the ceiling of the module. Ejecting the canopy was not an option with the module upside down. Fortunately for me the module was equipped with egress tools. Removing the egress pouch from under my seat I took out a windshield breaking tool which was a small cylinder with one end open and a release button. As I positioned the open end against the glass I pressed the release button and a spring loaded steel rod shot forward from the cylinder, striking the glass and shattering it. Shards of glass fell to the ground all around the canopy and I stepped clear of the module that had saved my life.

Looking around I surveyed my surroundings. The module had come down in the middle of a swampy forest, surrounded by trees that were approximately thirty feet tall with oddly shaped ovoid leaves. Waist high underbrush twisted and intertwined below the trees and was zigzagged with small animal trails. The ground was a moss covered spongy loam with stagnating pools of water everywhere. Permeating the air was an odor of rotting vegetation.

Most people finding themselves in this situation would be ill prepared. Fortunately for me survival training was a way of life growing up in the mountain wilderness of Washington State. Many a day of my youth had been spent hunting and camping. It also didn't hurt that as a Navy pilot I had been required to attend the six week Survival Escape Resistance and Evasion course in San Diego, California. So surviving in a hostile environment was not as intimidating to me as it would be for most.

The first thing that I needed to do was to ensure that I had shelter. It was just past midday and I did not want to be caught without protection from the elements when the sun went down. Not knowing what kind of dangerous animals were indigenous to this swamp I preferred to not become an easy meal. The ground was way too moist to provide comfort for the night so I looked to the trees.

I did not want to get too far away from the module until I was ready. Nearby was a stout tree with sturdy branches about eight feet from the ground. Close enough that I could jump up and grab hold then pull myself up. My goal was to just build a platform across two branches just high enough that I would be protected from any creatures that should wander by in the night.

The platform construction went quickly as I lashed together the branches using parachute cord that I had salvaged from the modules arresting parachute. Having no idea if it would rain during the night I also lashed leaf covered branches above my sleeping platform to hopefully direct any precipitation away from me while I slept.

The only weapon that I had was a short boot dagger that had been part of my flight uniform since my early days on active duty. In those days a Smith and Wesson .45 caliber pistol was also on my side but my current job as a test pilot did not have me flying over enemy territory and my pistol had been collecting dust in my gun safe at home. I wish that I had that sidearm with me now.

Not being hungry or thirsty I opted to forego foraging until the morning. Taking a few minutes I fabricated a half a dozen small animal snares with the remnants of parachute cord that were left over from my platform construction. First thing in the morning I would place the snares at strategic locations along the animal trails that I had seen earlier and with any luck I would have something to eat by lunch time.

Making a fire would also have to wait until morning. The trials of the day had left me exhausted and I knew that if I was going to make my way out of this jungle I needed to be well rested. With that thought in mind I grabbed the reflective space blanket that was packed into the egress kit and climbed onto my sleeping platform in the tree.

I had placed a long straight staff of wood on the platform after I had finished the construction. My thought was that I wanted to have something that I could use to deter any animals that may attempt to climb up to my perch. The staff was hard and stiff enough that I could jab with it and hopefully dislodge any tree climbing creatures that may visit in the night. Just for good measure I lashed my dagger to the end of the staff constructing a makeshift spear. While the staff alone was sufficient to accomplish what I needed it for I didn't think that it would hurt to have a sharp little sting at the end. Laying the staff down where I could find it quickly in the darkness I pulled the space blanket around me and lay down to try and sleep.

Sleep did not come easy even though I was physically exhausted. There was something that was bothering me about that morning's flight. Not quite sure what happened, I was sure that I had accelerated through the speed of light and yet I still existed. Not only did I exist but I seemed to be perfectly fine and felt no ill effects from it. Had I become light? If so how had I returned to my normal form? I was beginning to think that Einstein and every smart scientist that I knew had theorized inaccurately about the speed of light. I did not have all the answers but I knew that something was not adding up.

I lay their listening to the cacophony of insect sounds. That was one of the things that I had always enjoyed about swamps, the serenade of insects chirping and buzzing. The hypnotic effect of the rhythmic droning of the insects lulled me to sleep and I began to doze.

A screeching wail awakened me from my sleep. Listening intently I tried to determine the location from which it had come. Here is where my story begins. Quickly reaching out in the darkness I grabbed my makeshift spear. Quietly I peered over the edge of my sleeping platform so that I could see the ground below. I did not recognize the wail that had awakened me but instinct told me that I needed to be on guard. Staring intently into the darkness I slowly gained that semblance of night vision that allows humans to make out shapes and movements in the dark. While I could not make out any details I could clearly see any movement below.

Quietly I watched the open spaces below the tree. A shadow began to move along the trails next to the egress module making its way stealthily towards my hiding place. The shadow closed the distance until it was in the underbrush just below my tree. I still could not make out any details of my visitor.

The creature stepped into the open and raised its head sniffing the air. It knew I was there but still had not pinpointed my location. It appeared to be a large black feline type animal with a sleek muscular body that was roughly six feet long. Its body ended in a four foot long slender tail. The most striking feature that caught and held my attention was the eight inch long canines that protrude from its upper jaw. Saber teeth? Something was not right here. Saber toothed cats had been extinct on earth for ten thousand years. Yet here I was staring at one and hoping that it wasn't able to identify my location.

It appeared that luck was not with me this night for the cat raised its head and looked squarely into the tree where I hid. Bracing itself it leaped to the lowest branches of the tree and stared intently in my direction. It quickly became clear that I could not hope for the creature to ignore me and go about its business.

Rising to my knees I reached out with my dagger pointed staff and pricked the cat squarely in the chest. The feline roared in pain and leapt backwards falling from the branch. Pacing circles around the tree the cat tried to identify the best angle with which to attack me without having to come face to face with my pointed weapon again.

For a second time the cat leapt into the tree and jockeyed for a position that would give it an advantage over me. Reaching out again I violently jabbed the cat with my spear. Like a repeat of the first time the cat roared, leapt backwards and fell from the tree.

The cat sat there at the base of the tree looking up at me. It was after an easy meal and was perplexed at the pain that it had felt from my spear. For a seeming eternity that ferocious creature sat and watched my perch. Now that the creature knew where I was I did not dare sleep. Watching over the edge of my sleeping platform I waited for the next assault. That assault never came. After an hour or so the cat appeared to give up and disappeared back into the shadows. Had it moved on or was it waiting just out of sight for me to fall asleep again? I would stay awake and ready though just in case.

Watching for any sign of my visitor I noticed that moonlight was starting to makes its way through the branches above me. The moonlight also appeared to be coming from beside me at a much lower elevation. The angles of the light confused me and I positioned myself to get a better look at the moon. The conflicting angles of moonlight was explained quickly when low and behold above was a moon, just as I had expected but completely unexpected was a second glowing orb that traveled just above the horizon. This just could not be, there is only one moon, not two.

Like a blow to the forehead the realization hit me, this was not Earth. All the scientists had been wrong. Breaking through the speed of light had not turned me into light but instead appeared to have opened a doorway in space and transported me to another world. The existence of the saber toothed cat now made sense. While they had gone extinct on earth long ago I was no longer on earth and all the rules had changed.

My plight now became much more precarious because I could not expect a rescue helicopter to come hovering in low over the trees to extract me. The chances were that nobody at the test flight control center had any idea what had become of me. From their perspective I may very well have become light and disappeared. From my perspective my whole survival situation had now changed. I was alone.

Chapter Two

Survival

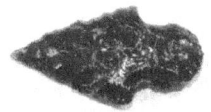

Sleeping very little during the night, I kept a watchful eye out for the saber toothed cat to return, my nerves were on edge. With spear ready at hand, I spent hour after hour scanning the moonlit underbrush watching for any sign of movement. The stinging tip of the staff had been a strong deterrent and the large cat did not return.

A halo of sunlight was starting to lighten the sky to the east. Sunrise was nearing and I had spent the larger portion of the night wide awake. Being confident that the cat that had menaced me earlier in the night had moved on I closed my eyes and allowed sleep to overtake me.

Sleeping fitfully I awoke periodically and listened for any sound that was out of the ordinary. Even sleeping in spurts I managed to get some rest. When I finally awoke I judged the sun to be at roughly nine o'clock and the morning was half gone. Sitting up on my sleeping platform I vowed to find a better way to keep predators from being able to harm me while I slept and pondering that thought I climbed down from my perch.

Once down on the ground I made my way to the egress module. It was important that I salvage everything that could possibly be of use to me in aiding my survival and transit out of this swamp.

It was getting very hot and muggy and I began to sweat profusely. Lowering the top half of my flight suit I tied it around my waist. Being in extremely good condition I was not concerned about the heat having a negative effect on me but I wanted to reduce my sweating as much as I could. Excessive sweating would lead to dehydration quickly and I still had not identified an available source of drinking water in the area.

Moving quickly I crawled inside the egress module and looked around. I did not want to be too heavily laden with equipment when I started traveling through the swamp. Keeping this in mind made it pretty easy to narrow down the items that I would salvage. The pouch containing the egress tool kit was an obvious choice. It also contained a small first aid kit and a compass. With some quick modifications I was able to attach a length of parachute cord to the pouch fashioning a makeshift shoulder strap and placed it over my head and left shoulder so that it hung at my waist on my right side. I placed the folded up space blanket and my animal snares into the pouch. There was little else of value within the module so kneeling down I exited. Passing out of the module the shards of glass that were the remnants of the modules canopy caught my eye. With a little work I could fashion the shard of glass into small points that could be affixed to arrows. Picking up twenty or so pieces of the broken glass that were large enough to work with I placed them in the pouch with my other survival tools.

Once back outside the module I looked around for anything else that might be of use. In a normal survival situation, where there was a realistic expectation of rescue, the brightly colored canopy of the arresting parachute would have been a valuable survival tool. In this instance I had no idea what I would encounter and decided to avoid carrying anything that would draw attention to me. I had a feeling that moving unnoticed and taking advantage of the natural camouflage of the terrain would serve me better. There was plenty of parachute cord still attached to the canopy though and I gathered up as much of it as I could and placed it into my makeshift survival pouch.

Having gathered everything that I thought would be of use I now turned my attention to getting out of the swamp. Removing the compass from my pouch I oriented myself to north. I already had a good idea in which direction east was from the travel of the sun but the compass verified it for me. What direction would lead me to the quickest way out of this swamp? Any direction would just be a guess so I opted to travel due east from my current location. I began threading my way through the intertwining underbrush referring periodically to the compass to ensure that I was continually travelling in the right direction.

It was slow going through the tangled growth of the swamp but I continued to push forward. As I worked my way through I kept an eye peeled for anything that I could use to fabricate more effective weapons for hunting and fending off predators. I had it in mind to construct a rudimentary bow and arrow but vegetation in a swamp tends to be twisted and gnarly, not well suited for a bow and arrows.

The ground over which I travelled was inconsistent. One minute I was traveling on firm solid ground and the next I was slogging through knee deep mud or waist high water.

There was an abundance of small animals everywhere. Many looked like a raccoon type creature while others were clearly rats. All of those that I had encountered were very skittish and scurried away well before I could get within striking distance with my makeshift spear. Snakes were in abundance, as well as, small lizard like amphibians. One could very easily mistake this swamp for many of those located throughout the continents of Earth.

The sun was directly overhead now and the temperature had been rising continuously throughout the morning. My estimation placed the temperature between ninety and ninety-five degrees. The humidity level had to be at 80 percent or higher. The moisture in the air was so thick that I felt like I was constantly immersed in tepid water. Still I pushed forward hoping to finally break clear of the swamp.

Pushing through an excessively thick wall of intertwining undergrowth I stepped out into a small open meadow of dry solid ground. It was a veritable oasis amidst the mud and stagnating water that surrounded it. A much needed break was in order and I sat down to rest my body and take stock of my situation. Looking around I contemplated the possibility of being able to defend this location from animals during the night. Twenty yards into the meadow was the upturned root system of a blown down tree. With some minor preparation and a couple of well-placed fires the blown down tree would work quite nicely as a backdrop for an easily defended campsite for the night. Having made up my mind to establish my camp in this meadow I set about making preparations.

The meadow covered roughly three acres, about the size of a supermarket parking lot back on Earth. Establishing my priorities I determined that first and foremost I needed to devote some effort to gathering food. Not being very fond of eating snake or lizard meat I was determined to catch one of the small raccoon like mammals that I had seen earlier. Removing from my survival pouch the snares that I had fabricated the night before, I began to walk the perimeter of the meadow looking for small game trails or tunnels. The prospects of game looked very promising with there being plenty of sign that the small mammals frequently used the meadow. Making my way around the edge and back to the blown down tree where I planned to make camp I managed to place all six of the snares that I had in my pouch. Now I just needed to forget about them for the time being and concentrate on my next objective, fire.

Not wanting to have too much activity in the areas that I placed the snares I worked my way back through the trail where I had pushed into the meadow. Gathering wood by the armloads I transported it back to my camp spot. It was important that I stockpile enough wood to last through the night. My hope was that by keeping strategically located fires burning throughout the night that I would be able to deter any predators from coming too close to where I slept. After twenty or so trips I felt that I had enough wood gathered for the night.

With only two hours of daylight remaining I wanted to see if I could find some drinking water. Further back into the swamp along the trail that I had travelled earlier I had seen a large bamboo type plant. If the plant had the same compartment like structure as the bamboo that I was familiar with I may be able to use it as a vessel for carrying and boiling water. Sterilizing water before drinking, especially the swamp water was vital to ensuring that I did not ingest some unknown microbial organism. I had learned the hard way during a camping trip in my youth when I had drank water directly from a slow moving stream and spent the next day sick to my stomach. This was a lesson that I had no desire to repeat.

Locating the plant I used my dagger to cut around the outside perimeter of the plant stalk. I was fortunate for this plant had the exact compartmented properties that I needed. Each section of the stalk was roughly a foot long and completely closed at both ends. Cutting out one section from the stalk I whittled one end away leaving an eleven inch cylinder that was four inches across and closed at one end. Drilling two holes in either side of the mouth of the cylinder I attached a short length of parachute cord creating a handle similar to the shoulder strap on my survival pouch.

Making my way back to the meadow I crossed through a knee deep stretch of water. Moving slowly to not disturb the sediment from the bottom I stopped in the middle of the pool. The top foot or so of the water was clear and seemingly drinkable. However, I knew better, I knew that millions of tiny bacteria swam in that water just waiting to be ingested by some unsuspecting creature. Not succumbing to the deception of the clear water I opted to wait until after it had been boiled before drinking it.

With my makeshift flask full of water I returned to camp. Kneeling down next to my large pile of firewood I found a short limb long enough to construct a fire bow using a piece of parachute cord. With the bow ready I split a short piece of wood lengthwise into two pieces and bored a cone shaped socket into both of them with my dagger. Selecting a short straight length of wood from the pile I rounded both ends and then shaved a couple more small pieces of wood into thin slivers. Now I just needed to spin the straight piece of wood between the two sockets with the bow until the friction had heated the bottom socket enough to create an ember that I could then coax into flame and place among the small slivers of wood. On a good day this process can take but minutes to get a fire blazing but I knew that in the humid environment of the swamp that it would take longer. After a full fifteen minutes of continuous sawing back and forth with the bow I was rewarded with the tiniest wisp of smoke rising from the socket. Continuing to work the bow back and forth I soon had a steady stream of smoke emanating from the lower socket. I tipped the smoldering ember out into my piled tinder and gently blew air onto it slowly breathing life into the flames. Once the flames took hold I slowly added progressively larger pieces of wood until I had a full blown fire roaring away next to the fallen tree.

Leaving enough room between the fire and the deadfall tree that I intended to use as a backdrop for my camp I proceeded to build two more pyramid shaped piles of firewood. I would light them later after the sun set and it was fully dark. I didn't want to waste the firewood that I had collected until it was necessary. My hope was that having the fallen tree at my back and a wall of fire to my front I would be protected from any animals that may desire to assail me as I slept.

Using three halfway straight lengths of wood and some parachute cord I constructed a tripod that I placed straddling the fire. Suspending the bamboo water container from the tripod I ensured that it was centered over the fire. As long as there was water in the container it wouldn't burn and the water would slowly come to a boil. After a good five minutes of a rolling boil and a short cool down period I would be able to slake my thirst.

Now it was time to check my snares and see if I would be eating tonight or going hungry. I retraced my path around the perimeter of the meadow checking each trap as I went. The second trap I checked had been sprung but had failed to catch whatever had triggered it. Resetting the snare I moved on to the next two traps only to be disappointed to find them untouched. In the fifth trap I was rewarded with one of the small rat-like animals. The snare had worked perfectly, quickly and efficiently putting the animal out of its misery. I removed the animal and reset the snare. Quickly skinning and eviscerating the animal I threw the remains as far into the swamp as I could to avoid attracting any unwanted visitors in the night. Drawing a blank on my sixth and final snare I took my prize and returned to the fire. Spitting the animal on a stick I placed it over the flames to cook.

The water was boiling when I returned and after allowing a generous five minutes to pass I removed the cylinder from the fire and placed it off to the side to cool. It was now fully dark and the symphony of insect sounds could now be heard reverberating through the swamp.

Removing a fiery brand from the fire I lit the other piles of firewood. With the security of the wall of fire I leaned back against the fallen tree and rested while my dinner slowly cooked.

This was my second night in the swamp and I was determined that I would not spend another night here. Coming across this dry meadow gave me hope that I was getting nearer the edge of the swamp and would soon be clear of this wet and muddy environment.

Pulling my flight suit back up around my shoulders I checked my meal. While it was charred on the outside and still a little raw on the inside I had become ravenous as a result of my exertions throughout the day. Leaning back against the tree I devoured the meat. It wasn't a very large meal but it was sufficient to beat back the hunger pains and lift my spirits. I washed it down with a long drink of still warm water from the bamboo container. I was not sitting at the local pub enjoying a cold beer as I would have been on Earth but either way I was quite content with my meal.

Salvaging a short leg bone from the remains of my meal I whittled it into a rough point. Removing one of the shards of glass from my pouch I began to slowly chip away at the edges alternating from one side to the other and back again. The shard began to take shape as I chipped one end to a point and shallow notches into the other. It was not a perfect arrowhead by any means but it was sufficient to tip an arrow and inflict damage upon whatever I cast it at. Working one shard after the other I soon had a dozen rudimentary points that I could fasten to arrows providing I could find the right materials to construct them.

The two moons were beginning to rise and I could see the light of both of them coming from different directions over the trees of the swamp. While seeing two separate moons transiting the night sky was disconcerting I could not help but be moved by the beauty of both as they crested the treetops and inched their way into full view. I could never have imagined a night sky being more beautiful than a full moon summer night on Earth but a second moon only doubled the wondrous beauty. As the sky grew darker the countless number of stars in the sky that were visible increased exponentially until the entire heavens were dotted with pinpoints of light in every direction. I could not help but wonder if one of those brilliant points of light was the familiar sun that warmed my beloved Earth. Holding out hope that I would ever know or that I would ever see and feel the caressing warmth of that sun again seemed futile.

With a halfway full belly and my thirst quenched I began to get groggy and knew that I would soon sleep. It was imperative that I wake up every few hours and ensure that my security fires had not died down to smoldering embers. After stoking all three fires I lay down, curled into a fetal position to retain heat and closed my eyes inviting sleep to escort me away from my current reality and into my mind full of memories from the past.

Chapter Three

Captured

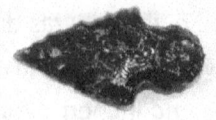

The night passed without incident. Waking up every couple hours I kept the fires stoked. Each time I would listen closely and peer into the darkness around the meadow. While I could sense that many animals lurked just out of the light in the edges of the swamp, none of them braved the fire to investigate.

Waking up just before the sun began to rise in the east I placed more wood onto the fires. In all of my adventures in the wilderness of my youth it always seemed to me that it became the coldest just before the dawn. That was the point when it was more comfortable to snuggle deeper into the blankets than to crawl out and start the day. I continued to lay by the fires enjoying the warmth while I could and patiently waited for the sun to climb into the sky.

My flight suit was becoming stiff from the baked on mud of the swamp. The pungent odor of the mud was now deeply rooted into the fibers. At the first opportunity I needed to bathe and wash my clothing. While I did not find the smells of the swamp to be particularly repulsive they did tend to wear on the nose after a while. My big concern was that my feet had not dried out since I landed here. My boots were continually saturated with water and I could feel the wrinkled up bottoms of my feet. It was important that I get both my boots and my feet dry at the first opportunity to prevent both blisters and a fungal infection from forming. Without the use of my feet I would not get anywhere.

The sun now cresting the tops of the trees to the east, I stood up and stretched the stiffness from my body. The thought of a little breakfast to start the day was very appealing and reminded me of the snares that I had set the night before. Picking up my spear I stepped outside the safety of my fires to check them. My luck of the night before had not held, for every trap I checked was empty. Disassembling the snares I placed them into my pouch as I went along. Clearing the last one I turned to return to the fire. Luck had truly abandoned me for no sooner had I turned back towards my makeshift camp and I was slammed to the ground by a large animal that had sprung from its concealing position among the trees at the edge of the swamp. The momentum of the animals leap from the trees carried it on over my body as I landed face first onto the soft ground. Quickly leaping back to my feet I found myself face to face with one of the large black saber toothed cats that I had seen my first night in the swamp.

Crouching with my spear in hand the big cat and I began to slowly circle one another as we both vied for an opportunity to dispatch the other. The cat charged and I stepped forward with my spear and stabbed viciously at its chest. The cat pulled up short and sprang backwards with a spine tingling roar. The tip of my spear had penetrated deep into its chest cavity. I could clearly see the animal's life blood pulsing from the wound and onto the ground. Still the large cat and I circled one another. It became apparent as we circled each other for a few minutes that the loss of blood was beginning to take its toll on the cat. It staggered slightly and nearly stumbled. The saber toothed cat was running on sheer animal instinct alone. Even as its life blood oozed forth from its body it could think of nothing but sinking its teeth into my flesh.

Again the cat stumbled, taking advantage I sprang forth with the tip of my spear leading the charge. Too little too late the cat sprang sideways trying to leap clear of my attack. In so doing it had sealed its fate, for as the large cat sprang it revealed its side to me and a well-placed stab with my spear pierced its heart. The cat fell onto its side with my spear sticking through its ribs. Landing full upon the cat I used the weight of my body to hold it down as it struggled to regain its feet. Weakening quickly as the blood rapidly leaked from its heart the big cat ceased to struggle and then ceased to breath.

Laying there across the body of the large cat I took deep breaths trying to calm myself from the encounter. I had never fought a large animal to the death in the wild before and my nerves were more than a little shaken. The noise of our struggle had attracted other animals. I could feel their hungry stares coming from the trees. Not wanting to repeat my earlier struggle I stood up and moved quickly returning to the safety of my fire.

Once again safely between the fires and the fallen tree I watched as first one large cat and then two more slipped quietly out of the trees and approached the carcass of the one that I had killed. Sniffing around the body the three cats roared ominously at one another. One cat watching the other two closely began to bite at the body. The other two approached and the first roared and swatted at them viciously with its claws. The second two cats moved back and took up positions watching the first. Patiently waiting for the first to finish its meal before moving in to dine on what remained.

Reluctant as I was to leave the safety of the fires I needed to get moving and get out of this swamp. Watching the actions of the three cats I slipped quietly around to the back side of the fallen tree so that it blocked me from their view. Keeping the tree between us I quickly entered the swamp and proceeded to put some distance between myself and the ravenous cats in the meadow.

When I felt that I was sufficiently far enough away from the meadow to not be detected by the large cats I stopped to catch my breath and take a bearing on my compass. I had originally been travelling to the east but at this time I determined that changing my direction to the northeast would increase the distance between myself and where I knew three large cats were enjoying a rather large meal. Taking up my new heading I slogged forward through the mud and muck of the swamp.

For two hours I pushed through knee deep mud and waist high water. I did not encounter any more of the large cats as I travelled. I continued to see large numbers of the snakes and amphibians that I had seen during my previous day of travel. As near as I could tell, the majority of the snakes that I came across were constrictors and not large enough to pose much of a threat to me. Once or twice I came upon snakes that had a short thick body that coiled up as I approached. Giving these snakes a wide berth I was not willing to risk my health to determine if they were venomous or not. My assumption was that if they were coiled to strike they should be treated as if they were the most poisonous things on this planet.

The trees were starting to thin out and the ground became drier, I was finally reaching the edge of the swamp. Continuing to the northeast the trees gave way to rolling grasslands. It was just passing noon and the sun bore down. Sweating profusely and smelling of swamp I came up a small rise and looked down the other side. At the base of the hill was a fast moving river dotted with shallow pools of emerald green water and fast moving stretches of whitewater. Suddenly I was very thirsty. Half running and half stumbling my way down the hill I reached the water's edge and dropping to my knees I submerged my face into the ice cold water. The fast moving water allayed any fears that I may have had about drinking it unsterilized and I began to drink slowly and steadily.

Having drank my fill of the cold water I sat back on the bank of the river and looked around. A few trees here and there overhung the banks. Large boulders were scattered everywhere with dark gray sand beaches in between. The sun continued to beat down and the heat grew as the day wore on.

Taking the opportunity to remove the stench of the swamp from both my body and my clothing, I removed my boots and undressing waded into the river. The water was frigid and my toes began to go numb from the cold. Pushing past the desire to avoid the cold water I jumped head first into the deepest part of the pool and swam under water until I had reached the far shore. Surfacing in chest deep water I found my footing on the bottom and waded towards the shore. Standing knee deep in water on the edge of a sandy beach I scooped up wet sand and began to scrub my body vigorously. Even the neutral odor of the wet sand was preferable to the acrid smell of the swamp that I was attempting to scour away. Massaging wet sand into my hair I tried to remove the oils and grease that had built up over the past two days. Already I was beginning to feel much better.

With my body covered in wet sand I again dove into the deep water and rubbed my body to rinse the sand free. Running my fingers through my hair while I was submerged I attempted to flush as much of the gritty sand as possible from my scalp. Satisfied that I had done so I surfaced and struck out for the shore where my clothes lay.

Once on shore I dug a hole in the wet sand and let it fill with water. After the water had seeped in I placed my clothing into the hole and stirred them around with a short stick. I didn't hold out much hope that the soaking would remove the foul odors as much as I would like but anything would be better than putting the dirty clothing back on. Tying the laces of my boots together I draped them over either side of a submerged rock so that the moving water would flow into and out of them, hopefully taking any smells and bacteria with it in the process.

While my clothes soaked I wandered the edge of the pool peering into the depths for any sign of fish that may be present. Still having not eaten anything today a shore lunch of roasted fish would go nicely. Shadows deep down in the water flittered here and there and gave away the presence of small fish that were darting for safety at the sight of my shadow. Using my short spear I knelt at the edge of the water and patiently waited. Sitting very still gave the fish the impression that I had moved on. My shadow remained stationary and didn't move, thus not giving the fish an early warning that danger was near. Slowly I slid the tipped end of my spear into the water and prepared to strike when one of the fish came into range. Just as I had my quarry lined up with my spear and was preparing to stab it I heard the loud cracking of a branch behind me.

Turning swiftly I found myself facing half a dozen warriors. Forming a half circle around me they had cut off all escape. They were trapped in leather harnesses decorated with hammered gold and ornately colored feathers. Each wore a loincloth made of an ebony black fur and matching calf length boots. More importantly I noted that each was carrying iron tipped spears, bows and arrows and short swords.

Crouching low with my spear in hand I prepared to defend myself. Not about to give up without a fight I fully intended to make them pay dearly for my life. One warrior stepped forward and said something unintelligible to me. Nothing of what he said made any sense to me. Frustrated the warrior pointed his spear at me and repeated the words. Again I looked at him without understanding. The warrior crouched and came menacingly towards me. With his spear in one hand and a short sword in the other he began to circle to my left. Jabbing viciously with his spear he attempted to impale me. Blocking the thrust with my own spear I jumped back just in time to miss being disemboweled by the short sword in his left hand. While I had some martial arts training under my belt I had never been trained in the use of sword and spear, but now seemed just as good a time to learn as any. Twirling my spear in front of me I feigned a blow to the right side of his head and when he lifted his spear to block it I stabbed down swiftly impaling his foot with the dagger tip at the opposite end of my spear. I pulled it back quickly as he yelled in anger and lifted his bleeding foot. The second he looked down to survey the damage that I had done I caught him with an upward swipe of my spear to his chin. He fell backwards into the river, out cold.

Two more warriors charged me. Stepping quickly to the left I changed the angle of approach so that the warrior nearest me now blocked the second one from being able to engage me. Spinning and ducking quickly I swept out with my spear and caught the warrior nearest me in the shin. Jumping backwards he stumbled over the second warrior and went down. Taking advantage of their disarray I charged forward and dealt the second warrior a rib cracking blow with the side of my spear then stepped back quickly.

The two warriors found their footing and this time approached me more slowly and deliberately. They split up with one circling to my right while the other circled to my left. Knowing that if I allowed them to get on either side of me one would strike while I fended off the blows from the other. Jumping quickly to the top of a nearby boulder I hoped to gain a height advantage over them that would even out the fact that they had me out numbered. The warrior on my left swiped his spear at my legs attempting to take my feet out from under me. At the same time the warrior on my right swung his spear at my head. Ducking the blow to my head I slammed my foot down firmly trapping the spear of the warrior on my left between my foot and the boulder. Kicking out violently my foot caught the warrior on the left square against the side of his head. Knocking him off balance it gave me the chance to jump down from the boulder and again face the two on even ground.

From the looks on the faces of the two warriors I could tell that they were getting angry. One thing I had learned over the years is that an angry person will not make wise decisions and one that fights with anger rather than calculated skill is destined to lose. My attack had gained the upper hand on them and they did not like it.

Again they circled to either side of me trying to split my attention. Using the boulder for advantage would not work again. Waiting for them to come to me really was not my style and as I turned towards the warrior on my left I stepped in and jabbed sharply at his face with the tip of my spear. In this split instant the other warrior had charged. Turning again sharply I moved purposefully toward the charging warrior and closed the distance between us quickly. My actions caught him by surprise and he could not react quickly enough to prevent me from catching his spear in my left hand while I slipped the tip of my spear between his ribs. Looking squarely into my eyes I watched his life fade away as he slumped to the ground. As he fell my spear jammed between his ribs and was jerked from my hand. Reaching down I grabbed his short sword and turned just in time to deflect the blow of the short sword from the other warrior.

Falling backwards over the body of my fallen foe I scrambled to quickly regain my footing. Making it to one knee I fended off blow after blow from the second warrior.

Making it to my feet I began to weave a curtain of steel between him and I. Jabbing in with his spear he hoped to extend his reach past the length of the short sword that I was now wielding. Striking down sharply I cut the tip from his spear and he dropped it to the ground. Now we were evenly armed and even though I was not an experienced swordsman I liked my chances. I began to press the warrior back towards the river. Thrusting and slicing with the sword I kept him on the defensive and waited for the chance to thrust my steel through his chest. My whirling sword continued to push him backwards when suddenly he stepped into the hole that I had dug to soak my clothing. Falling backwards onto his back he raised his sword to defend himself. Raising my sword over my head I prepared to strike the death blow that would reduce my adversaries by yet one more man. My arms came forward and down and like a flash I felt a blow to the back of my head and all went black as I fell forward onto the downed warrior.

Chapter Four

Princess Marlen

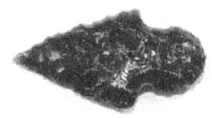

It did not surprise me when I regained consciousness that I was bound hand and foot. What did surprise me was that I regained consciousness at all. After reducing the party of warriors by two I had expected that the others would have killed me out of revenge. This was not the case and I lay on the hard ground with my hands tied to my ankles behind my back.

Looking around I determined that I was still on the bank of the river. The warrior that guarded me I recognized as the last warrior that I had fought before being struck from behind. Another warrior stood on a large boulder and watched down river. There should have been two more warriors but I was unable to determine their location. A few short minutes had passed when I saw the two missing warriors returning. They were travelling from downstream with one on either side of the river. Stopping at the boulder the one on the near side of the river waited for the one on the far side to wade across the bottom end of the pool. When they both faced the one standing on the boulder I could hear them talking but was unable to understand them. From the shrug of their shoulders as they spoke I assumed that they had been looking for the warrior that had fallen into the river but their search had not turned up anything.

The warrior jumped down from the boulder and the three walked towards where I lay. This one I had identified as the leader of this small group. The way the other two warriors deferred to him and fell in behind him as they approached provided ample evidence that I had discerned correctly.

As the three approached the leader barked an order to the warrior that guarded me. Kneeling down next to me my guard untied the leather lashing that bound my ankles to my wrists and grabbing my arm lifted me to my feet.

The leader of the group looked me in the eye and uttered something menacingly to me that I did not understand. Growing frustrated with me the leader backhanded me across the face breaking open my lip and jarring my teeth. Refusing to give him the satisfaction I held my footing and stared back at him. The taste of blood spread throughout my mouth as I gritted my teeth and held my ground. One day I would return the blow that this warrior just dealt me and return it tenfold.

Realizing the futility of trying to get me to speak the leader barked orders at the other three and they proceeded to gather up their weapons in preparation to move out. One of the warriors lifted my clothing from the hole in which I was soaking it. He looked the flight suit and undergarments over and seeing no value he threw them into the river. The leader lifted my pouch and dumped it onto the sand. Picking up the compass he eyed it quizzically but failing to recognize the purpose of such a strange device it to was thrown into the river. The parachute cord and knapped arrow heads were transferred to his pouch and mine was discarded. There was no sign of my short spear and dagger. My survival now would depend on those items that I could gather from this world for virtually everything that I had salvaged from the egress module was now gone.

The small band of warriors headed out with me in tow across the shallow end of the pool in which I had swam earlier. Crossing the river we climbed the small hill on the other side. Not being familiar with this land I had no idea where our destination lay but judging from the angle of the sun I was able to surmise that we still traveled in a northeasterly direction. As we travelled up and down ever larger hills I spied the occasional animal in the distance. As near as I could tell, these animals were similar to the plains antelope of my world. They were small in stature and very fleet of foot as was evidence by the speed with which they lit out as we grew near.

We continued to travel from hill to hill throughout the remainder of the day and nearing late afternoon we crested a small hillock and looked down into a camp. From this viewpoint I was able to see three or four small leather tents and six more warriors dressed identical to those that held me captive. There were multiple fires smoldering around the camp and a drying rack in the center from which hung what I believed to be the carcasses of three of the small antelope like creatures.

The warriors in the camp came out to meet us as we came down the hill. Approaching us one spoke to the leader of the small band and pointed at me. The leader responded with a few words and two of the newcomers grabbed me by my arms and escorted me into the camp. In front of one of the small leather tents they shoved me to the ground and shackled my ankle with a short length of chain that was connected to a stake that had been driven into the ground. Reaching down with a dagger one of the warriors sliced through the leather lashing that bound my wrists. Here they left me to contemplate my fate as they returned to the duties of the camp.

Sitting up I began to survey my surroundings as I rubbed the circulation back into my hands. A few warriors had left camp shortly after our arrival and were now returning with armloads of wood for the fires. A couple more warriors had spitted out two antelope rear hams over a fire and had started preparing the evening meal. The smell of the cooking meat began to gnaw at my empty stomach.

The sun was beginning to set in the west and the light was fading fast. Along with the sunlight went the heat. As the sun became lower and lower in the sky the temperature began to drop as well. The warriors stoked the fires and now firelight was beginning to take the place of the rapidly waning sunlight.

Presently I heard a noise coming from the inside of the tent near which I sat. A shadowy figure made its way out of the tent, stood up and stretched. Sitting there I looked up into the eyes of the most beautiful young woman that I had ever seen. She wore an ornately decorated leather harness that barely covered her well rounded breasts and a short brown leather skirt. Her skin was tanned a golden olive brown that accentuated her shimmering black hair and sea green eyes. She too was securely shackled by the ankle to another stake driven deeply into the ground near the mouth of the tent. She looked down sympathetically into my eyes and then surveyed the encampment.

She looked the camp over from one end to the other as if making a mental inventory of where everything and everyone was located. Seemingly satisfied she knelt down next to me and spoke softly. Clearly not understanding a word that she said I was mesmerized by the soft rhythmic melodies of her voice. She repeated her words and I stared blankly back at her. Realizing that I did not comprehend what she was trying to tell me she held her finger to her lips and softly shushed me to remain silent. She took up her post next to me and sat quietly watching the warriors going about their evening routine.

Sitting there quietly I watched her, admiring her beauty and pondering how she had come to be in the clutches of these warriors. The firelight reflecting off of her face highlighted her beauty and a glow seemed to emanate from her beautifully complexioned skin. Who was this woman? I could not understand a word that she said and I knew absolutely nothing about her but from the instant that I saw her I knew that I would do anything to protect and defend her.

Following her advice to be quiet I turned and joined her in watching the happenings of the encampment. The warriors were now eating the meals that they had prepared on the fire. It appeared that they were telling jokes back and forth as they were all laughing loudly. What appeared to wine bags were being passed from group to group and tankards were filled to over-flowing. This brought to mind the cold beer that I would stop and enjoy after work each day and my mouth began to water. With this thought I realized that I was extremely thirsty. As near as I could recollect I had not had anything to drink since my arrival at the river earlier in the day.

The smell of the roasted meat awakened a grumbling deep within my stomach. Not only was I thirsty but the day of traveling had left me ravenously hungry as well. The girl and I continued to remain quiet and patiently waited for the warriors to feed us.

It was now fully dark and the only light in the encampment was the flickering flames of the firelight. Finally, after what seemed an eternity a warrior approached the girl and I. He kicked me in the leg and said something that I did not understand. Handing each of us a plate and tankard of liquid that I hoped would be wine or some form of ale, he walked away and returned to the nearest campfire.

The woman and I sat quietly eating and watching the actions of the warriors. The food was not particularly appetizing, the meat being a little dry and over-cooked. It had a similar taste to venison and tasted exactly as I would have expected a small antelope to taste.

Also on the plate were a couple of roasted tuber type plants similar to a sweet potato. The sweet starchy flavor of the plant was a welcome addition to the meal. At least something on the plate had some actual flavor which is much more than I could say for the meat. I was beginning to miss the array of spices that were available back on Earth that allowed an individual to take a tasteless piece of meat and turn it into a gourmet meal.

The tankards proved to be a disappointment as well. In my mind I was expecting the sweet taste of wine when I touched the vessel to my lips. Instead I was greeted with the warm stale taste of water that tasted as if it had been sealed in a cask for weeks and allowed to sit in the sun. Even as stale as the water tasted it was as honey on my thirsty tongue.

Finishing our meal we continued to sit and watch the warriors. Presently another warrior approached us and threw down in front of me what appeared to be a leather harness and plain leather loincloth. The harness bore no insignia and was in a state of disrepair but I was thankful to have something with which to cover myself.

Standing up I slipped into the leather loincloth and attempted to strap on the leather harness. Apparent that I had no idea what I was doing the girl stood up and with a sly smirk assisted me. Although not knowing why the girl assisted me I was very thankful for her guidance. I could see that I had a lot to learn if I was going to survive in this world.

We watched as the warriors arranged their sleeping furs around the campfires and began to settle in for the night. It was starting to get really cold for the evening and the girl obviously sensing my discomfort arose from her sitting position and entered the tent. She returned shortly and draped an animal fur about my shoulders then again sat down next to me pulling another fur about her body as she settled in.

Again the girl attempted to speak to me. With a total lack of understanding I looked blankly at her and shrugged my shoulders. I did not know how to communicate with her that I could not understand her language. It turned out that I did not need to communicate that message to her because through intuition she had already reached that conclusion.

Pointing at herself she said, "Marlen."

I still did not understand. Then a little more forcefully she poked herself in the chest and again repeated, "Marlen."

It finally clicked in my head and I realized that my education in the language of this world had begun. Imitating her actions I poked myself in the chest and said, "Jack." She pointed back at my chest and repeated what I had said. I pointed at her chest and repeated her name. To some extent I guess at this point we had now been formally introduced.

My education continued until late into the evening. Marlen pointed out various objects around the camp and named them. Repeating her actions and words I was beginning to establish a basic vocabulary of the items that existed in this world. Without a doubt I had a long way to go but I was motivated to learn by the desire to be able to speak and converse with this lovely goddess.

At the first opportunity that presented itself I intended to escape from my captors and I very much wanted to take Marlen with me, but I had to be able to communicate my plans to her.

Two warriors guarded the perimeter of the camp remaining on opposite sides from each other and walking in circles. Their job was to keep the fires stoked and ensure that no dangerous animals such as the large black cats entered into the camp while the other warriors slept. Glad for their presence, I did not want to repeat the experiences of my first night on this world and I did not relish the thought of waking up to the scimitar like fangs of a large cat closing on my throat.

The rumbling snores of the sleeping warriors could be heard throughout the camp playing a rhythmic serenade with the sounds of the night time insects. It was now getting to be quite late and Marlen rose and placing a hand on my shoulder bid me what I believed to be good night as she turned and entered the tent and pulled the flaps closed behind her.

Stretching out on the ground in front of the opening to the tent I pulled the fur closely around my neck. It did not seem appropriate to share the tent with such a beautiful woman that I had barely met today. Instead I was content to lie in front of the tent and guard the entrance flap to ensure that nobody was allowed to enter. Hard pressed to explain it I had an overwhelming urge to protect this young woman and do everything that I could to ensure that no harm came to her. The droning of the insects lulled me into a state of semi-consciousness and I began to doze off.

Having barely slipped into a deep sleep a loud roar and a scream peeled through the night. Instantly the entire camp was awake and all the warriors were arming themselves and looking about trying to determine the direction from which the screams had come. On my feet now I too tried to identify the source. As I stood there looking around the perimeter of the camp scanning the edges of the firelight I sensed that Marlen was standing next to me and holding my arm. Together we watched the warriors scramble around checking in with the watches, one of which was missing. The remaining watch was pointing in a direction on the opposite side of the camp. Gathering up torches the warriors began to search in that direction for their missing comrade.

After what seemed to be hours but in reality was probably only ten minutes the warriors returned. Dragging behind them were two large objects and as they entered into the firelight I could make out that one of the objects was the disemboweled body of the missing perimeter guard. The other was the lifeless carcass of one of the large black cats.

Two of the warriors strung up the cat from a drying rack and expertly skinned the fur from it. Two other warriors wrapped the body of the fallen warrior with leather skins and prepared the body to be laid to rest the following morning. The guards again resumed their perimeter watch of the camp with one of the previously sleeping warriors replacing the one that had died.

For the second time this night the camp began to settle down. The adrenaline of the unexpected hunt for the cat carried on and it took much longer for the warriors to return to their sleeping furs. Marlen and I sat down and again watched the warriors settle in for the remainder of the night. She sat very close to me and clung to my arm. Without thinking I placed my arm around her shoulder and draped my sleeping fur about her. She did not pull away and only snuggled closer into my shoulder. My heart raced at being so close to this beautiful woman and we sat there with my protective arm encircling her.

The camp was now quiet again as the warriors returned to their slumber. It was not long before I could hear the quiet steady breathing of Marlen and I knew that she had fallen asleep in my arms. Not wanting to wake her I gently laid her down and snuggled up next to her pulling the furs around us letting the warmth of my body comfort her and keep her safe. For the moment content and comfortable I soon followed her into a deep slumber.

Chapter Five

Ronar

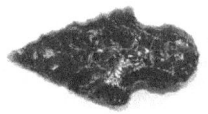

I woke up with Marlen wrapped safely in my arms. A little uncomfortable at what she might think when she awoke I was pleasantly relieved when she opened her eyes and looked up at me smiling. The warriors had risen well before dawn and had started packing up the camp. From all the indications I concluded that we would be moving out today. The tents were all struck and bound up like backpacks. All the dried meat was stowed into large leather pouches and the drying racks were disassembled. The fires had been kicked apart and the band was nearly ready to move out.

While the majority of the warriors prepared the camp to move two others had set about building a wooden platform and surrounding it with fire wood. My initial thought was that they were building a storage location for the firewood as if they intended to return to this location at some point. When they placed the body of the dead warrior from the night before atop the platform I realized that my original assumption was incorrect. What the warriors had constructed was a funeral pyre to honor their dead comrade.

Marlen and I were still shackled to the stakes as all the remaining warriors gathered around the funeral pyre. The leader of the band spoke first to the warriors and then holding a torch in one hand he raised his gaze skyward and spoke to whatever entity they believed in and then placed the torch among the piled wood. Tendrils of smoke spiraled upwards from the pyre as small flames spread rapidly. Within minutes it was engulfed in flames. The warriors stood watching the fire and then as one they saluted their fallen comrade by crossing their right arm over their chest with short swords in hand. Returning their swords to their scabbards they prepared to move out.

Two warriors approached Marlen and I, removing the shackles from our ankles they tied long leather leashes around our necks. Leading us to where the camp gear was staged they strapped backpacks onto both of us. The packs were heavily laden with tents and equipment. The party had lost three of their number in the last day, two by my hand and one to the saber toothed cat leaving fewer people to carry the weight of the camp. I wished that I could heft the load that had been strapped to Marlen so that such a lovely woman would not be burdened with the weight. Nothing could be done about it as our captors were not showing any leniency towards Marlen.

Pulling on our leashes the band of warriors set out towards the northeast. Travelling up and down the hilly terrain the group moved in single file with two warriors guarding the column. Marlen stumbled under the weight of her backpack and nearly fell. The warrior holding her leash pulled her violently nearly upending her. Lashing out I grabbed her leash and pulling back jerked the warrior from his feet. Jumping up the warrior turned to strike at me in anger. Catching his forearm in my left hand I planted my fist square against the side of his jaw knocking him to the ground. Moving forward to strike him again I felt the leather collar tighten on my neck as my handler jerked me backwards off my feet. Landing on my backpack I looked up to see my handler pulling his short sword to dispatch me. Before he could strike Marlen threw herself over my body shielding me from the warrior's sword. Fear coursed through me that he would strike anyway injuring Marlen but before the blow had fallen I heard the leader of the band yell threateningly to the warrior. Instantly he dropped his sword to his side and returned it to its scabbard. I don't know what the leader of the band had said but I was thankful for his intervention. Marlen and I helped each other to our feet and after a few minutes the forced march resumed.

Still only a captive of these warriors I felt that I had made the point that I would risk everything to ensure that no harm befell Marlen. Looking back over her shoulder she caught my eye and flashed me a sly knowing smile. While I could not explain the attraction that I had for her just seeing her smile and looking into her eyes sent my heart racing. She had not expressed that she had a similar attraction or that she was even in the slight bit interested but I was content to serve her as I could.

The band traveled throughout the morning without further incident. Nearing noon the leader called a halt to the march to allow everyone to rest, rehydrate and eat some food. We were allowed to remove our backpacks and stretch out our sore muscles.

While we rested my language lessons continued. Marlen would identify objects, tell me their name and then I would repeat her words. She not only taught me the names of objects but was starting to teach me various verbs as well. Learning quickly I had been practicing all morning, talking to myself as we marched. Fervently I hoped that it would not be long and I would be able to at least carry on a rudimentary conversation with her, to know more about her, where she came from, and how she ended up as a captive of these warriors. If I expected to survive in this world I needed to learn more about it and being able to communicate clearly was critical to not drawing attention to the fact that I was a stranger in this land.

At a command from the leader everyone again picked up their packs and resumed marching. We continued to travel to the northeast to what destination I could not fathom. The heat from the sun increased throughout the afternoon and the sweat ran down my forehead and into my eyes. Appreciating the sparse clothing worn by the denizens of this land, the harness and loincloth allowed the sweat to evaporate rather than saturating clothing. If I had been wearing my flight suit still I had no doubt that it would be soaked through. One thing that I did miss though was my flight boots. My feet had been spoiled by a lifetime of being wrapped in protective coverings. The constant marching up and down the hills was wearing blisters onto them. Occasionally stepping on a sharp rock I would wince in pain at the tenderness of my feet. It irritated me to feel the pain and recognize that my feet were a physical weakness that I had to overcome. Eventually the blisters would turn to calluses and I would be able to walk on anything barefoot without experiencing any discomfort.

Towards late afternoon we started seeing signs of habitation. We now followed a well-worn trail that had been rutted by the feet of countless generations of travelers. It was getting to be late afternoon and the sun was getting low in the western sky. As the band of warriors rounded the base of a small hill what appeared to be a very large village came into sight. The spires of thatched roofs could be seen over the crest of a high barricade wall. The wall was constructed of tall straight trees that had been buried deeply into the ground leaning outward at their top. The entrance to the village was a large wooden gate that currently hung open. The barricade surrounding the village would have been little defense against other humans but was sufficient to ensure that any dangerous animals in the area would be kept at bay.

Approaching the gate to the village we were greeted by women and children. Following them were other warriors of the village whose attire replicated that of my captors. There were many loud cheers and embraces as the women and children welcomed the warrior's home. After greeting the warriors they turned their attention on Marlen and me. Poking and prodding us with fingers and sticks it was apparent that my pale white skin was a novelty to them. Having not been on this planet long enough to have developed the golden olive tan that was present on every human that I had encountered since my arrival. The children pinched my arms and legs in disbelief that an individual could possess such a white complexion. Seemingly satisfied that my skin tone was real the children returned to the warriors and women. As one the entire band moved through the gate and entered into the village.

My captors led us down a wide lane that was bordered by street vendors on both sides. The vendors were selling everything from fresh fruit and meats to weapons and leather trappings. Acting as the central market place for the village the avenue was packed with shoppers, vendors and people just sight-seeing.

Pushing through the crowds our captors escorted us to the middle of the village. In the center of town was a large multi-tiered hut that was heavily guarded by warriors. These warriors were trapped similar to our captors but instead of having loincloths and boots constructed of sleek black fur these warriors wore loincloths and boots of a golden brown fur. I took these warriors to be the chief's personal guard. It raised questions why the chief of such a large village would need a personal guard around his domicile but I guess even a mighty chief could have enemies amongst his own people.

Expecting that Marlen and I would be escorted into the presence of the chief I was disappointed when the group turned left just before we reached the chief's hut. Continuing down a side street we arrived in front of a small hut that had reinforced windows and a door. At the entryway we were relieved of our heavy burdens and two warriors removed our leather leashes and pushed us roughly through the door. The door to the hut slammed shut behind us and the sound of a metal lock being slipped into place reverberated through the empty building.

Marlen and I were now alone as we heard the warriors move on down the street. It wasn't clear how long we would be kept locked away in the hut but I planned to make the best of the time by continuing to practice my understanding and usage of the language that was native to this planet.

The twilight of dusk could be seen filtering through small cracks in the walls of the hut and the dim light was sufficient for me to make out that there was no furniture in the hut with us. Against one wall I could see a pile of furs so at least we would be warm for the night. Walking the inside perimeter of the walls I tested the integrity of its construction and evaluated if there were any weak spots that could be exploited to aid our escape. To my consternation I found that the hut was constructed quite solidly. The dirt floor was pressed dirt worn smooth and there was no way that I would be able to dig my way out without the use of tools. Not being able to identify anything of use to us I picked up the furs and returned to where Marlen sat against the base of the wall opposite the door. Sitting down next to her and draping the furs across our laps I began testing my newfound language skills by trying to converse with Marlen. Once I had burned through my repertoire of nouns and verbs she continued to introduce new words and phrases.

Until it became fully dark outside the people of the village could be seen passing back and forth traveling down the side street. They all passed oblivious to our presence locked away inside the hut.

Marlen and I practiced my usage of her language until the night wore on and we both became tired. Lying down with my back against the base of the wall Marlen snuggled in front of me backing her body up against mine. Wrapping the furs closely about us we fell asleep almost immediately.

We had been asleep for only a few minutes when I heard the lock on the door being unlatched and I bolted to my feet. When the door opened five warriors entered with spears drawn and menacing me with their points pushed me against the back wall. Two of the warriors grabbed Marlen by the arms and exited the hut. The remaining warriors backed out of the door ensuring not to turn their backs towards me. An overwhelming feeling of despair swept over me as the door slammed shut and I again heard the lock being latched into place. Rushing forward I pounded on the door with my fists yelling Marlen's name. I faintly I could make out a yell coming from the distance. It may have been my imagination but to me it sounded like Marlen yelling my name.

Helpless to assist Marlen I waited anxiously for her return. Pacing back and forth in front of the door I listened intently for any sound signaling the approach of warriors. Not understanding why they had taken her, I just knew that for the sake of the warriors no harm had better come to her or vengeance would be mine.

After what seemed like hours I heard footsteps coming down the lane from the direction of the chief's hut. The lock was unlatched and pushing their way into the hut with their spears the warriors threw Marlen to the ground and then closed and locked the door as they left again.

Springing to Marlen's side and using what I knew of her language I blurted out, "are you okay my love?"

"I am fine Jack," she responded looking at me in surprise. "They only took me to see the chief."

"Why would they take you in the middle of the night?" I asked with confusion.

"For verification," she replied. "Many years ago the chief appealed to my father's court for an alliance against the pirates of Marduk. My father had agreed and during a dinner celebration the chief proposed that the alliance be sealed with my marriage to him. My father was outraged and had the chief and his troops thrown from the city. It is not safe for me here he will make me his wife if I cannot escape."

"Don't worry Marlen, I will find a way to get you out of here," I replied with confidence.

I settled Marlen down into the furs and redoubled my efforts to find a way out of our cage. Again I checked every nook and cranny of the walls to no avail. Checking the doors and windows yet again I found the hinges and locks were all on the outside of the building and afforded no access. The hard packed dirt floor was not an option. In defeat I lay down next to Marlen and stared at the ceiling while I listened to her quietly sleeping. How were we going to get out of this place? Maybe I could ambush the warriors when they came into the hut to get us. Realizing that would not work, because I would be severely outnumbered and I could not risk Marlen getting hurt.

Lying there looking up at the ceiling I had lost all hope of being able to escape. Just when I started to doze off I had a revelation that sat me bolt upright. The ceiling, I had not checked the ceiling for a way out. The construction was flimsy with wooden ribs extending from the top of the walls to the ceiling and meeting at a center point at the pinnacle of the roof. The whole thing was over-lain with thatched roofing materials. Standing up I moved to the wall that contained the window. Jumping up I grabbed the top of the wall and pulling myself up placed a foot onto the window sill to allow me to stand. Reaching up to the thatch material I pushed against it and to my surprise my hand slipped right through. My excitement began to rise as I pulled at the thatching material until I had a hole large enough to permit me to pull myself through. It took but a second and I was sitting on the roof of the hut looking out over the village.

I had to get Marlen. Returning to the inside of the hut I jumped down to the floor and quickly went to her side. Whispering to her quietly I urged her awake, "Marlen, hurry you must wake up, we have a way out."

She woke up disoriented and I gave her a couple of minutes to wake up and compose herself. When she was ready I explained my plan to her and lifted her up until she could reach the rafters in the ceiling. With a boost from me she was able to make her way onto the outside of the roof. With a short spring I retraced my steps and followed her. Once we were both outside on the roof we moved around to the shaded side of the hut and I quietly lowered her into the shadows at the back of the building and jumped down next to her.

Not knowing which way was the shortest route to the barricade that protected the city I was sure that we did not want to go in the direction of the market street. Moving away from the direction of the chief's palace hut we slipped from shadow to shadow. More than once we hunkered close to the ground under the cover of the shadows as groups of warriors passed us by.

We were nearing the edge of the village and I could see the barricade wall in the distance. A large open area separated the huts of the village from the wall and we would have to cross this space in plain view of anyone that may be paying attention. Looking around we prepared to make a run for the wall. The outward leaning poles that made up the wall would be easy to scale from the inside if we could just get too them. Stepping into the open and moving briskly we headed for the wall.

No sooner had we stepped into the open and I heard a warning yell from behind, "Halt. What are you doing there?"

Looking over my shoulder I saw a small compliment of warriors stepping out of an adjoining lane. At the warning from behind I urged Marlen into a run. The warriors could be heard approaching rapidly from behind and we were nearly at the wall. My hope was that once we got over the wall we could lose them in the jungle. Just short of the wall Marlen stumbled and went down. My momentum carried me to the base of the wall and when I turned to go back for her I saw that the warriors had reached her. As they grabbed her I came charging back and throwing my body amongst them I took them from their feet. Fists swinging in all directions I was determined to cause as much damage as I could. Blow after blow rained down on my head and body as I continued to dish out as much as I was taking. The warriors crowded in on me and it became impossible to continue to throw blows at them. Through sheer numbers they finally managed to overpower me and pin me to the ground.

Looking around quickly my eyes located Marlen. She had not been harmed and was now being held fast by a warrior. Feeling that I had failed her, my best efforts were not sufficient to succor her from the clutches of these warriors. One warrior started barking orders at the others, this one I took to be the leader of the group. "Get him on his feet," he said. "Do not hurt him the chief has plans for this one." Leaning in close he sneered a knowing smirk. "I hope you enjoyed your freedom stranger however brief it was. The chief has plans for you. When the sun rises in the east you will wish that we had killed you now," he said.

Without further conversation the group escorted us back to our prison hut. Removing the latch from the door they kicked it open wide. "Bind their hands," ordered the leader. "Do not attempt to escape again. My warriors will be waiting to spit you with their spears if you so much as poke your head through that roof and it would be a shame to deprive the chief of his entertainment." With that they pushed us through the door and locked it behind us.

Chapter Six

Sodan

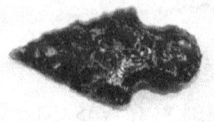

A violent kick to the ribs woke me from a deep slumber. "Wake up dog, the chief commands your presence."

After Marlen and I had been thrown back into the hut the previous night we had curled up among the furs and talked quietly. It was clear that escape was not going to be possible at this time so I had her tell me everything that she could about the chief of this little village. Expecting that the following morning we would be escorted to the chief I wanted to know what I could expect from him.

Marlen again recited what her personal experiences had been with the chief and then shared what she had learned about him through others. It was said that those that were unfortunate enough to be taken prisoner by the chief were never heard from again. It was not clear what happened to them because nobody had ever escaped to share the tale. I was not feeling good about the upcoming meeting.

Shortly before dawn we had gone to sleep and resigned ourselves to whatever the morning would hold for us.

The warrior kicked me again and then grabbing me by the arm jerked me to my feet. Another warrior had already drug Marlen upright. Our hands were still bound from the night before and my fingers had gone numb a long time ago. We were forced out the door and into the sunlight, the brightness of which forced me to squint and I struggled to see clearly through watering eyes. Dragging us down the street we were prodded on by the sharp points of spears wielded by the warriors. Passers-by stepped to the side of the avenue and watched our procession pass.

At the entrance to the chief's hut my escorts were challenged by the royal guard. "Halt, What business have you here?" the guard said.

The leader of our escort appearing to be offended by the challenge snapped back, "Our business is with the chief not his guard," he replied. There seemed to be some underlying tension between these two. Maybe a jealous rivalry because one guarded the chief of the village and the other was a common warrior. "Let us pass, the chief awaits us," said our escort. The royal guard parted and we moved to pass through the entryway. Pausing for a short second in front of the leader of the guard our escort leaned in and growled in a low tone, "It should be I guarding the chief Jarad not you. Your days are numbered my friend." With that he led us on through the entry gate and into the chief's palace of a hut.

Once inside we were escorted down a long narrow passageway that ended in another set of doors that were also guarded. As we approached, the two guards swung open the doors. There before us was a large high ceilinged throne room. People were milling about visiting with each other and at our entry they parted and cleared an aisle for us that lead to the foot of a set of small stairs. Atop the stairs was a high backed throne constructed of twisted and gnarled pieces of wood and carved beautifully down the front and around the seat back. Upon the throne sat a wrinkled up old man that had clearly passed his prime long ago. His fur loincloth and boots were died a royal purple and on his brow sat a thin golden crown inset with what appeared to be bright green emeralds. Around the circumference of the crown were placed the fangs of the saber toothed forest cats like I had seen in the swamp.

The chief eyed us suspiciously as we approached. In his left hand stood a stout spear embossed in gold and across his lap sat a gold inlaid short sword. Our retinue stopped before the throne and our escorts all knelt to one knee in reverence. Marlen and I both stood strong both refusing to show deference to the chief. The leader of our retinue looking up noticed that we still stood and became enraged. Swiping out with his spear he caught Marlen in the shins instantly dropping her to her knees. Standing up he approached me, "kneel before the chief," he said.

Using what I had learned of their language I responded back, "I kneel before no man," I responded. At least I think that is what I said. I could very well have said something derogatory about his mother's parentage for all I knew. Either way it had the same result. His face reddened and beginning to froth at the mouth he reached out with the butt of his spear and jabbed me a savage blow in the stomach. Instantly I was doubled over but still refused to touch my knee to ground. The second blow fell and caught me in the back of the knees. The next strike hit the back of my head exploding in flashes of light crossing my vision like fireworks and the next thing I knew my face was planted nose first onto the hard packed clay that made up the floor.

Not sure why I always insisted on doing everything the hard way, I attributed it to my independent nature that I had developed growing up in the Northwest. Some days I pondered if being so stubborn was really worth all the pain that I received as a result of it. Would it have changed anything to have knelt before the chief? In hindsight I would be in a lot less pain and the chief would still be a withered old despot. Surely I must try to remember this.

"Finally, you grace my court Princess Marlen," spoke the chief.

Looking up from her position on her knees before the throne Marlen responded with fire. "You cannot hold me here Padek, my father will come for me."

Chief Padek smiled at her and began to laugh wickedly. "That he may Marlen but he won't find you here. You had the chance to rule by my side but now you will disappear among my harem and no one will ever see you again. You will just be another nameless woman among many," he replied.

"Never Padek, I would rather die than become a member of your harem," she responded venomously.

"That can be arranged my dear but long before that you will be mine," he sneered back at her.

"Ludor, who is this other that you bring," he asked the warrior that escorted us.

"He is another that we captured along the edge of the vast forest oh great chief. He does not seem to be of this land. His skin is pale and he was without harness or markings when we found him. He speaks very little of the language but has proven to be formidable in battle. When first we found him he killed two of my best warriors before he was subdued," the one I now recognized as Ludor stated.

Padek looked squarely at me. "Who are you stranger? Who sent you to my land and what business do you have here?" he asked.

"My name is Jack Wilde," I said clearly. "I am but a traveler in your land. I was sent by no one and am only passing through. I wish that you release Marlen and me now and let us be on our way."

The entire throne room rang out in laughter at my words. Looking around at the assembled warriors and ladies I saw no humor in my statement. Again I spoke, more loudly this time to be heard over the din of the laughter. "If you release us now I assure you that no harm will befall you. My only ask is that we be provided with weapons and food and escorted to the gate of your city and we will no longer be of concern to you."

The crowd laughed louder still and the chief nearly fell from his throne in mirth. Raising his hand for silence he attempted to calm the crowd so that he could speak. "You will never leave Jack Wilde, alive that is. You have fire and my people will enjoy seeing you put to death in the pit of battle. Prepare him for battle and take him away," he barked to my escort.

Two warriors grabbed me by my elbows and began to drag me kicking and yelling from the throne room. They dragged me toward the doors through which we had entered. I saw Marlen kicking and fighting with the warrior that held her. She was screaming my name as the doors closed between us.

Taken out of the chief's hut I was forcefully dragged down a side street. After passing a dozen huts of various shapes and sizes we entered into an open arena surrounded on all sides by a low wall and gradually ascending seating. Here I expected to be put to death without even having a chance to fight for my freedom, but at the center of the arena one of the warriors kicked around in the dirt until he found a half buried length of rope. As he pulled on the rope I could see that it was attached to a wooden trapdoor. The warrior raised the trapdoor and flung it over revealing a dark hole beneath it. In one swift move I felt a knife sever the lashings that held my wrists and a foot in my lower back as I was kicked forward into the hole.

Spinning in the air I fell. Anticipating a long drop I was pleasantly surprised to land on soft sand after a short fall of only ten feet. Lying on my back in the sand I massaged my wrists and looked up at the warriors that had placed me into the pit. Satisfied that I had survived the fall they closed the trap door leaving me in complete darkness.

Continuing to lie in the cool sand I listened intently for any sounds. More than once I thought I heard the shuffling of an animal. Based upon my surroundings I surmised that the sounds that I heard were coming from some sort of a small vermin such as a rat. Having no desire to have rats crawling over my prostate body I made my way to my feet. The blackness of the dark was complete and I could make out nothing in any direction. Standing still I waited for any sign that would indicate to me a direction of travel. The shuffling sound of the animals continued to get closer and closer. Beginning to recognize the soft coolness of a draft blowing onto the back of my neck and having no other direction in which to travel I turned to get the breeze upon my face and reaching my hands out into the darkness in front of me I began to gingerly move forward.

Continuing to move in the direction of the breeze I came up against a cold dirt wall. Feeling along the wall with my hands I kept moving slowly in the direction from which the breeze was coming along a passageway or tunnel with a low overhead. Reaching out I was able to touch both walls with my outstretched arms. Traveling for what I would estimate to be about fifty yards a faint light became discernable in the distance. Beginning to move a little faster but still taking care to not stumble, I wanted to get into that light. Something about the unknown of the darkness can be unnerving and I wanted to again be surrounded by light.

Rounding a corner in the tunnel I stepped into a lighted chamber. Sitting around the base of the wall throughout the chamber were other men. On the far wall was a barred gate. Arrayed at intervals around the wall were small oil lamps which provided a dim illumination throughout the chamber. Those men that were awake turned to look at me as I entered the room. There were ten other men in the room besides myself and crossing to the far wall I tested the gate shaking it violently. It did not move. Turning back toward the center of the room I looked around for any other way out. Just then one of the other prisoners spoke, "It's no use my friend. Each one of us has done the same thing and there is no way out until they let us out."

"What about back down the passageway," I asked.

"Nothing, I have explored it myself and there are no other passages that way other than the trapdoor through which we have all been dropped," he said.

Sliding down the wall I slumped next to the man to which I had been speaking. "Why are they holding us all captive here?" I asked.

"We are all here for one reason and one reason only, Chief Padek's entertainment. When they are ready we will be released into the arena to fight one another, wild animals, or the chief's best warriors. All that sit around this room are dead men for no one ever survives the chief's entertainment games," he responded solemnly.

"Well I do not intend to die for anyone's entertainment and as long as I still breathe they will pay dearly for this injustice," I replied.

Smiling at me the man responded, "You have fire in your heart my friend. I am Sodan of the city of Valcot. Your pale skin color belies your origin from where do you hail?"

"My name is Jack Wilde and I come from a place called Earth," I said.

"Earth, I have never heard of it. How did you get here?" he asked.

"It is a long story Sodan. Suffice it to say that I am a long way from my home. By what name do you call this world?" I asked questioningly.

"I don't understand," he said. "Everyone knows this is the continent of Astor on the world Phoria. You ask strange questions Jack Wilde but I like you metal."

"I must offer my apologies Sodan, I am new here and am still learning," I responded evasively.

Our conversation was abruptly interrupted by the arrival of a group of warriors at the locked gate. The gathering of men in the room rose to their feet and shuffled forward to the gate where the warriors passed wooden bowls filled with a thick gruel and tin cups filled with water through a horizontal slot. As each man received his bowl and cup he returned to his position along the wall. When it came my turn at the gate I accepted my share of the food and water. Before turning away I tried to engage the warriors in conversation. I desperately wanted to know what had become of Marlen. Of her the warriors knew nothing but I was able to find out from them that the chief had ordered the games to commence the following day. They were to be held in celebration of the Princess of Pendak being added to his retinue. I was greatly disturbed by this information and felt my face flush with anger towards Chief Padek. Angrily I returned to my place along the wall next to Sodan.

"What is wrong Jack?" he asked questioningly. "You seem as if the guards have angered you."

"They have my friend," I replied glumly. I did not know how much I could trust Sodan but at this point I had very little to lose, so I shared with him the story of my capture and of Marlen.

After I had shared my tale Sodan sat quietly in contemplation eating his food. Taking this opportunity I too began to eat. The gruel was terribly plain and flavorless. It was comprised of grain similar to wheat and had been prepared solely with water. The gruel bore many similarities to the oatmeal of Earth but could have benefited greatly from a dab of cream and sugar. Eating as quickly as possible I wanted to get the meal over with as soon as I could. Forcing the last finger full of the gruel into my mouth I washed it down with the warm water from the tin cup.

Placing the cup and bowl on the ground I rested my elbows on my knees and buried my head into my hands. Many of the men had returned to sleeping as was evidenced by the din of snores that reverberated through the room. Sodan shifted position next to me and clearing his throat began to speak. "I do not know how the games are conducted here in Ronar and I expect that any opportunity for escape will be slim. The arena will be heavily guarded but fighting together we may be able to win through to freedom."

"I cannot leave Marlen in the hands of Padek," I blurted out angrily.

"Relax my friend," he said calmingly. "You cannot help Marlen if you are dead. If you stay and fight that is the inevitable result. If you are free we may yet devise a plan that will allow us to free Marlen from the clutches of Padek."

I knew in my heart that he was right but I still felt a pain in my chest at the thought of abandoning Marlen. "You are right Sodan," I acknowledged. "I cannot help Marlen if I am a prisoner in this pit or worse, lying dead on the sands of the arena. I am with you my friend. How may we affect our escape from this wretched village?"

"We must be prepared to react at the first opportunity," he said. "Preparing for battle is the best thing that we can do because no matter how much we try to plan the fight the fight will go where it leads. A battle lives and breathes with a life all its own and those that do battle must react on instinct and hope that their preparations have been sufficient for them to carry the day. The best thing that we can do right now Jack Wilde is to prepare, and preparation right now means to rest. We will talk more later."

I lay down on the sand of the chamber, thinking of Marlen and hoping that she was safe I drifted into a fitful slumber.

Chapter Seven

The Arena

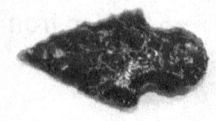

The lack of rest that I had since arriving on this planet had finally caught up with me. Sleeping through the night I was awakened the next morning by Sodan informing me that the warriors had arrived at the gate with our breakfast. All the men in the chamber shuffled forward to the gate to await their turn to receive the meager offerings of food. Again we were served the thick tasteless gruel of the night before. My guess was that there was no sense in wasting the good food on men that were very likely going to die soon.

The warriors were in a festive mood and joked and laughed with each other as they doled out our meals. Much of their conversation was centered on various bets that were being placed among the warriors as to who would survive the longest in the arena. For my sake I hoped that they were wrong in their estimations as I had not fared well in the betting pool.

Once again I tried to engage the guards into conversation to garner any hint of information about Marlen. Just as in my previous attempt from the day before they either knew nothing or would not deem to share any information with me. Frustrated I returned to my spot next to Sodan.

While we choked down the vile gruel Sodan and I entered into conversation with two other men that were sitting next to us. The two men both seemed to be in rather jovial spirits considering the predicament that they were in. To my surprise I learned that both of these men were from the city of Pendak. My ears immediately perked up at this information. They had been dispatched as part of search party by the king of Pendak to locate the missing princess.

While searching along the edge of the great swamp they had been set upon by a group of warriors from Ronar. Most of their party had managed to fight their way to freedom and these two alone had been taken prisoner. After their capture they had been interrogated extensively by the chief's royal guard. The guard had been trying to determine why they were present along the territory of Ronar.

With the number of individuals that I had met, myself included, who had been interrogated it was apparent that Chief Padek greatly feared invasion from neighboring cities. He tried at every opportunity to gain intelligence from the prisoners that may give forewarning of invasion.

Choosing not to reveal how much I knew about Marlen or that she in fact was being held prisoner within the village. Since I could not be confident enough that these two men would support any plan that I may have to rescue Marlen since I was not of their city. Sodan shot me a quick glance of recognition at the mention of princess. With closed mouth and a quick nod of my head I signaled to him my desire to remain silent on the subject of the princess.

Still I didn't understand the jovial attitude that the two men were exhibiting and even with deft questioning I was unable to get them to reveal what they knew. Something was amiss with these two but try as I might they were not giving up their information. The only scrap that I could gather was that the king of Pendak was convinced that Chief Padek was responsible for the disappearance of his daughter. What that meant for the village of Ronar I could only guess.

Leaning back against the wall I began to formulate plans in my mind that might be useful if the time came. The most important part of every scenario that I bounced around in my mind was that I needed to get Marlen over the wall and into the forest. I firmly believed that if I could get her out of the village then we could elude any pursuit and avoid recapture.

My musings were interrupted by the return of the warriors. Something was different with this visit though because the number of warriors was double that of when they brought our food. The warriors lined both sides of the passageway outside the gate with three blocking the end. The leader of the group slipped a key into the lock on the gate and with a click released the mechanism that freed the gate and allowed it to swing free. Pulling his short sword he kicked the gate wide and directed us to exit. In a single file line the men exited the chamber. Once all the prisoners were out three warriors fell in behind and the entire procession began to move down the passage. They kept us surrounded at all times with short swords and spears and every side passage that we passed was guarded to prevent escape.

The tunnel that we were being escorted down ended abruptly at a set of stairs leading upwards. My estimation of the direction of our travel placed this stairway below the center of the arena. There was a large wooden trapdoor at the top of the stairs and to the right of the base of the stair was a doorway that opened into a heavily guarded armory. Here were stored the tools of the arena. In racks along the walls were spears and tridents. Arrayed in clay barrels throughout the room were quantities of short swords with an occasional long sword mixed in. Bows and arrows were not used for the arena since they allowed one to kill from a distance. The whole point of the arena was hand-to-hand combat and killing. Short swords and spears seemed to be the weapons of choice.

The leader of the warriors pushed the first two prisoners up the stairs. The trapdoor in the arena was raised and a dusting of loose sand blew into the passage.

The two men ascended the stairs and stepped into the open arena. Two warriors from the armory ascended the stair behind them and each carried a short sword and spear. At the top of the stairs they threw the weapons into the sand and descended back to the armory with the trap door closing behind them.

The anticipation was building as my adrenaline began to rise. While I did not relish the idea of having to fight to the death I was not going to let anyone stand in the way of my rescuing Marlen. If that meant that I would have to fight to the death then I hope the people of Ronar were ready for a show of fighting skill like they had never seen.

A faint clanging of metal on metal could be heard through the wood of the trapdoor. I yearned to be out in the open of the arena and out of these dank passages. Captivity did not sit well with me and given the opportunity to fight for my life or be at the mercy of another I would choose to fight every time. Excitement was starting to set in and I found myself beginning to fidget and move about in anticipation.

The trapdoor rose again two more men were pushed into the arena with weapons thrown in behind them. Again the trapdoor slammed shut. Sodan and I were next in line to enter the arena. Having only just met Sodan I liked his character and dreaded the thought of having to fight him to the death.

Leaning close to Sodan I whispered quietly, "I cannot fight you to the death my friend."

"Nor I you," he responded. "I say we give them a good show and when the opportunity is right we strike at the heart of these people."

"Agreed," I replied.

The trapdoor opened and Sodan and I ascended the stairs. Stopping at the top we looked around the arena at the multitude of citizens that crowded into the stadium seating. Stepping forth onto the hot sand my eyes struggled to grow accustomed to the bright sunlight. Two warriors stepped forth from the trap door and threw two long swords onto the sand at our feet. The sand had been stained a deep crimson from the fresh blood of the previous battles.

Sodan and I retrieved the swords from the ground and tested their weight in our hands. Never before had I held a long sword in my hands and my experience with swords was limited to some dabbling in fencing that I had done in college. Sweeping the sword through the air in front of me I could tell that the weapon was well balanced and it felt like an extension of my arm.

Circling around one another we held our swords out between us. Sensing my hesitation in initiating the attack Sodan moved forward and engaged me. My lesson in sword fighting had begun.

Swiping his sword left and right at my body he forced me to block and parry his attacks. Backing slowly away from his onslaught we worked our way closer and closer to

Chief Padek's private box. Sneaking a quick look at the chief I saw that Marlen stood beside his throne with a leather leash about her neck At the sight of the chief so close to Marlen I began to see red and shifted from using my sword in defense to a more offensive approach.

Turning the tables on Sodan I began to feign striking at one angle with my sword then shifting my attack to come from another direction. He circled me as I began to press my advantage and I could see that he was increasingly hard pressed to defend himself from the tapestry of steel that I was weaving ahead of me. My aim was not to harm Sodan but I wanted to ensure that we were putting on a good show for the crowd so that nobody would question the validity of our battle.

Pressing forward I backed Sodan around to where he stood directly in front of the throne defending himself. We were now in a position to strike. My plan was to jump into the seats in front of the chief's box and fight my way to Marlen's side. I was preparing to strike when a fireball rained out of the sky. Not far from where we pretended to fight a flaming clay pot impacted the ground splashing flaming oil across the sand. Where had the pot come from? Instantly the stands erupted into chaos as the people struggled to get out of the arena.

Fiery clay pots continued to rain down around the arena. Instantly taking advantage of the diversion we vaulted the wall into the stands. Fighting our way to the chief's throne box his warriors drew weapons and attempted to stop us as our momentum cut a swathe through their midst. Reaching the throne I caught a glimpse of Chief Padek disappearing down a stairway behind the throne with Marlen in tow.

Getting so close to reaching Marlen's side I refused to have her snatched from under my very nose. Yelling to Sodan I descended the stairs following them. At the bottom of the stair I caught up with the chief and his personal guard who I recognized as Ludor and four others. They immediately turned to attack me. Ludor barely had a chance to raise his weapon as a flash of lightning that was my sword reached out and plucked his head from his shoulders. The speed of my attack startled the remaining warriors and it caused them to delay just long enough for me to be in their midst. The long sword that I wielded had a decisive reach advantage over the short swords with which they attempted to defend themselves. Two more men fell under my sword before the remaining guard turned and ran. Padek turned to run with them and almost simultaneously Marlen stumbled and fell. When she struck the ground the impact was enough to jerk the leash from Padek's hands. He hesitated only a second while he contemplated trying to retrieve the leash. Seeing me cut my way through his guard decided it for him and he turned and ran following his guard down the passage.

Rushing to Marlen's side I took her in my arms and checked her over to see if she had been harmed in the fall.

She looked up into my eyes and said, "I knew that you would come for me Jack."

"I'm here now but we are far from safe," I said. "We need to get out of the city while the Ronar are distracted by the attack."

Sodan fought his way to our side and stood guard over us while I prepared Marlen to move. Getting her back on her feet I asked Sodan which way he thought we should go. He advised that we not go back through the arena as the attacking army had entered the arena and full scale war was being waged on the sands. Having little other choice we proceeded to follow down the passageway where chief Padek had gone.

We encountered very little resistance as we travelled down the passageway. Those warriors that we did encounter elected to turn and run rather than to engage us in fight. After having travelled only a short distance Marlen pulled us to a halt adjacent to an open passageway on our right. "This one," she said. "This is the passageway that I entered through with Padek. It leads to the city streets. Padek had walked the streets in parade this morning with me in tow to show me off to his subjects and brag about me being added to his harem. At the end of a long avenue we descended a set of stairs that led to this passage."

Having very few options I looked at Sodan who gave me a shrug of his shoulders and taking Marlen by the hand we moved into the new passageway. Moving through the darkness we had gone what I estimated to be about two hundred feet when my toe struck hard against something on the floor. Pulling Marlen and Sodan to a stop I knelt down to determine what I had struck with my foot. Reaching out with my hand I felt the bottom step of a flight of stairs that ascended upwards. In the darkness I could faintly make out a thin crack of light coming from above through closed doors.

Slowly we ascended the stairs until we stood before a closed wooden doorway. The sounds of fighting came from the other side and gingerly I pushed it open a crack to see what was happening beyond. If we had barged through the door without first looking to see what was on the other side we would have emerged in the midst of a large contingent of warriors from Ronar and would have been no better off than when we had started.

Immediately I pulled the door tight and with Sodan's help we held it as warriors on the other side tried to pull it open seeking an escape from the avenue. In the brief glance that I had when I peeked through the door I had surmised that the attacking warriors were pressing hard on the Ronar who were slowly falling back against the onslaught. They had no way of escape except into the buildings that lined both sides of the avenue or through the doorway that we currently held fast.

The sounds of men dying could be heard coming through the door then began to fade into the distance. The remaining warriors must have escaped into the buildings and their attackers had followed. When no sounds of fighting could be heard in the immediate vicinity outside the door I again slowly opened it to look around.

The bloodied bodies of warriors from both sides of the conflict lay scattered throughout the avenue but none living could be seen. Pushing the door wider I stepped out into the avenue with Marlen and Sodan following. Pressing up against the wall of the buildings to the right of the door as we exited we moved along the wall swiftly and quietly until we reached a cross street. Turning onto the street we could see individual battles occurring between soldiers for the length of the street. What immediately caught my eye though was the sight of the village wall about five city blocks in the distance. Our goal was in sight.

Threading our way down the street the fighting warriors took little notice of us as they were preoccupied with their individual battles. We had reached the end of the last block without incident when one of the warriors of Ronar dispatched his opponent and turned to look at us. He stood between us and our chance at freedom. As he moved to intercept us, I pushed Marlen behind me and stepped out to confront him. This needed to be quick because I did not have time to delay for fear that other warriors of Ronar would come to his aid. Still carrying the long sword I took advantage of my greater reach and quickly reaching out struck at his left thigh. When he blocked the blow I spun quickly and bringing the blade down on his right shoulder I sliced him clean to his left hip.

As he fell to the ground I signaled Marlen and Sodan forward. Now we needed to get across the open area between the buildings and the log wall without being seen. Looking both directions I couldn't see anyone that was not engaged in battle. I was banking on the fact that they would be too occupied with their own fights to take notice of us slipping over the wall.

Stepping into the open and moving swiftly towards the wall we heard a yell from behind. Looking back up the avenue which we had just traversed I saw a handful of warriors of Ronar running to intercept us. Sodan immediately turned to defend our escape. Stopping I joined him preparing to sell my life dearly to help Marlen get clear of the city.

"No Jack, you must go," Sodan said. "Take the woman and get her to safety, I will delay them long enough for you to get away."

"I cannot leave you here Sodan," I replied. "They outnumber you three to one."

With a wry smile across his face he responded back with, "That is good my friend, for they may have a chance that way. Now go and get over the wall before they get here."

With extreme trepidation I grabbed Marlen by the hand and turning sprinted towards the wall. The outward leaning logs made it easy to scale and we very nearly ran right up the wall. Reaching the top I lowered Marlen down as far as I could then dropped her the last six feet to the ground. Kicking my legs over the wall I prepared to drop down beside her. Looking one last time before my head passed below the top of the wall I saw Sodan surrounded by warriors. He was taking a toll on their numbers with his long sword but I feared that they would eventually over-power him and he would be lost. There was nothing left for me to do but get Marlen as far away from Ronar as I could. Sodan's sacrifice would be for naught if we were to be captured again.

Dropping to the ground next to Marlen I took her hand and we sprinted for the forest that surrounded Ronar. Entering into the forest we crossed a well-worn path leading to the northwest. All I knew was that it was leading away from Ronar and that is the direction that we needed to go. At a steady trot Marlen and I proceeded to put some distance between us and the battle that raged in the village.

Chapter Eight

Fleeing Pursuit

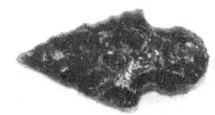

Pushing Marlen through the afternoon we were able to put a great distance between us and the city of Ronar. Often we checked our back trail to ensure that we were not being followed and each time there was no sign of pursuit.

Having not had the opportunity to make too many friends on this planet it pained me to lose one and I regretted the loss of Sodan. As we travelled away from Ronar my mind would return to the last sight that I had seen of him surrounded by warriors. Sodan was a warrior and I know that they paid dearly for his life.

The path that we had followed away from Ronar became grown over from disuse a little over a mile from the village. The forest closed in on the trail and we were forced to wend our way through the tangled underbrush of the forest. We continued to travel to the northwest although our speed had slowed considerably without a trail to follow. The thick forest was both a hindrance and a blessing both slowing our travel and also providing us with cover from anyone that may be pursuing us.

It was mid-afternoon before I deemed it safe enough for us to stop and rest. In a small opening in the forest we sat down and leaned against the base of a large tree. After catching our breath I spoke to Marlen of the presence of her father's army in Ronar.

"Do you think that the army of Pendak would have been victorious in Ronar," I asked.

Taking a minute to contemplate my question she responded, "My father's army is well trained and I have no doubt much better equipped for war than the warriors of Ronar. While the fight could not have been easy for them I am sure that they would have emerged victorious."

"That is good then," I said excitedly. "If we circle to the south we can meet up with the army of Pendak and you will soon be returned safely to your father's court."

"No," she blurted out abruptly. "There are those in leadership positions among the army of Pendak that would benefit from my disappearance. I would hardly be any safer with them than if I had stayed in Ronar."

With my face clearly showing my confusion I asked her what she meant.

"What I meant Jack," she began to explain. "Is that there are many factions within the city of Pendak that would seize the opportunity to overthrow my father while he is distracted by my disappearance. That safest thing for us and my father's kingdom is for me to return unannounced and without fanfare."

Beginning to understand Marlen's concerns I scrapped any idea that I had of returning her to her father's army. "Rest assured Marlen," I stated bluntly. "I will do everything that I can to get you safely home to your father."

"I know you will Jack," she said with confidence that bolstered my ego. "My safety and my life are in your hands and I know that you will protect them both with your very own."

My chest swelled with pride at the compliment from this beautiful woman and I knew that she was right. I would do anything to protect her and keep her safe.

"Come my dear," I said with a smile, "We have only a couple more hours to travel before we will need to stop for the night and prepare our defenses to protect us from the dangers of the forest."

Rising to our feet we continued our trek through the thick forest. Conversing quietly as we travelled I attempted to learn from Marlen the best direction for us to travel.

"In what direction does Pendak lay?" I asked.

She took a short second to judge the direction of the suns travel then answered, "Pendak lies directly to the south."

"Directly to the south may be a big problem for us," I responded. "Between us and Pendak is the great forest and swamp where we were captured. What lies to the northwest?"

"If we continue to travel in our current direction we will hit the coast sometime tomorrow," she said.

I much preferred to travel down the coast than to try to navigate our way through the swamp I also knew that if need be I could construct a raft that may help us to travel faster and have some safety from the carnivorous land animals.

"I don't relish the idea of crossing through the swamp," I told Marlen. "Let's continue on to the coast and then make our way to the South from there."

Marlen responded confidently, "I follow where you lead Jack. I trust you with my life."

Continuing to travel through the forest we moved up and down tree and brush covered hills. Towards late afternoon the underbrush began to thin and the trees grew farther and farther apart. Anticipating that we would not have to travel much farther and we would be clear of the forest, I began to grow concerned because I wanted to have enough forest around us that we would be able to have cover from passing eyes and the materials that we needed to build a shelter of some sort. My decision was to stop and prepare a camp for the night.

"Let's stop here for the night," I said. "We can gather some firewood and I will work on someplace for us to sleep for the night."

We moved around gathering every scrap of dry wood that we could find and piled it at the base of a large tree. Using my long sword I cut a number of larger pieces of wood into smaller more manageable sizes. I hated using the sword for cutting wood and I wanted to preserve its edge but there was no other option. Using the sharp edge of the sword I split some of the pieces of wood in half lengthwise for use in building a fire.

The smaller dry twigs that we had gathered were piled up and finding a straight stick about two feet long and a fingers width in diameter I began to spin the stick by hand in a notch that I had cut into a split piece of dry wood. Directing Marlen to gather handfuls of dry grasses I continued to spin the stick until a wisp of smoke began to rise from the notch. When she returned with the grass I tipped the charcoal ember that had developed in the notch onto it and gently blew it into flame. Placing the flame among the pile of small sticks I nursed the fire to grow until it was large enough to put off plenty of heat.

Once the fire was started we sat down to rest. With our backs leaning against the great tree we sat between the fire and the trunk. We had no furs to use for the night and would have to rely on the fire and the heat of our bodies to keep us warm and comfortable.

Marlen leaned her head against my shoulder and was soon sound asleep. It had really bothered me to push her so hard to travel throughout the day but the greater the distance between us and Ronar the safer I felt that she would be. The travel had taken its toll on her and now I knew that she needed all the rest that she could get.

Surrounded by the warmth of the fire I sat wishing that I had taken the time to gather some food while we travelled for the pangs of hunger were beginning to grumble through our stomachs. I regretted that Marlen should have to go to sleep hungry but for now there was no other option. Tomorrow was another day and as we travelled I would keep my eyes peeled for anything that we could eat along the way. There had to be some kind of fruits or berries within this forest that we could sustain ourselves with while we travelled.

Keeping the fire stoked I ensured that the flames remained high enough to ward off any predators that may be prowling nearby. My confidence from my previous experience camped out in the swamp assured me that the animals of the night were quite scared of the fire and would not approach our camp.

While Marlen slept I sat contemplating the life-changing events that had occurred to me over the last few days. If anyone had tried to tell me a week ago that I would be sitting in an arboreal forest on a primitive world with a beautiful princess leaning against my shoulder I would have laughed at them and recommended that they stop drinking. Yet here I was and my whole perception of life and my whole identity had been turned upside down.

Everything that I had seen of the technology of this planet thus far made it clear to me that I was here for the long haul. The chance to return to my own world would not be coming any time soon, if ever.

In a sense I was very fortunate though. My identity would become whatever I made it to be. Based upon what little I had seen of this world so far, honor and courage were the foundations of a person's identity. Both of these qualities I considered myself to possess in excessive quantities. While I had learned many methods of fighting throughout my years of service in the military I rarely had an opportunity to use a sword or spear. Both of these weapons were the tools of honesty and courage in this savage environment. My skill with weapons was in its infancy but just like with everything else the value of my skill would be measured by the value of the practice that I put into perfecting it. There was a lot that I had to learn.

What of the beautiful princess that sat next to me? The more time I spent with her the more my heart longed to be with her forever. While the honorable thing to do would be to return her to her father's court as quickly as possible I did not relish the day when I would and she would no longer be with me and by my side all the time.

The hair on my neck rose as the roar of a saber toothed forest cat peeled through the night air interrupting the rhythmic sounds of the insects.

Gently leaning forward so as to not disturb Marlen's sleep I placed more wood onto the fire building the flames up higher in an effort to ensure that the large cat would stay away.

Remaining ever vigilant I watched as the two moons of Phoria slowly wended their way into the sky. Just as on my first night on this planet I was amazed at the clarity of the night time sky and the number of stars that could be seen twinkling brightly against the black backdrop of the heavens. I took this as evidence that an industrial revolution had not yet occurred on this planet or if it had it was still in a small enough quantity that it had not negatively impacted the environment. The smog and light pollution of my own world obscured the view of many of the dimmer stars in the night sky.

Beginning to drift into a half sleep, that semiconscious state where you are not fully asleep but at the same time not fully awake and aware I was still able to hear the things that were going on around us but still gain a measure of rest. While I would have preferred slipping into a full blown slumber I could not take the chance that the fire would die down and leave us unprotected from the animals of the night. At all cost I must stay awake to protect Marlen.

As Phoria's largest moon crested the midnight sky and started its descent Marlen awoke and stretched. Looking at me she said, "You need to get some sleep Jack. We have a long way to travel tomorrow before we will reach the coast. You rest and I will stand guard and keep the fire burning."

With her gentle coaxing I slid my long sword over to her and allowed myself to slide deeper and deeper into that slumbering sleep that I so desired.

I do not know how long I slept but I was awakened by the sizzling sound and tantalizing aroma of cooking meat. Opening my eyes I could see the predawn light beginning to spread throughout the sky. Looking at Marlen I saw her tending the fire over which was spitted portions of a large snake. Instantly regaining my faculties I immediately jumped to the conclusion that Marlen had left the safety of the fire in order to obtain food for us.

Noticeably upset I asked her about it. "Did you leave the safety of the fire?" I asked.

With a big smile she calmly responded and said, "Relax Jack, I have not left the fire."

Confused I asked, "Where did you get the snake?"

"It came to us," she said.

"What do you mean came to us?" I asked.

"While you slept the snake slithered in close to the fire seeking the warmth. Taking advantage of the opportunity and your long sword I put it out if its misery and turned it into breakfast for us," she said.

Her resourcefulness amazed me. Somehow along the way I had forgotten that she was a native of this savage planet and was not the helpless princess that I had made her out to be in my mind. She obviously had a lot more survival skills than I had given her credit for and was likely better suited to survive in this hostile environment than I currently was.

Admonishing me for my over-protectiveness she clearly pointed out that she was able to take care of herself and any doubt that I may have had melted with the aroma of the cooking snake.

She directed me to sit down and eat. "You must eat Jack," she said. "You need to keep your strength up if we are to reach the coast today and I am not able to carry you if you should fail to keep up." With that she laughed wryly and handed me a portion of the cooked snake.

Feeling put in my place I sat down and did as she bid. Beginning to chew on the meat that she had given me I was surprised that it had much better flavor than the meat from the antelope type creature that we had eaten before. Evidently the snake had enough fat in its body to actually create some flavor while it was cooking.

As I ate I asked Marlen to forgive me for being so protective. I needed her to know that I only wanted to ensure that she was safe.

She responded gently, "that is okay Jack just remember that I would do the same thing for you."

Feeling rested and with full stomachs we again set out on our trek for the coast. The thick forest grew ever thinner the farther we travelled and eventually turned into rolling coastal foothills. Making our way through the thigh high grass we travelled up and down the hills continually making our way to the northwest.

As the sun reached midday we crested the top of a large hill and could clearly see the ocean in the distance. Blue expanses of water rolled on to the horizon.

With growing excitement we pushed on anxious to reach the sea. After another hour of travelling up and down the hills we reached a high bluff overlooking a wide expanse of sandy beach below. Just offshore was a barrier reef that protected the beach from the onrushing tidal surges that battled to pull the beach away. High up on the bluff we tried to find a way to get down. Looking down on the beach it seemed as far away as ever. We began to travel south paralleling the beach while we continued to look for a path that would lead us down. I would have given anything for a length of stout rope that we could use to rappel down.

After travelling south for what seemed to be miles but in all actuality probably only measured half a mile at the most we came upon a trail that led out of the tall grass and into a cut between two hills. The path looked to be well worn by the hooves of animals making their way down to the beach to lick at the salt deposited by the surf. Turning again to the west we followed the path into the cut.

The path narrowed between two cliffs and squeezing through we stopped on the edge and surveyed the sheer drop to the beach below. The height was intimidating but the overpowering desire to reach that water bolstered our courage and we continued along the path. Descending rapidly along the cliff face to the south of the cut the path was barely wide enough to support our feet. With our faces pressed against the cliff we made our way one step at a time closer to the beach. In many places we clung to the path with the tips of our toes and with scratching fingers struggled to find hand holds.

After many long minutes of strenuous effort we reached the soft sand and sitting down hard I lay back breathing heavy. Marlen dropped down next to me and there we lay trying to catch our breath and willing our hands and feet to stop shaking. The physical effort expended descending the cliff had pushed our bodies to the limit and I did not even want to move.

We lay there on the dry sand for a full twenty minutes before we had recovered enough to get up. Rising Marlen reached her hand down to help me to my feet. Hand in hand we walked down to the edge of the surf where stabbing my sword deep into the sand we waded in and together fell face first into the cold water.

Chapter Nine

The Beach

Emerging from the cold water of the ocean surf I instantly felt as if the sweat, grime and weariness of our travel that day had been washed away. With a splash Marlen popped to the surface of the water next to me. As she stood up the sun scintillated off the rivulets of water that ran down over her ample bosom. In that very instant right there I wanted to take her in my arms and declare my love to her forever. Yet instinct told me that the time still was not right. So instead of wrapping her in my love I lay backwards into the water with a splash and let the low surf roll over me.

I felt Marlen grab my hand as I lay in the surf relaxing. Regaining my footing on the sandy bottom I stood up. "What is the matter?" I asked questioningly.

"Come, we must not tarry in the surf too long," she said.

A bit confused I asked her why.

"Just trust me Jack," she said. "We must not stay in the water for very long. The creatures of the sea will come soon."

Having no idea what she was talking about I trusted to her native instinct and decided that the wisest thing to do until I knew more about these sea creatures was to follow her lead. Hand-in-hand we walked out of the surf and back onto the dry sand.

Pulling my long sword from the sand I placed it over my right shoulder and turning slowly surveyed the beach. Looking first to the north I could see no prominent features of land jutting into the sea. The beach faded around to the northeast. Expanses of white sand and the occasional grove of palm trees framed the base of the cliff as far as I could see. Turning to the south the beach continued on for what I estimated to be about ten miles then turned to the southwest. At the far extreme of my vision the coastline appeared to end and turned back towards the south and out of view. Since Pendak lay to the south we began to move in that direction.

Still having a few hours of daylight left I wanted to get as far down the beach and away from the Cliffside trail as we could before we stopped to set up camp for the evening. There had been ample evidence along the access trail that many animals used it as a path to reach the beach. While I had no idea what animals had been using the trail I could only assume that if the prey animals were using it then so to would the predators.

~ 99 ~

A half mile to the south of our location I could see a thick grove of palm trees that stretched from the high water mark in the sand to the base of the cliffs above. From this distance the grove appeared to have everything that we would need to fabricate both shelter and fire for the evening.

As we headed toward the grove of palm trees sea birds could be seen soaring effortlessly low over the surf. They darted in and out of the waves and occasionally would dive head-long into the water and bobbing to the surface with small fish in their beaks they would gulp them down their throats before again taking flight.

Scattered sporadically throughout the soft white sand were the cast off shells of small crustaceans. About the size of my open hand they very closely resembled the horseshoe crabs of my own Earth. Among those were also the empty shells of small clams. They were not large, perhaps two inches across the shell but if a person were to gather enough of them they would make for a very fulfilling meal. My mouth watered at the thought of having a seafood meal for dinner and brought back memories of my youth gathering clams from the sand and among the rocks with my family.

We arrived at the grove of palm trees without having seen another animal along the beach. The wind-blown sand obscured any sign that predators had travelled this way and left me wary of what I may find hiding within the grove.

Surveying the grove of trees I realized that they were date palms. While I would have preferred coconuts for their flavor and nutritional value I was not in any position to be choosy and dates would go wonderfully with seafood.

Quietly we entered the grove of trees and began to thread our way through them. Marlen staying close to my heels as we warily searched the grove for any signs of life. Working our way to the base of the cliff we then paralleled it. Midway across the grove at the base of the cliff was a small stream of water seeping down the cliff face. The water pooled in a small basin before being absorbed by the sand. Dropping to my knees I tasted the crystal clear water. It had a fresh clean flavor and thankfully was free of salt. My concern that the springs close proximity to the sea would have imparted a saltiness that would have made it undrinkable was unfounded. Informing Marlen that the water was safe we knelt beside each other and taking our time we drank our fill. Not having a container to carry water, I would have to devise something before we moved south tomorrow. Once we had satisfied our thirst we continued along the base of the cliff until we had reached the southern edge of the grove and turning back to the west we moved back through trees to reach the beach where we had entered.

Driftwood lay scattered everywhere throughout the grove. Feeling secure that the grove was empty we both collected firewood as we went. With an armload of wood I knelt down to gather another large piece and as I grasped it I froze in place. Turning slowly I directed Marlen to kneel down and be very still and quiet. In the sand next to the piece of wood that I had in my hand was the unmistakable paw print of a large forest cat.

Looking around through the trees the hair on the back of my neck stood up as I could feel eyes watching me. I needed to locate where the cat was hiding before it attacked. If not it would be too late. Scanning every shadow and piled up bunch of driftwood I searched in earnest for any sign of the great cat. Finally amidst the shadow of a small grouping of trees I caught the tiniest glint of sunlight off the over-sized canines of the cat. It lay quietly in the shadows watching us. We very nearly had walked right into it and would have had no warning before it had pounced for the kill. It was by the merest of chances that I had seen the track in the sand. Very faint and without clarity I could very easily have overlooked it and paid the price with my life, as well as, Marlen's.

Very quietly I explained to Marlen what I had discovered and directed her eyesight to the hiding place of the great black cat. We had walked a big circle around the cat when we had entered into the grove it was sheer luck that we had not come directly upon it as we meandered through the trees.

Still kneeling down in the sand I directed Marlen to drop her firewood and rise slowly. Following suit I dropped the firewood that I had in my arms and stood as well. So too did the great cat. Abandoning all attempts at stealth the cat stepped clear of the shadows and started stalking its way towards us.

Keeping myself between Marlen and the saber toothed cat I readied my long sword and crouched into a fighting position in preparation for the attack that I knew was coming. Continuing its approach the great cat crouched low in preparation to spring. The one advantage that I did have over the cat was that I knew it would try to sink its great teeth into my neck on its initial attack and I was ready.

Trusting to my instincts I stepped forward to close the gap between us just as it sprang and left its feet heading towards me. I hoped that by shortening the distance between us at the very instant that the cat leaped it would not have an opportunity to change its direction until it landed. While the cat was in midair I struck like a viper. Thrusting at the cat with my long sword as we came together the keen edge sliced a deep gash across the animal's well-muscled shoulder. Roaring in pain it leaped to the side trying to avoid my blade.

Pressing my advantage to prevent the cat regaining its footing I sprang towards it once again slashing at its neck with my sword. The cat leaped back again to avoid my blade as it swiped out at me with its razor sharp claws slicing four shallow slits across the calf of my left leg. Blood began to pour down my calf and around my ankle but I couldn't tell how deep the cuts were nor did I have time to evaluate the seriousness of my wounds. This great predator would not allow me that luxury and I needed to dispatch the cat quickly and tend to my wound.

Remaining on the offensive I slashed and stabbed at the cat repeatedly to keep it off balance. With an awkward sideways spring the cat leaped towards me lashing out with its paws in an effort to decapitate me and take me out of the fight. Sidestepping quickly I ran my long sword through its ribcage. The blade penetrated through to the far side of the ribs then pulled free from its body as it leaped away more in shock than in pain. Finding its footing it prepared for one last leap but before it could do so the powerful heart of the beast that would normally give it a strong advantage in any encounter proved to be its undoing. As it crouched to spring its massive heart pumped blood out both sides of its body and quickly emptied its life into the sand. Staggering the great cat fell over onto its side, dead.

Falling to my knees I sat breathing heavily as Marlen approached and immediately began tending to the wounds on my calf. To get the wound to stop bleeding Marlen packed it with the white sand and bound it up with fibers from a palm frond that lay nearby. Not sure how well the sand would help I could feel the coagulating blood around my ankle that had mixed with sand begin to stiffen like a coarse plaster. I'm sure this wasn't the ideal dressing but it would have to work until I could get to the water and clean it out and properly dress it. Thanking her for her assistance we again gathered the armloads of firewood that we had dropped earlier and started making our way back through the trees to the ocean side of the grove.

Upon reaching the beach we piled the firewood between two palms and then headed for the surf. I needed to clean the wound on my leg as quickly as possible. While the claws of the great cat had sliced cleanly through the skin there was no accounting for the myriad of germs that those claws contained. In this savage world I could ill afford to be laid up with an infection in my leg.

Walking knee deep into the surf I scrubbed the coagulated blood and sand from the wound. The salty water stung as it washed through the cuts but I endured the pain because I knew that it was washing away the contaminants with it. Surveying the wound I found it to be more superficial than dangerous. The cat's claws had not penetrated deep enough to sever any major blood vessels or arteries. Back on Earth the flight surgeon would have insisted upon stitching it up, to cause me more pain I think, but it would heal fine without stitches. In the end I would have four parallel scars running horizontally across my calf but I could chalk that up to my first battle scars on this planet. I expected that there would be many more before I was done.

With the wound on my leg taken care of I decided that it was time to address our food situation. Pointing to the array of shells that scattered the sand I asked Marlen where they could be found. Once I clarified for her that I meant the live animals and not just the empty shells she led my by the hand out of the surf until we were standing on just wet sand. After just a few minutes of searching around on the wet sand she pointed out a small divot at her feet. I had a hard time seeing what it was that she was pointing out to me but after a closer inspection I was able to discern a nearly imperceptible dimple in the sand. After I acknowledged that I had seen the dimple she dug her fingertips into the sand on either side of the dimple. Bringing her hands together grasping the sand she lifted them revealing a squirming mass. The articulated legs of a small crab reaching in an attempt to dig itself deeper into the sand could be seen.

Noticeably impressed with her capture of the crab I started to look around the wet sand as well to see if I could find any of the hidden creatures. It took me much longer than Marlen but finally I was able to identify one of the small dimples. Following her example I dug my fingertips into the sand on either side of the dimple just as she had. Closing my hands together I was greeted with the wiggling movement of life that heralded my success. It didn't take us too much searching and we soon had a half dozen crabs collected for our dinner.

Still curious about the small clams I pointed at one of the empty clam shells and asked her about them. It took a little longer to find the clams but she finally pointed out another small divot in the sand. This time though there was a small star in the base of the divot. Repeating her crab catching skills she soon produced one of the small clams. Smashing the clam against my long sword she broke it open and pulled forth the animals body. Holding it up for me to see she pointed out the tip of the clam's neck that was clearly in the shape of the small star that I had seen in the dimple. That was good to know since in my mind I was questioning how she had known the difference between the dimple created by the buried crab and the dimple created by the clam. Her clam anatomy lesson had cleared that up for me.

With a bit more searching and digging we had rounded out our meal. Now it was incumbent upon me to get a fire going to both cook our food and provide a measure of protection for the evening.

Returning to where we had placed the firewood I began to prepare the fire. Taking my long sword Marlen pried loose a piece of dry bark from the nearest palm tree and using the hilt of the sword smashed the bark separating the fibers. When she had finished she handed me a handful of stringy bark fibers that resembled a bird's nest. Using the same hand drill method that I had used before, I quickly coaxed a burning ember to life and nestled it among the strands of bark. Blowing gently I breathed life into the ember until it burst into flame then placing the flaming bark among the pile of driftwood I soon had a respectable fire going.

Other than the palm trees there was not a lot of cover to provide us refuge from the marauding animals of the night. To provide us some safety I built numerous small pieces of wood into a circle around our camp. Transferring flames from the main fire I soon had a ring of fire built up as a safety barrier while we slept.

I took care of the fires while Marlen placed the crabs and clams onto a bed of coals that she had pulled from the original fire. It wasn't long before the cherry red coals had turned the crabs a bright orange color and the clams had all opened up with their muscles relaxing as they cooked. When they appeared to be fully cooked Marlen, using two pieces of driftwood like large chopsticks, pulled them from the fire and placed them onto a green palm frond that she gathered from nearby.

Stepping clear of the ring of fire I found a nearby palm from which hung a large bundle of ripened dates. Using the long sword I sliced the bundle loose and carrying it over my shoulder rejoined Marlen. We now had our meal complete and sitting side-by-side looking out over the ocean we partook of the feast that we had prepared.

Enjoying our repast we sat quietly and watched as the sun descended below the horizon and as darkness set in we completed our seafood dinner. Lying back I relaxed as the warmth of the sun baked sand penetrated my body. Marlen snuggled down beside me and placing her head on my shoulder we made ourselves comfortable and settled in for the night.

Chapter Ten

Unwanted Company

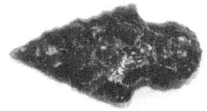

At sunrise I opened my eyes and looked up into a clear blue sky. Marlen was still sleeping soundly with her head resting on my shoulder and a leg thrown over mine. Lying there quietly so that I didn't wake her I held her in my arms and enjoyed the warmth of the morning sun beating down upon us.

Waking periodically throughout the night I had kept our safety fire going. It had been a quiet night without any sign of danger and evidently the saber toothed cat that I had killed had been the lord and master of this grove of palms and had kept all other predators away. If they had known that the great cat had met his demise I expect that we would have had more company during the night.

Enjoying a sense of fulfillment holding Marlen close to my chest I slept very well during the night. We had needed the rest to recover from the great distance that we had traveled since we had left Ronar.

The warmth of the morning sun continued to increase and was becoming uncomfortably hot. Beginning to get thirsty I thought about the cool spring at the base of the cliff. Marlen's head resting upon my shoulder was restricting the circulation of blood to my hand and my arm began to tingle as if being poked with a thousand needles and I needed to move.

She looked so beautiful and peaceful as she slept and I hated to wake her. Taking just a few more minutes I absorbed the beauty of her face. Her olive tanned skin highlighted her luscious pink lips. Her perfectly spaced eyes were lined with long curly lashes and led the eye down the length of her well sculpted nose. She was beautiful.

Craning my neck forward I kissed her gently on the forehead. She snuggled closer to me and after a few seconds opened her eyes.

"Good morning my love," I said rather boldly.

"Good morning," she responded with a smile. "We have slept long, but I feel much better."

"Me too," I said. "I could use some cold water though and we need to get moving as soon as we can."

"Yes," she agreed. "We still have a long way to travel to reach Pendak."

"Well let's start with some water and then we will determine the next leg of our journey," I said.

Agreeing we both sat up and stretched the stiffness from our bodies. Panic spread over me instantly as I looked south and about a half mile down the beach I saw nosed into the sand and resting at the edge of the surf a wooden ship. Leaping to my feet I grabbed Marlen by the hand and pulled her into the cover of the trees.

From the security of our camouflaged position we watched the ship and tried to ascertain if our presence had been noted by those onboard. The ship had a high prow that was carved into the head of a dragon. The stern was half as high and appeared to be the dragon's tail. There was a single mast located mid-ship with a sail secured neatly to the yardarm. Down the side of the ship were attached circular shields. They were brightly painted with reds and yellows and had large metal bolsters affixed to their centers.

Standing near the bow of the ship were five men. Their clothing was unfamiliar to anything that I had seen on this planet thus far. They wore tunics of woven linen and some were dyed an olive green color and others brown. They all wore baggy white pants with reddish colored leggings wrapped from their ankles to their knees and short leather boots on their feet. Around the waist of each was belted a scabbard with a short sword and on their heads sat shiny metal domed helmets.

The five men appeared to be watching the southern end of the grove of trees in which we hid as if waiting for someone. The ship was too large to be effectively sailed by the five men that we could see. These must be the ones left to guard the vessel and the rest of the crew must be in the grove gathering food and water.

The ship bore a strong resemblance to the ancient Viking long ships of my home world. Remembering back to the history lessons of my youth I estimated that the crew of the ship was at least twenty people. Eight shields were attached to the gunwale of the ship and associated with each shield was a hole that measured about eight inches in diameter. These holes were oarlocks and based on these numbers it would take sixteen people to man the oars used to propel the ship when the wind was not favorable. It would take one man to steer the vessel and at least two to attend to the sails. Lastly would be the captain of the vessel whose job would be to give the orders that would direct the actions of the crew and control the movements of the ship. If my numbers were accurate there would have to be at least fifteen crew members unaccounted for and foraging within the grove.

Turning my attention from the ship and its guards to the surrounding trees I scanned from left to right looking for any sign of movement among the boles of the palms. Seeing none I quietly shared my concerns with Marlen. "I believe that there are at least fifteen men here in the grove with us. We need to find cover and remain out of sight until they leave," I said.

"They seek water," Marlen replied quietly. "These are warriors from Valcot. My people trade with them regularly for weapons and armor. This vessel however is a warship not a trader."

"Is Valcot allied to Pendak?" I asked.

"We are not at war with Valcot but we are no allies either," she said venomously. "The Valcot are sea-going raiders that sail up and down the coasts of Astor preying upon small villages and other ships. The distant location of Valcot on the northeastern coast keeps our trading relationship civil and makes war between our two cities unlikely."

"So asking them for passage to Pendak would not be wise?" I asked.

"Not wise at all Jack," she answered. "The Valcot trade in slaves as well as weapons and the minute they are aware of our presence we will be slapped into chains and sold into slavery."

I had no intention of allowing Marlen to fall prey to these slavers from Valcot. Leading her by the hand I began to quietly sneak through the grove looking for a location that would allow us to remain hidden. We had moved into the grove only about twenty yards when I stopped short at the sound of a sword hitting against a palm. Immediately dropping to the ground we peered in the direction of the sound trying to determine what had caused it. Farther back in the trees I could barely make out the shapes of three men as they gathered dates from the trees. Moving slowly to a tuft of low palmettos we took refuge from the sight of the men. Our camouflage would not last long as the men worked their way closer to us harvesting dates. We had to move before they spotted us.

Peeking around the edge of the palmettos we waited until the attention of the warriors was directed away from us. Once all three warriors were looking elsewhere we moved from the cover of one tuft of palmettos to another. We needed to get to the north end of the grove and as far away from the ship as possible. The farther north we could get the less chance there was that any of the warriors would stumble upon our hiding place as they worked their way back to the ship. We didn't get very far when the yells of warriors made it clear that our efforts at stealth were no longer necessary.

Looking back I could see that the three were now in pursuit of us and holding Marlen's hand we broke into a dead run. Zigzagging our way through the palms we attempted to put some distance between us and the warriors. Tripping in the sand Marlen stumbled and fell and as I helped her to regain her footing I could see that the three were gaining on us rapidly and eluding them would not be possible. Drawing my long sword I took up a position between the warriors and Marlen. They may capture us but I was not going down without a fight. My cold steel would taste their blood before they ever put their chains on us.

The three warriors split as they approached. One came directly at me while the other two moved to flank us on either side. Marlen had backed against a tree and I stood in front of her prepared to do battle. The warrior in front of me stopped short and began to speak. "Drop your sword and it will go much easier for you," he said.

"Not today my friend," I replied. "We are no threat to you. Let us be on our way and you may live to see tomorrow."

The three warriors laughed hysterically. I failed to see the humor in my words and did not let their overconfidence concern me. The warrior in front approached and striking downward at my head with his short sword attempted to remove it from my shoulders. Blocking the blow with my long sword I reached out and planted my left fist to the right side of his chin. He crumpled face first into the sand. As I turned to confront the warrior to my right the one on my left moved in to attack me from behind. Before he could strike a blow Marlen threw a handful of sand directly into his face. He began yelling and struggling to wipe the sand from his eyes. With two men out of the fight I devoted my concentration to the one remaining warrior.

Stepping in close to him I feigned a cut to his left arm and when he raised his sword to block it I quickly changed the direction of my blade pricking his thigh with the tip of my long sword. He became angry that I had drawn blood so easily and began slashing and cutting furiously with his short sword. My long sword gave me a distinct advantage over the reach of his short sword and I blocked his thrusts and cuts effortlessly. Reaching out I pricked his left shoulder drawing blood, then his right. It was clear that even with my limited skill I was the better swordsman. My opponent was beginning to get winded and his breathing was heavy. I could have dispatched him at any time but I was finding it hard to kill one that I had so severely mastered with the sword. His arms were tiring and he was finding it harder and harder to hold his sword up to defend himself. Letting his sword slip low one too many times I took advantage of the opening and striking him a blow to the side of his head with the flat of my sword I put him on the ground, alive but unconscious.

Turning with my sword raised I barely managed to deflect a blow aimed at my back from the remaining warrior. Managing to clear the sand from his eyes he had rejoined the fight. As I moved in closer to engage him I heard a yell come from deeper within the grove.

"Halt, that is enough," the voice said clearly. My last opponent immediately lowered his sword and stepped back away from me. Obviously the order had come from his captain. The sound of our clashing swords had drawn the attention of the rest of the warriors and they had all moved towards the sounds. I kept my eyes glued to the warrior that I had just been fighting. The other two warriors that I had knocked out had regained consciousness and made their way to their feet. Again clearly outnumbered I lowered my sword and turned to look in the direction of the voice. As I turned Marlen joined me and grabbing my left elbow stood close by my side. Looking down into her eyes I flashed a futile smile. She smiled back then her gaze drifted in the direction of the voice and her eyes went wide in amazement.

Quickly looking to see what had shocked her so, I caught sight of the leader of these warriors and my jaw dropped in amazement and disbelief. There before me walking through the trees was Sodan.

Approaching us Sodan ordered the men to stand down and return to gathering provisions. They hesitated not knowing what to make of the situation. Again Sodan barked, "back to work dogs, these are friends not our enemies."

Scowling with venom in their eyes the three warriors that I had bested reluctantly walked off and returned to gathering dates.

Sodan came forward and smiling broadly embraced both Marlen and I. "I see you two managed to avoid the Ronar and stay alive," he said.

"Sodan I thought you were dead. The last I saw you were surrounded by warriors. How did you get free?" I asked.

Laughing and patting me on the shoulder he replied, "There were only ten so I took it easy on them. Actually a number of warriors of Pendak showed up and drew their attention away. While they were busy I slipped over the wall and headed west towards the coast. I happened upon this ship and her crew and was taken onboard," he said.

"They treat you as their captain, how can that be?" I asked.

Chuckling again Sodan responded, "Jack I am not their captain I am their prince."

Marlen and I were both taken aback. We had both believed that Sodan was a common warrior from Valcot. Never would I have guessed that he was a prince.

A little confused I asked, "You are a prince of Valcot? You mean heir to the throne type prince?"

Obviously finding humor in my confusion Sodan responded, "Yes Jack heir to the throne type prince, although the lines of succession run deep in Valcot. I have two brothers that stand to inherit before I do but that works in my favor because it frees me up to enjoy the world without all the responsibilities of ruling a city."

As we talked we made our way towards the spring at the base of the cliff. Arriving at the crystal clear water there were two men filling wooden casks. Kneeling down next to them we drank our fill and then accompanied Sodan as we walked through the grove towards the waiting ship.

"What is your destination?" Sodan asked.

"I have promised Marlen that I would return her safely to her father's court so our destination lies to the south," I replied.

"Travel to the south will be impossible without a boat," he stated. Pointing with his finger towards the south, "Just around the point there the great swamp begins and a person cannot travel by foot."

"Will you and your crew take us to Pendak?" I asked.

"Sorry my friend, we cannot," he responded. "This ship is a man of war and as such would draw unwanted attention from the navy of Pendak. You are welcome to sail with us to Valcot and I will personally accompany you on a trading vessel to the city of Pendak."

"What do you think Marlen?" I asked.

"I think that the trip will take much longer but at the same time be much safer," she replied. "I think that we should accept the hospitality of Sodan."

Replying to Sodan, "Very well my friend we will accompany you."

"Wonderful," he responded enthusiastically. "We will set sail as soon as we have finished taking on provisions."

Having not yet eaten Marlen and I walked to the edge of the grove and found a hanging bunch of ripe dates and cut them loose. Sitting in the shade of the palms we watched as the captain of the ship barked orders to the crew as they returned with the food and water that they had foraged. When the last small group of men had returned Sodan called out and waved to us. It was time to set sail. We returned to the side of the ship and climbed over the gunwale and took our places in the stern next to the steersman and Sodan. The crew pushed the vessel clear of the sand and then piled aboard. Taking their places the men deployed their oars and began to backstroke the ship into deeper water. Once clear of the surf they changed direction and began to propel the ship forward. With a rhythmic splash, pull, lift and push the crew moved the ship at great speed into the open ocean.

At an order from the captain the crew shipped the oars and unfurled the sail from the yardarm. Securing the sheets and the braces to hold the sail firm it began to fill with the heavy wind of the ocean breeze and the ship leaped forward with a jerk. Settling in on the decking at the rear of the vessel Sodan took a seat next to us. The crew lounged across the deck from bow to stern. With the ship under sail the oarsmen were without an immediate job so they assisted where they were needed to trim sail and ensure that all lines remained fast.

Sodan spoke loudly to be heard above the wind and splashing of the water past the hull. "It will take us a day and half to reach Valcot. Until then rest and enjoy the ride." Leaning back against the gunwale Marlen and I rested as the misty spray of the salt water kicked up by the bow tempered the heat of the sun as it beat down upon us. We were now safely on our way to Pendak by way of Valcot.

Chapter Eleven

Underway

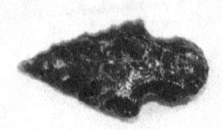

The ship made really good time as a strong wind out of the west propelled it forward. The square rigged sail remained taut as the force of the air whistled through the rigging. The fine mist splashed off the bow and kept us wet most of the day. Fortunately the sun remained hot and with no shade to deflect it we stayed comfortably warm even though we were soaked with salt water. Remaining low within the hull of the ship we tried to stay clear of the crew as they moved about attending to their duties. Often Sodan would come and sit with us and I would talk with him about the details of the vessel. While I had spent lots of time on boats back on earth this was my first time to have ever sailed on a long ship. I was fascinated with the details of the vessels construction and the machinations of the crew that made it sail. Sodan promised to go into more detail about the vessels sailed by his people while we were in Valcot.

With the sun getting low on the horizon the crew furled the sail and lashed it to the yardarm. Deploying the oars they began to row towards the shore. Sodan was sitting with us and I took this opportunity to ask him why we were moving to shore. His explanation was brief and made sense.

"We are pulling into shore for the night to allow the crew to rest and walk on solid ground," he said. "We normally do not sail through the night unless we are at war or executing a nighttime raid. When the moons are full it is easier to navigate at night but since we are in no hurry we will spend the night safely ashore."

Understanding the wisdom of this choice I acknowledged the sense of the decision. Besides I knew that Marlen and I both could use some time on shore to stretch our legs and freshen up.

The crew rowed strong through the surf and we soon felt the forward momentum stop as the keel sliced into the sand. A number of the crew jumped over the gunwale into knee deep water and began to pull the ship further up onto the sand. After setting anchors into the sand to ensure that the ship did not drift with the tide the crew began to offload the items that would be needed to prepare a beachside camp for the night.

A short distance up the beach from where we had grounded was a small grove of palms. Half of the crew set up lean to type shelters while the remainder entered the grove to gather firewood.

Jumping over the gunwale and into the water we made our way onto solid ground where we stretched our stiffened muscles to try to limber up the cramps that had set in while we had sat aboard the ship. Sodan joined us on the wet sand.

"I have placed some leather sleeping sacks in the stern of the ship," he said. "For your protection I would like for you and the princess to sleep aboard tonight. The crew will sleep on the beach and protect the ship."

Thanking him I asked what we could do to help get the crew settled in for the night. He responded that once they had the security fires built everyone would eat and then taking guard shifts sleep for the night. Well the one thing that I knew we could do was to help gather some food. So in the waning sunlight we set about gathering crabs from beneath the sand in the surf line. By the time that we had gathered thirty crabs or so the rest of the crew had returned with the firewood and had strategically lit fires in a half circle around the bow of the ship. Returning to the inner circle of the fire we shared out the crabs with the crew and finding a spot near one of the fires began to prepare our meal for the evening.

Thanking us for our contribution to the crew Sodan joined us to eat.

"How much longer before we reach Valcot," I asked Sodan curiously.

"We have another full day of sailing," he said. "This time tomorrow we will be eating comfortably at my father's table."

Defaulting to my main concern I asked about passage to Pendak. "How long do you think that it will take for us to book passage on a trading ship to return Marlen to her home?"

"It should take us no more than a week to find a vessel heading back south. At the most a fortnight," he replied. "Once we find a captain bound for Pendak it will take another two weeks underway to reach the southern peninsula."

The timeframe that he outlined was much longer than I would have preferred but under the circumstances would have to do. The important thing was being able get Marlen home.

It was fully dark now and after a couple hours quizzing Sodan on the ships of Valcot, his city and his people, and as much as he could tell me about Astor we bid him a good night and crawled back aboard the ship. Making our way to the stern we found the sleeping sacks that Sodan had left for us and crawling inside of them reclined on the deck.

"I'm sorry that it will take so long to get you home," I told Marlen apologetically.

"Do not be concerned Jack," she replied. "I don't really care how long it takes as long as I am with you."

"Nevertheless Marlen, even though I feel the same way and am happy wherever I am as long as I am with you," I said. "I promised you that I would get you safely home to your father and that is exactly what I intend to do."

"And I have no doubt that you will do just that," she replied with confidence.

"Tell me about Pendak," I urged her. Since that was her home I anticipated spending a lot of time there and the more I knew about her city the better I would be able to fit in and be accepted by her father and his court.

"Pendak is a beautiful city," she began. "It sits at the southern tip of the Noral peninsula. The peninsula is protected from attack to the north by a great high wall that runs from coast to coast. The city itself is surrounded by a rock palisade wall and the land in between the city and the peninsula wall is cultivated farmland. As a young girl my father would take me on rides through the countryside to the wall and back. Stopping along the way we would visit with the farmers and would often be invited for lunch with their families. I envied them their small cozy hovels that they called home. They just seemed so much warmer and lived in than the large drafty castle where I grew up."

"That sounds beautiful Marlen," I said. "I can't wait to see it for myself."

"I am looking forward to showing you around the city when we get there," she replied. "The cobbled city streets all lead to the great square surrounding the palace. The streets are lined with homes and shops, and every manner of building that you can think of. The people of Pendak are friendly and greet you with a warm heartfelt good day as you pass on the streets."

"Pendak sounds like a wonderful place," I responded. "It sounds like quite a contrast from the savagery of Ronar."

"The two cities are like night and day Jack," she replied proudly. "My father is a just ruler and the people of Pendak love him."

"I have never heard mention of your mother," I said.

She replied somberly, "I never knew my mother. She died in childbirth when I was born. My father tried hard to compensate for her loss but I was raised more by the chamber maids of the castle than by anyone else."

"I'm sorry," I replied genuinely saddened. "I did not know."

"That is okay Jack," she said. "I regret that I never had the opportunity to know her but have made peace with that fact long ago. We have a busy day tomorrow let us rest now, good night my Jack."

"Good night my princess, sleep well," I responded quietly. Laying back on the deck I watched as the two moons of Phoria climbed into the sky and observed the different congregations of night time stars. Among all the constellations that I could see not one was familiar to me. For all of my life I had the security of the big dipper in the sky to guide my direction. Now all I could see were nameless stars dotting a blackened canvas. I would have to remember to ask Sodan more about the constellations. One of them had to be the equivalent of the Earth's big dipper for use in navigation.

The crew of the ship was now quiet. A crackling sound could be heard as the flames of the fire slowly consumed the wood. An orange hue of light silhouetted the dragon on the prow as the firelight struggled to illuminate as far as it could. The last thing I remember before drifting off to sleep was the impression that the dragon headed prow moved as the flickering light appeared to animate it then sleep finally overtook me.

The sound of activity roused me to full wakefulness. The half-light of dawn was spreading its way across the sky as the crew stowed their gear onto the ship. The night passed quietly but all too quickly. The security of having twenty armed men standing guard had allowed me to sleep deeply and I had awakened well rested.

Marlen was already up and about. She stood with Sodan near the mast watching as the crew made the final preparations to get underway. Once all the gear was properly stowed and made fast the crew pushed the ship clear of the soft sand and scrambled to their places at the oars.

Crawling out of the leather sleeping sack I stretched my back and legs. Reaching over the side of the ship I scooped up cold saltwater with my hands and splashed it onto my face to wash the sleep from my eyes. Enjoying a strong cup of coffee when I awoke in the morning was something that I really missed. Marlen seeing that I was awake came and stood by my side while the crew transitioned from the oars to the sail.

"Today we will reach Valcot," she said. "And then we will be one step closer to Pendak."

Smiling at her I placed my arm around her shoulder and pulled her body close to mine and looked out over the rolling swell towards the horizon wondering what else lay out there beyond that thin line in the distance.

Sodan approached and placing his hand on my shoulder said, "Today my friend we will arrive in Valcot. The canals, the great market place, and the cold ale await us. When we arrive I will treat you to the finest meal and ale that you have ever had."

"That sounds great my friend," I said. The thought of the meal and cold ale reminded me of my early days as a pilot flying aboard aircraft carriers. My mouth watered at the memories of that first meal after the ship pulled into port. After months of eating mass-produced food for every meal I had developed the routine of finding the first steak house I could find and enjoyed the largest steak I could buy and as I savored every last bite I washed it down with a cold beer. I was looking forward to arriving in Valcot.

Marlen and I took our positions in the stern and settled in to pass the time as we sailed throughout the day. Near noon the wind died down to a mere breeze and the forward progress of the ship began to slow. At an order from the captain the crew snapped to and began furling the sail. Once the sheet had been secured they took up their positions at the oars and with the rhythmic beat of a hide drum being tapped by a crew member in the bow they began to pull us closer towards Valcot.

Growing tired of the inactivity of sitting on the deck and waiting for time to pass I rose to my feet and approached the crew member manning the rearmost oar on the starboard side. Of all the crew members this one had to be the first one that I had bested back in the large palm grove. He looked up at me with a scowl as if challenging my presence near the oarsman.

Speaking firmly I declared my intentions to take my turn at the oar. With a low laugh he directed me to join him. Taking up a position outboard of him I grabbed hold of the oar and began to follow his lead synchronizing the movement of the oar with the rhythmic cadence of the drum. Once he felt that I had learned the movements and was in synch with the rhythm of the drum he let loose of the oar. Holding his position next to me he observed closely to ensure that I was continuing to operate the oar correctly.

The mindless rhythm overtook me and my thoughts began to wander as my body developed the repetitive memory of the motions. Dip, pull then lift and push, again and again I repeated that motion until the movements were automatic.

Many of the crew manning the oars had seen me take up position next to the crewman. Initially the glances that they shot me were tainted with humor and quite possibly contempt that I should even try to hold my own with them at the oars. After the first hour of sweating under the load of the oar the blisters began to develop across the pads of my hands. The sweat seeped into the broken skin and stung but the looks from the crew had turned from contempt to looks of admiration. Over an hour into my turn at the oar I was continuing to hold my own and maintain the rhythm with the other oarsman. At the two hour mark the captain called a halt to the oars to allow the crew an opportunity to catch their breath. The wind was still light but the crew quickly unfurled the sail anyway. The forward momentum under the sail was slow but it was enough to allow the steersman to hold our heading.

After the oars had been stowed and the sail set the crew began to mill around the deck. More than one approached me and patted me on the back commending me for my efforts at the oars. Even those crewmen that I had made enemies of in the palm grove came forward and with a smile declared their truce with me as they acknowledged my efforts.

Returning to the stern I took up a position next to Marlen and Sodan to rest and catch my breath.

"Very well done Jack," Sodan commended. "A strong sign of a good leader is the willingness to dig in with the crew and get your hands dirty. By joining them at the oars you have bonded with them in a way that will guarantee that if you need their swords they will stand by you. Men will follow those that are not above walking in their boots and have earned their admiration. That level of respect cannot be commanded, it must be earned."

Marlen passed me a water skin and tipping it back I swallowed a great draught to quench my thirst. The water had a light hint of saltiness from being on the ship but it did not matter. My thirst was such that the water could have been laced with vinegar and I would still have swallowed it with relish.

The afternoon wind began to pick up and the ship once again began to move forward under the insistent push of the air. My body was beginning to stiffen from my effort at the oars and I stretched the muscles to keep them from binding up. Once I had limbered up I found a place against the gunwale in the stern and leaning back against the side of the ship rested while I watched the activities of the crew. Taking this opportunity I made a mental note of every action and movement of the crew that was needed to keep the ship upright and running smoothly across the long swell of the sea.

Paralleling the beach the steersman kept the ship just within sight of land. Keeping the cliffs that overlooked the beach in sight eliminated the need to use more traditional navigation aids. Although keeping the sun on the starboard bow would have sufficed to ensure that we were sailing in the appropriate direction it did not hurt to have more than one means of determining our heading.

Mid-afternoon the beach turned sharply away from us to the south. The steersman immediately took a ninety degree starboard tack and the ship slowly entered into a large harbor. Once we had cleared the point of the headland on the starboard side the propelling wind was blocked from pushing the ship forward. Again the sail was furled and secured to the yardarm and the oars were deployed. The crew pulled the ship ever deeper into the harbor and in the distance I could barely make out the masts of other ships. As we moved closer to the other ships I could just start to make out the silhouettes of buildings in the distance. The anticipation among the crew could be felt like electricity in the air as we closed the distance to the city.

Joining Sodan in the bow, Marlen and I both craned our necks around the dragon headed prow trying to catch the first glimpses of a city that neither of us had ever seen before. As we got closer it became easier to make out the details of the other ships and the city. People could be seen walking the decks of the ships as we drew near and passed them. Finally the full effect of the city came into view.

As we looked at the growing city with a sense of awe Sodan said proudly, "Welcome to Valcot."

Chapter Twelve

Valcot

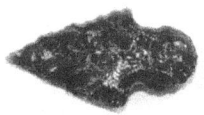

The mouth of a large canal could be seen directly ahead. It was spanned by a heavily fortified bridge. To either side of the bridge, running in both directions, was a high wall constructed of piled and cemented stones. The buildings of the city could be seen over the ramparts of the wall and the structures were a mix of both masonry and wooden construction.

The crew continued to propel the ship forward with the oars and my concern began to grow as we approached nearer to the bridge. It was evident that the height of the mast would not clear the bottom of the bridge yet Sodan appeared to not be worried. Maybe we would anchor off shore from the city and a smaller boat with no mast would be used to ferry us up the canal. My concern was answered as the captain barked out an order and the aft oarsmen, five from each side of the ship, pulled their oars in-board and stowed them. The remaining ten oarsmen continued to move the ship towards the city.

The ten crewmen, now free of their burden of propulsion, set about making preparations to lower the mast. The yardarm was lowered first. A block-and-tackle was used to raise and lower the yard with one half of the block attached to the yardarm while the other half was mounted high up on the mast. A line routed back and forth through the pulleys provided the necessary mechanical advantage for a minimum of manpower to raise and lower it. The end of the line had been secured to a cleat on the gunwale. Unfastening the end of the line four men began to slowly feed the line through the block mounted high on the mast and the yardarm slowly descended toward the deck. When it had reached the point where it was still the height of a full grown man from the deck, the remaining crewmen began to slowly turn the yard until it was parallel with the ship and once aligned with the keel the yard was lowered the rest of the way to the decking.

There were six shroud lines, three to port and three to starboard, that were used to keep the mast from shifting side to side. The forestay line ran from the top of the mast to a forestay rigging block in the bow. It was the tension on the forestay that kept the mast firmly locked into the socket in the keelson and against the mast fish. On the aft side of the mast was a large wooden wedge that forced the mast against the mast fish. The wedge served as a locking device to ensure the mast stayed firm in the upright position.

The wedge was knocked loose from its seat with a large wooden hammer and six crewmen manned the shroud lines while the remaining four manned the forestay line in the bow. Lowering the mast was a balance of allowing the mast to fall slowly towards the stern of the ship while maintaining enough side tension with the shroud lines to keep the mast centered on the deck. The four crewmen in the bow began to feed line into the forestay block and the top of the mast began to slowly descend towards the deck in the stern. The six crewmen manning the shroud lines slowly fed line through the shroud blocks while maintaining enough tension to keep the mast from straying too far to either side of the ship. In a matter of minutes the mast was nearing the deck and not a moment too soon as the ship passed below the fortified bridge.

Transiting beneath the bridge I could see on the underside the sharp points of an iron portcullis that had been raised and secreted deep within the brickwork of the bridge. The gate could be lowered during an attack to prevent seagoing assailants from entering the city by way of the canal.

Once inside the wall I could see that the city itself had been constructed utilizing the natural canals that transected a great marshland. Bridges spanned canals connecting one part of the city to another and it would have been virtually impossible to have moved the ship about the city without having first lowered the mast. Wooden piers lined both sides of the canal down which we slowly moved. Tied to the piers were many ships similar to the one on which we stood but wider and with more rounded lines depicting cargo vessels. Wooden carts pulled by small burro like animals moved down broad avenues that paralleled the canals. Men, women and children of all ages scattered the streets. Some were shopping at stands along the avenues, others were obviously on their way to somewhere else, and children darted to and fro playing the many games of tag and such that occupy the days of youth. All were dressed similar to the crew on the ship wearing tunics with cotton pants and leggings. The women however wore linen dresses fronted with small waist aprons.

The buildings were a mix of alternating wooden structures and sod houses. The crew waved and exchanged hails with people on the other ships and the shore as we passed.   Standing in the bow with Sodan, my arm draped around Marlen's shoulder, we took in the sights of the city of Valcot.

Veering hard to port the steersman guided the ship into the mouth of another canal that lead into the center of the city. To either side of the canal were shorter canals that angled away in the direction of our travel. These short finger canals were lined on both sides with vessels of war, long ships similar to the one we were on. Here were moored the fighting vessels of Valcot.

Nearing the end of the canal a large wooden structure came into view. It was by far the largest building anywhere in the city which led me to the assumption that this was the home of the king of Valcot, Sodan's father.

With great skill the steersman brought the long ship at a quartering angle towards an empty slip at a pier near the end of the canal. At an order from the captain the oarsman on the pier side of the ship immediately pulled their oars inboard and stowed them as the outboard oarsman began to back paddle to slow the forward momentum of the ship and swing the stern close in to the pier. Crewman jumped to the dock both fore and aft and secured the vessel to large wooden bollards.

After giving direction to the captain to stand down the crew after they had made the ship fast Sodan leaped over the gunwale of the ship and landed firmly on the pier. Following his lead I too leaped over the rail and assisting Marlen we soon both stood next to Sodan.

Signaling one of the crew forward Sodan dispatched him to the palace to inform the king of his arrival. "Come," he said. "Let's make our way to the palace."

"We are your guest my friend," I replied. "Lead on."

Entering the avenue Sodan led us towards the large wooden palace. He was very popular among the people of Valcot. Many stopped to greet him as we passed and asked about his health. Prince or not Sodan took the time to talk to each and every one of them as if he had known them forever. I was beginning to realize that even though Sodan was third down as the heir to the throne of Valcot he was the front runner in the hearts of the people and justified my trusting my instinct that he was an honorable man.

Shop keepers tossed him fruit and many young beautiful women flirted with him in passing. Sodan humbly acknowledged each one. To say that Sodan was a bit of a celebrity in Valcot would have been an understatement of an overly obvious fact. Marlen and I had no problem keeping up with him as we travelled down the avenue. In fact more than once we had to stop and wait for him to exchange pleasantries with people before we could move on. Waiting was not a problem, we took the opportunity to see as much of Valcot as we could and my light complexion along with our savage dress drew as much attention to us as did the fact that we accompanied Sodan.

Finally, with much fanfare, we reached the palace gates. The guards recognized Sodan immediately and allowed us entrance without any ado. They greeted Sodan with welcoming gestures and many a pat on the back. He was obviously as well liked by the palace guard as he was by the people of the city. A messenger was waiting to escort us to the throne room of the king.

Following the messenger we proceeded down a long hallway and past many rooms that were used for various purposes of running a palace. We arrived in a great room where nearly a dozen people surrounded a tall wooden throne and as we approached the people parted and I could see the king, Sodan's father, as he leaned forward expectantly awaiting his son. As Marlen and I prepared to bow to his majesty the king arose and rushing forward embraced his son with open arms. This seemed to be a serious breach of royal protocol even to me who knew very little about protocol. Marlen and I glanced at one another then remained standing, foregoing the bow of reverence.

"Sodan my son," said the king, "I had thought that you were lost."

"Not lost father," replied Sodan, "merely detained for a short while."

Other men stepped forward and embraced Sodan. The resemblance was unmistakable and I surmised that the two men were Sodan's older brothers.

One of them spoke. "The last we heard little brother you had been taken prisoner by the Ronar."

"It is true," replied Sodan, "I was taken prisoner by the Ronar while I hunted in the great swamp and was the guest of Chief Padek for a period of time but alas he made the mistake of placing me in the arena fully armed. Now I am home."

Turning in our direction the king greeted us. "To whom do I owe the honor?" he asked. "Obviously you are friends of my son and as such are welcome in the city of Valcot."

Stepping forward Sodan apologized for his manners and introduced us to those gathered in the throne room. He introduced Marlen first, "Father, please welcome the Princess Marlen of Pendak. Princess Marlen, this is Jodan the King of Valcot." Bowing his head slightly Jodan took Marlen's hand and welcomed her. Sodan then introduced me. "Father, this is Jack Wilde. Jack, this is Jodan the King of Valcot. Jack assisted me in fighting clear of the arena in Ronar and I assisted him with rescuing the Princess Marlen in the process."

The king turned to me and taking my hand thanked me for assisting his son then looking at me quizzically he asked, "From where do you hail Jack Wilde? Your light shade of skin is unknown to me in Astor."

Unaware of the cultural beliefs of these people I did not know how they would react to finding out that I was from another world and I wasn't quite sure how to respond to his question. Without going into great detail I responded frankly, "I am not from Astor your majesty. I hail from Earth."

"I have never heard of Earth," replied the king. "It must be on one of the other continents of Phoria."

Again I responded evasively, "Yes my lord, Earth is a long distance from Phoria. My ship ran aground near the great swamp and I was taken prisoner by the Ronar." Here I had not really lied. My ship had crashed into the ground in the great swamp and I just left out the details that it was a ship that flew through the air and not one that sailed upon the sea with which they were familiar.

Seemingly satisfied he thanked me again and then introduced his other two sons as Daval and Tarnat. Both were older brothers to Sodan with Tarnat being the oldest and the heir to the throne of Valcot. Marlen and I greeted them both with bowed heads and open hands.

King Jodan returned to the throne and summoned a page. "Jack, Marlen, you are both welcome in Valcot and our hospitality is yours for as long as you would require. My page will escort you to rooms where you will be able to freshen up and rest from your journey. Please join us for the evening meal tonight for I would love to hear more of both Pendak and Earth," he said.

The page motioned for us to follow. Hesitantly I looked to Sodan. He smiled and responded quickly, "it is okay my friends. I will seek you out later after I have caught up with my father. Please go and enjoy the hospitality of Valcot," he said.

Placing my hand on his shoulder I thanked him and then Marlen and I fell into line behind the page and followed him out of the throne room.

Staying close on the page's heels we zigzagged our way through numerous passages and up a couple flights of stairs before we finally arrived at a closed wooden door. Opening it wide he motioned us forward and inside was a lavishly adorned suite that was fit for a king. He identified that this was to be Marlen's room and that mine was directly across the hall. Reluctant to leave Marlen alone I followed the page into the hallway closing the door behind us. Across the hall the page swung open another wooden door and inside was a room as lavishly adorned as the one in which we left Marlen. Bidding me to make myself comfortable the page informed me that the chamber maids would arrive shortly to prepare a bath for me. Thanking him I explored the room more as he exited and closed the door behind him.

On the far end of the room was a large bed covered with plush pillows, linen blankets and heavy furs. On the right wall of the room sat a reclining divan and a small desk and chair. Adjoining the left wall was a small antechamber that was in effect the bathroom with a low wooden tub and a wash basin that sat atop a small cabinet. Returning to the main room I heard a low knock on the door. Opening the door is saw two beautiful young maidens carrying pails of steaming hot water. Stepping back I let them enter. After dumping the pails of water into the tub they quickly exited.

Taking this opportunity I stepped into the hallway and knocked gently on the door to Marlen's room. It gently swung open and Marlen greeted me cheerily.

"I just wanted to make sure that you were okay," I said.

"Do not worry Jack," she replied. "The handmaids are filling my bath now and when I am going to soak the saltwater from my skin and then lay down to take a nap before dinner."

"That sounds like a really good idea," I said. "If you should need me, please do not hesitate to call upon me. I am just across the hallway."

"Rest assured Jack that if I am in need you will be the first person that I call upon," she replied smiling broadly.

My face flushed red but I was quickly saved from my embarrassment by the return of the handmaids. Two pushed their way past me and into Marlen's room and I quickly opened the door for two more that entered my room.

"Now go and get cleaned up and get some rest," Marlen urged. "I will see you soon for dinner."

Taking heed of her words I returned to my room just in time for a third handmaid to arrive with clean clothing. Laying them on the bed she quickly ushered the two other handmaids from the room and following them out closed the door.

Looking down at my body I was in agreement with Marlen that a good soaking in the bath would do me some good. The remnant crust of the salt air combined with the accumulated dust and dirt very nearly gave the appearance that my skin was darker than it actually was. Removing my harness and loincloth I headed for the bath.

Entering the room I could see that fresh linen towels had been laid out for me along with a sharp razor and a bar of lye soap. The washbasin had been filled with steaming hot water as well as the bath tub. Rubbing my hand over my chin the week long stubble of beard growth pricked at the palm of my hand and my fingers. A shave wouldn't hurt and lathering my face with the soap I scraped the thick layer of hair away. Rinsing the remaining soap from my chin I was already beginning to feel much better.

Now for the rest of me, stepping gingerly into the steaming hot water I entered the tub. Sitting down was a little painful to begin with because of the temperature but my body rapidly grew used to the heat. Laying back I slowly submerged my body into the water and exhaling a deep breath closed my eyes and allowed my body to relax for a few minutes. The heat of the water slowly pulled the stresses, aches and pains that I had accumulated since my arrival on Phoria from my body.

After a good fifteen minutes of soaking I lathered up and scrubbed my body clean. Not knowing how much time I had before we would be summoned to dinner I wanted to be prepared. Rinsing the soap from my body I stepped out of the tub and using the linen towels dried off. Taking this opportunity I threw my harness and loincloth into the soapy water in the bath. Giving them a quick washing to remove the dirt and grime I hung them on a hook on the wall to dry and entering the main room I picked up the clothing that had been brought. The linen was soft and pliable. The tunic was the olive drab color that I had seen before and the pants were white linen. The leggings were scarlet red. Once I was dressed I lay down on the bed and closed my eyes wanting to get some rest before dinner. It took but a matter of seconds and a deep slumber overtook me.

Chapter Thirteen

Hospitality

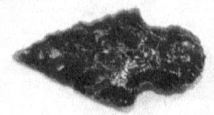

As I slept a loud pounding pried its way into my subconscious mind. Initially I thought the pounding was a sound within a dream but then the realization struck me that someone was actually at the door to the room in which I was sleeping. Awakening with a start I jumped up out of bed and rushed to the door and quickly swung it open, my gaze was met with the surprised look of the page that had been sent to fetch Marlen and me to dinner. She was just coming out of her room as I greeted the page. Wearing the garb of the local women which consisted of a linen dress and a waist apron she was absolutely beautiful.

Entering the hallway we proceeded to follow the page to the dining room.

"Did you rest well," I asked Marlen.

"Yes I did," she replied. "Not only did I rest but the bath was wonderful. After scrubbing the travel grime from my body I felt like a new person."

"Me too," I responded. "Now I am famished and looking forward to dinner."

The page led us into a dining hall containing a long wooden table. Already seated there were Sodan and his two brothers along with half a dozen royals of the court of Valcot and another more savagely dressed wearing a leather harness, a loincloth and furs. The king had not yet arrived. Seeing us enter the room Sodan stood and greeted us warmly.

"I trust that you rested well," he asked.

Marlen and I both acknowledged that we had as he led us to the two seats next to him that had been reserved for us. He sat at the right hand of the king and his two brothers sat directly across from us. The seats were in positions of honor and I was flattered by the recognition. All stood while Marlen was seated and then return to their places.

Sodan filled silver goblets that sat before us with local ale. "Here my friend is the ale that I promised you and may it be the first of many," he said.

Thanking him I raised the goblet to my lips and tasted deeply of the sweet malty liquid. "That is a superb draught," I responded. "And I agree, may it be the first of many."

A page entered the room and announced the arrival of King Jodan. Everyone rose to their feet and waited for the king to walk the length of the table and greet each person pleasantly. Upon arriving at his seat he immediately sat down and all those around the table followed suit.

The table was arrayed with a vast variety of foods. There were legs of antelope and some sort of fowl slightly smaller than a chicken. Baked fish was spread across great platters of silver. Carved wooden bowls contained a mix of vegetables some of which I recognized as carrots and the potato like tubers that I had eaten when I had first been taken prisoner by the Ronar. Also in the bowls were green tufts of some sort that I assumed were similar to broccoli or cauliflower. Breads and cheeses were abundant as were large silver tankards containing the warm ale. My mouth was watering voraciously at the assault on my senses of sight and smell. Patiently I waited, following Sodan's lead, until the king had prepared his plate. Once he had completed his selection of food he signaled for the rest of those seated at the table to join in.

All those around the table began to fill their plates with the succulent pieces of meat and vegetables. My mouth was salivating profusely at the anticipation of the flavors that I was about to experience as Marlen and I joined in.

The king had already begun to eat his meal by the time everyone else had gathered the food that appealed to them thus there was no more waiting. He was the first to get his food and the first to eat as custom would dictate and all others at the table were only allowed to eat after him.

The conversation around the table was light hearted and tinged with mirth. There were discussions about the current prices of trade goods. Others regaled those next to them with stories of their travels. In between large bites of food I carried on a conversation with the king and the royal brothers. The king wanted to know more about how I had come to be in the arena with his son. Starting with my first night on Phoria and leaving out the minor details about the technology that brought me to this planet I narrated my short tale up to the point of encountering Sodan and the ship's crew on the beach. They were noticeably impressed with the parts of the story where I had faced the forest saber toothed cats with a dagger lashed to a stick and then with my long sword.

The conversation then turned to Marlen. She too told her story from the time that she had been taken prisoner by the Ronar on the edge of the great swamp until now. While her story was not overly filled with amazing exploits the way in which she told it had captivated the attention of all those nearby. Everyone at the king's end of the table was enthralled by her tale and none more so than the savagely dressed gentleman sitting across the table from us.

The hair on the back of my neck stood up as I watched this gentleman hanging on every word that Marlen spoke. Instinct warned me that I needed to keep a close eye on this scoundrel but observing protocol as a guest of the king I held both my hand and my tongue and determined that this one would bear watching.

The ale continued to flow as those at the table had eaten their fill. The king rose and began to address all those present. "Tonight we feast in honor of the safe return of my youngest son Sodan from the clutches of the Ronar and Chief Padek. We also feast to welcome Jack Wilde and Princess Marlen of Pendak to the city of Valcot. Lastly we feast to celebrate our new alliance with Chief Tallis of the Tagus tribe. The rest of you that are present represent the largest trading houses in Valcot and directly impact the economic well-being of the city. Chief Tallis is here to discuss trade agreements with you that will help to guarantee markets for your goods. Please relax and enjoy the comforts of the fine ales of Valcot and welcome to all."

Now I knew a little bit more about this savage individual that leered longingly at Marlen. He was not of the city of Valcot and I did not trust him.

At this point in the evening Marlen took her leave from the table and thanking the king for his hospitality returned to her room.

Marlen's exit signaled a relaxing of etiquette and a host of musicians and dancing girls entered that hall. The musicians began to play as the girls circulated around the room filling tankards with the sweet ale. Many a guest at the table took liberties with the girls that would have been inappropriate had Marlen stayed in the room. Many a cheek was grabbed by the guests and just as many had been slapped in return by the girls. The royal dining hall did have some limits after all.

The dancing girls did not wear the traditional garb of the women of Valcot. They were dressed in varying colors of diaphanous silks and taffetas that billowed around their bodies with every movement. Once everyone's tankards were filled the girls began to dance and sway in time with the music. The rhythmic movements of their arms and hips mesmerized me and I found it hard to take my eyes from them. The beauty of their bodies and skill with which they danced was like nothing that I had ever seen before.

Watching one of the dancers closely I noticed that she had a scar high up on the left side of her lower back in the shape of a "V". Not paying much heed to the scar I didn't even give it a second thought until later in the evening as the girls rotated around the room I noticed that each and every one of them had the same identical scar. It suddenly dawned on me that this was not really a scar but a brand. These women had all been identically branded.

Contently enjoying the hospitality of Valcot I had completely forgotten what Marlen had told me about the two mainstays of Valcot's economy, weapons and slaves. I now realized that the dancing girls were the products of the business of Valcot and not employed as entertainers for the palace. Curiosity was getting the better of me so I decided to ask Sodan about the brand. "Why do all of these women have a "V" branded onto their lower back," I asked.

"Because they are the slaves of the royal house of Valcot," he said nonchalantly.

It would be wise for me to remember that I was no longer on Earth. While my own moral beliefs and values screamed out that owning another person was wrong I needed to respect the culture of the world in which I now found myself. Although I did not have to support it I did have to respect it.

My jovial mood of earlier had now turned somber as I began to pity the situation that would force them into slavery. Redirecting my focus to a subject less depressing I looked around the room to see what everyone else was doing. The king was in heavy conversation with his two older sons regarding the safety of their borders. Tallis was holding court at the far end of the room discussing trade issues with the merchants. Sodan's attention was being raptly held by a young blond dancing girl sitting on his lap. If being royalty on Phoria meant living like this I could be very content with this lifestyle.

The strength of the ale was beginning to cloud my thinking and having always been one to know when enough was enough I thanked everyone for their hospitality and made my way back to my room. Rejoining my sleep where I had left off earlier came easy after the relaxing effects of the ale. Flopping face first on the bed I was once again fast asleep.

The next two weeks were extremely busy for Marlen and me. My mornings were spent on the practice fields learning the finer arts of swordplay from Sodan. Surprisingly the art of the sword came naturally to me and after the first week of heavy practice I was holding my own against him. By the second week I was forcing his hand and making him work hard to defend himself against my blade. The long sword began to feel like an extension of my own arm and seemed to move of its own volition. My instincts were being honed to a sharp point and my rough edges in fighting were slowly being smoothed out. My survival in this world was beginning to feel more probable every day.

My afternoons were spent in the company of Marlen. Often we would walk the avenues of Valcot interacting with the people and talking with the shop owners. We were welcomed at every turn. Our midday meals were enjoyed at various inns around the city. Places that catered to travellers and traders and were frequented by the seedier types known in every large metropolitan area. There was one inn in particular called the "the One Eyed Banda" that we enjoyed. The music was slow and mellow and the food was hot and plentiful. The feature that I found most attractive about the inn was that it was the only one that I had found that served ale cold. Granted it wasn't iced up like I preferred from my local pub back home but it was considerably colder than room temperature.

Once I had asked the proprietor as to how he kept the ale cold and he described a method of convection where water dribbled over wooden casks of ale while they were fanned by slaves. The water running over the casks removed the heat from the ale while the airflow from the fanning removed the heat from the water. Traditionally on Phoria ale was enjoyed at room temperature but the novelty of cold ale was a marketing ploy that appeared to be paying well for the inn-keeper.

Normally I would be concerned with taking Marlen into any inn that was not a safe reputable establishment but my new found skill set with the blade had instilled me with confidence that I could protect her from anything that may arise. It was custom in Valcot to never go anywhere unarmed. Sodan had provided me with a scabbard suited to my long sword that I kept strapped to my back. Attached to the belt at my waist was a common short sword and dagger. I was as heavily armed as any other cutthroat or brigand at the "One Eyed Banda."

Upon our first visit to the inn I inquired to Marlen as to what in the world a banda was and why having one eye would be notable for the name of an inn.

Laughing at my confusion Marlen explained that a banda was what the people of Phoria called the great saber toothed cat that I had grown so familiar with in my short time on this world. Feeling the healing scars on my leg I had developed an affinity for the inn and felt a sense of camaraderie towards its namesake.

Marlen and I sat eating our meal and sipping a cold ale one afternoon when through the door walked Sodan. Flopping down in an empty chair at our table he informed us that he had found a cargo vessel that was bound for Pendak. It was scheduled to set sail at dawn and our passage had already been secured.

"Wonderful," I replied. "How many days will we be at sea before we reach Pendak?" I asked.

"The captain of the ship estimates that trip at ten days," he said. "Cargo ships do not move with the speed of the long ships. It may take up to a week longer if the winds are not favorable."

The timeframe for the trip was not nearly as important as the fact that I would have Marlen on the last leg of the journey to return her home. "We must celebrate," I declared raising my voice to get the proprietors attention, "Innkeeper, bring us a tankard of your coldest ale."

"Right away sir," he responded quickly moving to fill my order.

The three of us sat and drank heartily listening to the music that lilted upon the air. As the sun set the inn began to fill up. People of all backgrounds began to fill the bar. Watching individuals as they came through the door I was getting proficient at determining who was harmless and those that I needed to keep an eye on. Late into the evening three men entered through the door and pushed their way to an empty table. I recognized their garb as being the same savage dress of leather harness and furs that had been worn by Tallis.

Continuing with our conversation Marlen and I expressed our gratitude to Sodan for his assistance and friendship.

"Please come with us," Marlen entreated Sodan. "I would love to have the opportunity to return the hospitality that you have shown us during our stay in Valcot."

"Maybe soon Marlen," Sodan replied. "The timing is not good right now. There are concerns about the integrity of the people of Tagus regarding our new trading alliance. My father believes that it is in the best interest of Valcot but I have my own misgivings. My gut tells me that trouble is brewing with the plains people and right now my sword is needed here. Rest assured though that one day soon I will be knocking at the gate of Pendak requesting an audience with the princess."

We all laughed heartily at Sodan's promise to come to visit and I began to get an uneasy feeling as the hair on my neck bristled. More than once I felt as if we were being watched during the evening but every time I looked around the room I was unable to identify anyone that was paying us an undo amount of attention.

"Sodan I believe that somebody is watching us," I said.

"You are correct Jack," he replied. "I have seen the men from Tagus watching us more than once and talking in low whispers. I believe that they are watching me for some reason and I don't trust them. Come and let us be clear of this place before I start a war with the plains people."

"Very well my friend," I said in agreement. "I think that you are right and something is not right with Tallis or his warriors. Maybe Marlen and I should stay to be of assistance if we can."

"Not to worry Jack I will be fine here in Valcot," he assured me. "If war should break out nobody is as well armed as the people of Valcot. Your concern right now is to get the princess safely home to Pendak."

Rising to our feet we moved out the door and headed for the palace. Sodan led us on a round-about return path to lose anyone that may be following us and after moving down the dark streets we finally arrived safely at the gate to the palace. We were immediately given entry and bidding Sodan good night we moved through the halls towards our rooms. At the door to Marlen's room I opened the door for her and after embracing her with a hug I wished her a good night's sleep and went to my room.

Closing the heavy wooden door behind me I crossed to the bed and kicking off my boots and tunic I lay down to sleep. Try as I might I could not drift into the dream filled slumber that I desired. Something was eating at my mind about the warriors of Tagus that we had seen at the inn. It bothered me that they even knew who we were. We had never met any of them except Tallis and I found it odd that they were able to recognize us. Something was clearly wrong but I couldn't put my finger on what it was. With a troubled mind I finally managed to find the sleep that had eluded me for so long.

Chapter Fourteen

Abducted

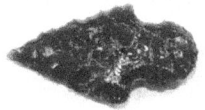

Awakening well before dawn the excitement of the coming journey to Pendak filled me with anticipation and I was looking forward to being aboard ship and underway with Marlen close at my side. Rising out of the bed I strapped on my leather harness and loincloth pulling the tunic and pants over the top. After I had wrapped the leggings around my calves I pulled on my leather boots and laced them tightly. Wrapping my belt around my waist I ensured the short sword and dagger were positioned correctly so that they would be close at hand if needed. Lastly I strapped my sword across my back where it hung comfortably between my shoulder blades.

Properly attired and armed I was ready to move out. Stepping into the hallway I approached the door to Marlen's room and rapped my knuckles gently upon the hard wood. Patiently I waited for an acknowledgement that she had heard and hearing nothing from within I knocked again a little louder and waited for her response.

As I stood listening at the door Sodan approached up the hallway.

"Good morning my friend," he greeted my jovially. "Are you and the princess ready to go?"

"And a good morning to you too," I replied. "I am ready but I am not sure about Marlen. She has yet to answer her door." With that I knocked even louder and yelled through the door. "Marlen it is me Jack. It is time to go to the ship. Are you ready?"

Still I heard no sound of movement within and with growing anxiety I tried the door. It opened to my touch and swung open. Quickly stepping into the room I looked around and found the entire room in disarray. The linen blankets and furs from the bed were scattered all over the floor and taking in the condition of the room instantly it was clear that a struggle had taken place. Moving quickly to the adjoining room that contained the bath tub I saw that Marlen was nowhere in sight.

Returning to the main room I found Sodan looking through the items that littered the floor. "Sodan she is gone," I said.

"She would not have left without you Jack," he replied. "Someone has taken her."

"I don't understand," I said. "Who could have done this?"

Having picked up something from the floor Sodan turned to me with an outstretched hand. In his palm was a small metal device such as warriors wear on their leather harness. While the device was oddly familiar I could not place where I had seen it before.

"It is the insignia of Tagus," Sodan replied with contempt.

Now I remembered where I had seen this insignia before. It was the same as I had seen on the leather of Tallis at dinner the first night and then again on the harness of the warriors from Tagus that had been watching us at the inn.

It was now becoming clear that the warriors of Tagus must have overheard us talking about leaving this morning to set sail for Pendak. My instincts had been right but I continued to berate myself for having not seen it before. The infatuated look with which Tallis had watched Marlen at dinner and the way that his men had been watching us at the inn, it was all clear now. My mind had tried to warn me and that is why I had such a hard time going to sleep. I wished that I had listened closer to my instincts but nothing could be done about that now. Right now the important thing was finding Marlen and getting her back.

"Quickly Sodan we must be after them," I stated.

"We must get to the gate before they do," he said. "Quickly follow me."

At a sprint I followed Sodan through the halls of the palace. He gathered warriors as we went and as we passed through the palace gate and into the street we had fully half a dozen men in tow. The streets were nearly empty at this early hour and we ran at breakneck speed with Sodan leading the way.

Approaching the gate Sodan called to the guard. "The delegation from Tagus, have they passed this way?"

'Yes my prince," replied the leader of the guard. "They passed this way shortly after midnight."

"How many were there? Was there a woman with them?" I asked excitedly.

"Yes my lord. There were fifteen of them and at least three of them were women," he responded fearfully.

"We must be after them Sodan," I said moving towards the gate.

"Wait Jack, they have at least five hours head start. We will never catch them on foot," he said. "Come, to the palace, let us prepare and I assure you we will be after them within the hour and be able to travel much faster."

I wasn't clear what Sodan meant but I realized the futility of trying to catch up to them on foot with the commanding head start that they had. "Okay," I said. "But we need to move quickly. Every second that passes they are getting farther and farther away."

"I know my friend," he responded. "Trust me and we will soon have her back safely in your arms." With that we headed out at a run for the palace.

Approaching the palace gate Sodan barked orders to the leader of the guard. "Send a messenger to the stables. Have two grall saddled, outfitted with provisions and brought here immediately. We will be back for them shortly."

I had no idea what a grall was but if they would help us to move faster in the pursuit of Marlen's captors I was all for it. Following him we ran into the palace and up the main hallway. Turning sharply we entered into a room that was arrayed with weapons and clothing of all types.

"We need to be properly attired for the plains," Sodan said. "We will need to blend in and wearing the tunics of Valcot we will stand out and draw too much attention to ourselves."

Quickly Sodan and I changed out of what we were wearing and into unmarked leather harness and furs. He had explained to me that harness without markings was common attire among travellers that were trying to keep their city of origin secret, as well as, for mercenaries or soldiers for hire. This would be the guise that we would assume as travelling mercenaries were common among the peoples of Astor and would draw little attention to us.

Strapping on our weapons we were nearly prepared to set out in pursuit of the Tagus. He handed me a long spear tipped pike and a long bow with a quiver of arrows. The hefty hardwood shaft of the pike reminded me of the makeshift spear that I had used to fend off the Banda in the great swamp when I had first arrived on Phoria. Archery had been a life-long hobby of mine and this was a weapon that I was familiar with.

Returning to the gate we found two large bovine type animals awaiting us. They were bulky and intimidating creatures and instantly I was reminded of the American bison. The creatures were over six feet at the shoulders, covered in a heavy gray fur and had a large wooly head that was armed with two horns extending a full three feet from each side and curved forward ending in sharp points.

Just back of the forward shoulder hump was strapped a small leather saddle and saddle bags. Leather reigns extended back from a large golden ring in the animal's nose and I assumed was used to steer the animal if such an animal could be steered.

Sodan leaped to the back of one of the grall. Following I leaped to the back of the other. With plenty of experience riding horses back on Earth the feel of the grall between my legs felt more like I was preparing for an eight second ride on a bucking bull rather than a trail animal. Tucking away my trepidation I treated the experience just like riding a horse and was pleasantly surprised to receive similar reactions from the grall. Placing our heels to the ribs of the animals we were instantly thundering down the streets of Valcot and headed for the main gate.

The guard at the gate recognized us as we rumbled up the avenue and swung the gate wide as we approached. Passing through the gate I followed Sodan into the open outside the city.

Surprised at the fleetness of the large grall I had expected that because of their size and great bulk they would be more of a slow lumbering animal. The reality was that they were extremely agile and quick. While they were easily directed with the reigns it was obvious that they were trained for battle. Relaxing the reigns and allowing the grall its own lead I was able to provide directional control by simply placing pressure to one side of the animal or the other with my knees.

Outside the gate we followed a well-worn road that meandered across sodden fields and through growths of trees. Climbing in elevation out of the estuary where Valcot lie we soon crested the surrounding hillsides. Stopping our mounts we looked to the south and I beheld for the first time the vast plains of Astor. I could not help but feel like I was looking out across the rolling grasslands of western Kansas of which I was familiar from my home world.

The road that we had been following continued on into the plains and dismounting Sodan and I searched the ground for any sign of the passage of the Tagus. The tracks of the hoofed feet of grall were everywhere along the road.

"They passed this way," I told Sodan. "There appear to be tracks of fifteen to twenty animals and they were moving fast."

"Tallis is trying to get deep into the plains," he replied. "My guess is that he will turn west at some point. The territory claimed by the Tagus is in the western plains at the base of the high mountains."

"We must hurry and catch them before they can gain reinforcements," I said.

Remounting, we again set out down the road and onto the plains. To begin with the tracks were easy to follow but the farther down the road we went the more the grass of the plains had reclaimed the road. We had travelled about a mile when the road completely disappeared having been absorbed into the terrain of the plains and the tracks left by the grall of Tallis were now harder to see amongst the tall grasses. Continuing on we caught a glimpse of a track here or a broken stalk of grass there and our rate of travel had slowed considerably.

Looking far out over the plains I could see nothing but rolling hills and grass. Desperation that we would not be able to catch up with Marlen's abductors was beginning to set in but still we travelled on following the meager scraps of the trail as we could find them.

Climbing a gentle rise in the prairie we were suddenly greeted by the full on rush of half a dozen mounted warriors that lay in wait for us. They had managed to hide themselves and their mounts in a low spot between rises. Their presence was a good sign though because they had been left behind to ambush us and slow our pursuit but I wasn't about to let them delay us for too long.

Sodan and I urged out mounts forward as we neared them I noted that he held his pike out in front of his charging mount similar in fashion to a knight in a medieval jousting competition and I now understood the importance of the pike and its razor sharp spear point.

Holding my pike as I had seen Sodan hold his we met the first two assailants leading the charge head on. As we crashed together I felt my pike bite deeply into the flesh of my opponent. My mount pushed on past his and as he fell the pike was torn from my grasp and followed him to the ground. It seemed that I would not get a second pass with that weapon.

Unsheathing the long sword from my back I turned my mount to meet my next opponent. This one being more wary than the first did not charge head long into my blade. It was this wariness that allowed him to live just a little bit longer. Circling our mounts around one another we both vied for an opening that would allow us to strike a fatal blow and this jostling for position was wasting valuable time that I did not have. Taking advantage of an opening I reached out with my sword and stabbed my opponents mount full in the neck. Hoping that the anatomy of these animals would be similar to those of my home world I targeted the large artery that ran up the side of the neck. I was not disappointed when in a spray of blood my opponents mount reared throwing him off balance. Losing his seat in the saddle he fell from his mount and my blade met him halfway to the ground removing his head from his body which landed with a thump quickly followed by his rolling head. Turning to find another opponent I heard the wounded mount fall heavily to the ground and wail in desperation as its life flowed out onto the grassland.

Quickly taking stock of the situation I saw that Sodan also had two opponents down and was heavily engaged in battle with a third. Zeroing in on the last assailant I charge my mount directly at his. The two mounts met head on with a sound eerily reminiscent of thunder. The impact threw both of us from our saddles and landing heavily on the ground I struggled to regain my footing. The wind had been knocked from my lungs as I hit the ground and I inhaled deeply trying to regain my breath. Turning around I could see that my opponent was in no better shape than I was and I had no intention of letting him recover before I attacked.

Holding my long sword in my right hand I pulled the short sword with the left and charged forward. My opponent barely managed to raise his sword to prevent me from decapitating him and he fended off blow after blow from one sword or the other as I pressed him backwards. While I led my attack with the long sword it was the short sword that quickly slipped in and pierced his heart when he let his guard slip to block an overhanded blow from the long sword. In the fraction of a second that he had left his rib cage unprotected I stabbed upwards with my left hand driving the short sword between his ribs. His body stiffened as he felt the steel slice into his body then fell hard to the ground.

Breathing heavily I turned about trying to see where Sodan was. As I turned I saw him standing there with a big smile on his face. He had evidently dispatched his opponents quickly enough to be able to observe my last battle.

"Very well done," he said. "I do not envy anyone that would be foolish enough to cross blades with you."

"Tallis knew that we would be in pursuit," I said. "If his intention was to remove us from his trail he should have left a lot more men." With a low laugh I walked towards Sodan. "There are now six less to oppose us when we catch up with him." Slapping him on the shoulder I returned to the first warrior that I had killed and freed my pike from his body. While I did this Sodan gathered our mounts and taking just a few more minutes removed the saddles from the remaining mounts of the Tagus and with a slap from the flat of his short sword he sent them running out across the plains.

"Mount up Jack. We must follow those grall for they will instinctively head in the direction of their herd mates that are with Tallis," he said.

Understanding his meaning I leaped aboard my mount and settled into the saddle. Once Sodan was mounted we urged our mounts forward in pursuit of the rapidly disappearing grall.

"Are you sure that we should follow them and not the tracks?" I asked questioningly.

"This will be the quickest way," he replied. "The grall are heavily herd bound animals and will travel in a straight line following their noses to return to their herd. By following them we will travel on a direct shot straight to Tallis. Following the tracks we would catch them eventually but not before meandering across the plain and this way will be much quicker because we will shortcut the trail and not waste time looking for sign. Plus we can travel as fast as we can ride. The grall will bed down just before dark without a rider to push them so we can get as far as we can before night sets in."

"Very well," I replied. "Let's ride."

Spurring our mounts to greater speed we moved across the plain like the wind in pursuit of the fleeing grall. For an animal so large their speed was absolutely amazing. Holding tight to the saddle I let my mind drift to Marlen hoping that she was safe even though she was in the clutches of Tallis. I hoped that she was being treated as the princess that she was and I hoped that when we caught them Tallis would fight with all his might to keep me from taking her because I intended to make him pay before I released him from his own misery.

Chapter Fifteen

The Pursuit

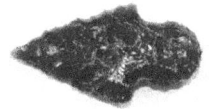

The grall of the Tagus maintained a stampeding sprint for a good five miles as they ran from the scene of their riders' demise. We kept up a steady pursuit pushing our mounts so that we could keep the fleeing grall within sight in the distance. Finally the grall began to slow to a lope as they caught their breath from their forced charge.

Taking the opportunity as they slowed we reduced the speed of our mounts to match. Maintaining our distance we feared that if we pushed the grall too hard they would continue to run into the night. Once the sun went down we would not be able to follow their trail in the darkness and we needed for them to feel safe enough to bed down by nightfall.

It was now midafternoon and continuing on vigilantly we followed the beasts hoping that we had made the right decision to follow them back to Tallis. Trusting Sodan's experience and judgment I placed my faith in the strength of our friendship and I instinctively knew that the decision to follow was the right one.

Keeping a watchful eye out across the plains we examined every dip and rise in the prairie watching for any sign of the Tagus. Looking behind us we continuously checked our back trail to ensure that we had not been flanked by an enemy sneaking up behind us, but no sign of Tallis or his men could be seen anywhere.

Without warning, the grall that we followed came to an abrupt stop and all turned to look to the right of their trail. Immediately Sodan and I stopped our mounts and strained our eyes to see what had drawn their attention. Looking intently at the grassland I could see nothing moving. Continuing to watch I finally made out the barely perceptible movement of the grasses as something stealthily moved towards the grall.

"There," I told Sodan as I pointed with my finger, "Just this side of the next rise something is moving."

Following the direction that I pointed he was able to pick out the movement through the grass that had caught my attention. Quietly we watched as the moving grass drew closer and closer to the grall. The animals were becoming agitated and began to paw heavily at the ground with their hooves and snort menacingly. In a matter of seconds the animal sneaking through the grass broke into a sprint and was in the middle of the grall before they could react.

The massive body of the animal came into full view as it leaped to the back of the nearest grall and to my surprise the animal was a large lizard, actually a lizard on steroids. It stretched a full twenty feet in length, ten feet of muscular body with razor sharp teeth and ten feet of thick tail. My estimation was that the creature stood a full three feet tall at the back.

"It is a mondor," stated Sodan. "Beware the bite for it can be deadly. Even a slight bite from this animal will lead to infection or death."

I did not relish the thought of meeting my doom as the result of being bitten by a lizard regardless of how big it was. "We must do something," I stated excitedly.

"Wait Jack," Sodan replied patiently. "The mondor cannot kill all five of the grall. Once it has bitten one it will withdraw to a safe distance and follow them. The injured grall will eventually lag behind the others and go down. That is when the Mondor will move in for the kill."

Just as Sodan had predicted the mondor had inflicted a vicious wound to the neck of the grall that it had leaped upon then jumping back to the ground it slipped off into the grass to await its inevitable meal.

"We will need to be careful as we follow the grall or we will risk running into the mondor," he said.

Putting some distance between us and where we thought the mondor to be we moved two hundred yard to the left of the trail. The grall again began to move and instead of following them we paralleled their course keeping them within sight. Constantly we looked about us keeping our eyes peeled for the mondor that we knew was trailing somewhere behind.

It didn't take long before the injured grall began to fall behind the others and noticeably limping the bitten animal stumbled often and finally went down. The last we saw of the doomed animal was it struggling to get back on its feet as the mondor arrived and began to tear large chunks of flesh from its rapidly failing body. It was a gruesome end for the animal but I was satisfied in knowing that the mondor would no longer be following.

It was late afternoon and following the grall for what I estimated to be another ten miles after their herd mate had fallen they began to slow and coming to a halt began to mill around and eat voraciously at the grass.

"It won't be long now and they will bed down," Sodan said. "We will camp here for the night and be back on the trail when they arise at first light."

Dismounting we stretched our legs while we kept an eye on the grall. One by one they finished eating at the grass and lay down to sleep. Removing the saddles from our grall we turned them out so they could eat. Our mounts, following the actions of their brethren ate heartily of the plains grass and then lay down to sleep. We decided to have a cold camp so that a fire would not give away our position in the odd chance that we were close to Tallis and his men.

Finding dried meat and linen blankets in the saddle bags we ate a cold meal and washed it down with stale water from a skin bag. "I will take the first watch," said Sodan. "I will wake you in four hours."

Not wanting to waste a second of rest I quickly curled up in the linen blanket and using the small saddle for a pillow under my head I quickly fell into the deep trance of sleep.

My four hours of sleep passed quickly and I was awakened by Sodan to assume the next watch while he got some sleep. The two moons of Phoria were slowly making their way across the sky and illuminated the plains for as far as I could see in any direction. Our sleeping mounts were piled up a mere twenty yards from where we slept and looking out across the moonlit grasses I could see the four dark humps in the distance of the grall that we had been following. All was quiet and nothing appeared to be moving.

My biggest concern during my watch was keeping my eyes peeled for mondor. I had already experienced the stealth with which they could move through the grass and any inconsistent motion drew my full attention. Assuming that the one full grown grall would be more of a meal than any one mondor could handle I hoped it would keep our visitor busy throughout the night.

The grall that we had been following started to stir as the sun began to rise in the east. Beginning to get a little bit anxious that they would move on before we were ready to follow I spoke Sodan's name in a raised voice to wake him. He immediately jumped up looking around to see what threatened us. Quickly allaying his fears I explained that the grall were preparing to move. Recognizing the meaning of why I had awakened him he moved to roust our mounts from their sleep and once he had them up and about he brought them to where I stood and we set about saddling them and preparing our gear to again be on the trail.

When the grall began to move we were in the saddle and ready to follow. Letting them put a quarter of a mile distance between us we spurred our mounts forward and settled into a matching pace to the rear of the animals. Under Sodan's advice we allowed the gap to grow ever larger between us and the grall. Anticipating that today we could come upon Tallis and his warriors the more distance between us and the grall the more forewarning we would have to prevent us from riding directly into the hands of the Tagus.

Watching the specks on the horizon that were the grall I was startled to see them begin to multiply and calling Sodan to a halt we quickly jumped from our saddles and urged our mounts to lie down on the ground. The bulk of the animals could not be completely hidden by the grass but getting them low worked to reduce the silhouette that could be seen from a distance. Pulling two wooden stakes from his saddle bag Sodan drove them into the ground with the pommel of his sword and lashing the reigns to the stakes we began to make our way through the grass towards where we had last seen the four grall.

Covering the distance quickly we kept low so as to not be seen by whoever or whatever it was that had joined the grall and in a matter of minutes we had closed the gap significantly and prostrating ourselves on the crest of a low hillock we were able to look down into a small ravine between long flat plains. There in the ravine was an encampment the size of which was too large to be the band of Tagus that we had tracked out of Valcot. Watching the activities below we tried to ascertain who it was that occupied the camp.

A total of twenty or more large leather tents made up the encampment and people could be seen moving in and around the tents. From our location I could see that they were all attired in a similar fashion to the warriors of Tagus. Still too far away to make out any insignia that was worn on their leather harnesses it was clear that these people were from one of the many nomadic tribes that made their home among the grasslands and after watching for hours we were unable to recognize anyone within the camp. I had hoped to catch a glimpse of Marlen to verify that we had found her but if she was in the camp she was being held inside one of the tents but we needed to figure out a way to search the camp and see if she was there.

"Sodan I have a plan," I said,

"I hope it is a good one Jack," he replied. "By my guess there are at least sixty people down there and we may be good with the sword but they still have us outnumbered significantly."

"Aw, but we still have the element of surprise," I said confidently. Over the next few minutes I laid out my plan to Sodan, then keeping my profile low I started to work my way back towards where we had left the grall staked out. Once I had reached them I turned towards the south and moving in a great arc I worked my way around to the southern end of the encampment. When I entered the camp I wanted to make sure that I entered from a completely different direction than the grall that we had been following.

With confidence, whether real or improvised, I walked directly into the camp and within seconds was surrounded by the guard with the razor sharp tips of multiple spears pressed against my flesh. The vigilance of the picket guards had been very lax and due to their inattention I was able to get will within the perimeter of the encampment before they had realized that I was not one of their own. I expected that somebody would be held accountable for my easy entry. Looking the guards over I quickly recognized that displayed prominently upon their harness was the insignia of the Tagus and any question that I had about whether or not we had found the right warriors was answered. Now I just needed to find Marlen.

"Whoa my friends," I said. "I do not mean anyone any harm. I was making my way to the foothills of the mountains to hunt banda when my grall was ambushed by a mondor. I managed to kill it but it was too late. My mount had already been bitten."

"You wear no insignia," one of the guards questioned suspiciously. "From what tribe do you hail?"

"I owe allegiance to no tribe in particular," I replied. "My sword answers to the highest bidder."

The guards that surrounded me continued to eye me suspiciously and I could tell that they were not fully buying my story but at the same time they were buying enough of it that they had not run me through. I was hoping that Sodan was still watching from his hidden vantage point overlooking the camp. There was not much chance that he would be able to provide me assistance if I needed it but knowing that he was there helped to fuel my confidence to continue on with the ruse.

"Your arrival here is suspicious," the guard that I took to be the leader said. "Consider yourself our prisoner until the chief has said otherwise." With that his men moved in and relieved me of my weapons. Forcefully grabbing my forearms they pulled them behind my back and lashed them tightly with a leather strap then leading me into the camp they forced me to sit down next to a fire pit. The leader of the group threw my weapons down by the fire and ordering two warriors to guard me he left. Nonchalantly watching him I followed his path with the corner of my eye to determine which tent he entered, it stood to reason that he was going to inform the chief of my capture and as he entered a large tent in the center of the camp he had unknowingly identified for me where I could find the chief.

Looking around the camp from my position by the fire I worked to commit every item and its location to memory. All of the tribe's stock animals were picketed out just north of the camp and piled neatly next to the fire was a mound of dried grall dung that was being used to fuel the fire. Wood was scarce on the plains and other than the tall grass which would burn quickly the only other option was dung.

The eastern part of the camp was bordered by a row of small wagons. These were designed to be harnessed to grall and used to move all the equipment of the camp from one location to another.

People moved about the camp attending to the chores and duties necessary to keep a camp of this size functioning and for the first time I noticed that mixed among the warriors of the tribe were women and children. This was not just a roving camp of warriors but a core encampment for the tribe. The majority of the people in the camp moved about completely ignoring me and the only ones that acknowledged my presence were a few children that stood nearby staring at me. Learning that the curiosity of children was consistent no matter where you went I flashed them a big smile and attempted to engage them in conversation but they immediately became shy and took off at a run. I laughed quietly as they disappeared among the tents.

Turning to the warriors that guarded me I asked them what the chief of the tribes name was and not surprisingly they ignored every attempt that I made to try to get them to divulge any information that may be helpful. Giving up on my attempts to get them to talk, I again looked around the camp taking it all in. Looking out of the corner of my eye I tried to determine the location on the crest of the nearby hill where Sodan lay hidden patiently waiting for my plan to fully develop. He was camouflaged well because even though I knew he was there I was unable to see any sign of him.

The leader of the guard returned. "The chief will see you shortly," he said. "When you enter the tent you must go in with your eyes down. Do not raise them until directed or I will personally separate your head from your body."

"Very well," I replied.

Maintaining control over my emotions and forcing myself to be calm I was beginning to get a bit irritated with the delay in being taken to see the chief. After waiting for what seemed an eternity but in reality was only five minutes the leader of the guard grabbed me by the elbow and lifted me to my feet.

"Come, it is time, the chief will see you now," he said.

Rising to my feet I moved towards the large tent in the center of the camp and at the entryway I lowered my eyes to the ground and trusting to the guidance of the guards I entered into the tent. Looking down at the ground all I could see as I entered the tent was an elaborately decorated hand woven rug. Walking up the length of the rug the guards came to a sudden halt and I fought the urge to raise my eyes and see who it was before me. The leader of the guard addressed the person that I took to be the chief and at his direction I lifted my eyes and looked full upon Tallis, the chief of the Tagus. He sat regally on a high wooden chair that acted as his throne and sitting on the floor at the foot of the throne was Marlen. A leather collar was tied snugly around her throat and attached to it was a leather leash the other end of which Tallis held firmly in his hand. Looking up at me with despair in her eyes, I immediately began to see red with rage and had my hands been free they would have been wrapped around the throat of this kidnapping slime.

Chapter Sixteen

The Tagus

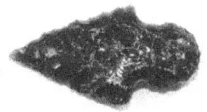

"**W**ell Jack Wilde, you got here much quicker than I expected," he said smugly. "It is too bad that all your efforts to get here have been in vain because you will never be leaving this camp alive. I assume that you have come for the princess."

"No Tallis, I am here for only one thing," I said menacingly. "To watch the light in your eyes go out as I kill you."

Tallis was a coward. I could see the fear in his eyes as I told him that I intended to kill him and he flew into a fit of rage. "Tie him to the wagons," he screamed. "I want him dead at sunrise."

The guards hit me violently with the butts of their spears and forced me back out of the tent. Pushing me in the direction of the wagons I was struck a savage blow to the back of my knees when I had reached the nearest wagon and sprawling forward on my face a number of warriors jumped upon me and when they finally let up I was bound hand and foot spread over a wheel of a wagon.

This was not quite how I had seen my plan going but regardless I had found Marlen and now I just needed to figure out how to get her out of this camp safely. First and foremost I needed to figure out how to get loose from the bindings that held my hands and feet but I knew that Sodan was still free and assistance was near at hand.

Having no desire to sit patiently and wait to be rescued like a damsel in distress I started working on the leather lashings that held me fast. One thing that I have learned about leather over the years is that unlike a synthetic rope, leather always has weak spots and whether it has been worn thin through usage or from the process of tanning, thin spots equate to weakness and a spot at which the leather fibers can be forced apart. Of the four lashings that held me in place one of them had to have a weakness that I could exploit.

Pulling on each lashing one at a time I applied pressure stretching the leather as far as I could. The two lashings that held my feet stretched very little and held tight and gaining leverage with the legs was difficult as the bindings were low on the leg near the ankle. My hope lay in the bindings that held my arms.

Flexing the muscles in my arms I pulled straight against the knots that held my wrist but while the leather stretched extensively it refused to part. Changing the angle of my leverage I braced my elbow against the hard wood of the wagon wheel and flexing my bicep solidly I twisted briskly at the shoulder in the same motion used by an arm wrestler. The leather around my wrist began to tighten cutting off the circulation to my hand but I was going to either get loose from that binding or make my situation even worse. Relaxing my arm I rested for a few seconds and then focusing my mind to push the muscles of my arm beyond their abilities I again placed a strain on the leather and snapping my shoulder hard forced the leather to its limits. Just as the pain in my shoulder began to be unbearable the knot in the leather at my wrist slipped through itself and in an instant my hand was free.

Holding my arm in place as if it were still bound I quickly looked around to see if anyone had noticed my efforts and it was clear that nobody was about to witness my escape. Fortunately for me once I had been bound to the wagon wheel the warriors that had escorted me out of the chief's tent had returned to their duties under the assumption that I was secure. Just one more mistake for which they would have to pay dearly.

Continuing to emulate being bound securely I waited for the sun to set. In order to remove the remaining lashings I needed the cover of darkness to hide my actions so that none of the warriors would again lash my free arm to the wheel. Patiently I stood watching as the shadows in the camp grew longer and longer. Standing immobile with my head down as if I were asleep and hanging in my bindings I counted away the minutes until I felt that it was dark enough to complete my escape without detection.

While I would have preferred to have waited until the majority of the camp had gone to sleep I wasn't about to take a chance that my attempted escape would be discovered.

Knowing that I would soon be fighting for my life against overwhelming numbers I hoped that the element of surprise would be on my side. The sun had now set and the long shadows created by the firelight hid my movements as I released the remaining lashings that held me tight. Once loose I quickly slipped behind the wagon wheel for cover as I determined my next course of action.

I needed to get to my weapons without being seen. Once I was armed I would be better equipped to fight back so my first priority was to make my way to where my weapons had been thrown near the fire outside the chief's tent.

Staying in the shadows I slipped quietly from under the wagon to the dark side of the nearest tent and just as I prepared to move to the next a loud noise came from the north end of the camp. Instantly warriors were yelling and rushing in that direction. It didn't take but a few minutes and the warriors came rushing back through the camp with the entire herd of grall right on their heels. Someone had stampeded their animals and in the back of my mind I knew who to thank for the distraction.

Taking advantage of the chaos I moved into the open and made my way directly to my weapons. Quickly I strapped on my swords and shoved my dagger into my belt. The Tagus were too occupied with trying to avoid being run down by their own mounts to even take notice that I was moving among them.

The spread of the grall's horns added to the chaos as the leather of tent after tent was hooked by a horn and ripped loose from the framework that supported it. The camp was beginning to look more like a war zone than an organized encampment.

I reached the chief's tent just as he exited to see what the commotion was. He stepped out just seconds before the covering was ripped open and the interior and all its occupants were exposed.

Fires were beginning to spread throughout the camp as the heavily hooved feet of the grall scattered the hot embers of the fires into the surrounding grasses. Confusion reigned throughout as warriors, women and children together tried to salvage as much of the camp as possible while avoiding the charging grall.

Through the now open skeletal structure that remained of the tent of Tallis I could see Marlen still bound by the neck and lashed to the throne where I had seen her earlier. Tallis stood before the tent structure looking to the north trying to make sense of the confusion overwhelming his camp. Charging straight towards him I rushed to free Marlen and as I neared Tallis he turned and immediately recognizing me he reached for his sword. Unable to slow down as I approached him it was impossible to bring the business end of my sword to bear to defend myself. Expecting me to confront him with steel Tallis was unprepared for my next move. Rather than stopping to fight I pushed forward even faster catching Tallis unprepared and as I passed by I struck him a savage blow to the side of the head with the butt of my sword. He immediately slumped to the ground.

Any lesser man would have stopped and cut Tallis's throat from ear to ear but I could not bring myself to kill a defenseless man as he lay unconscious. Immediately I went to Marlen's side and pulling my dagger cut the leather collar from her throat. Jumping to her feet she threw her arms around my neck and hugged me.

"I knew you would come for me Jack," she said looking adoringly into my eyes.

"We must hurry Marlen," I said. "We need to get clear of this camp before they realize what has happened."

Leading her by the hand we slipped through the side of the tent structure and quickly made for the darkness of the grasslands beyond. Running briskly through the grass we were nearly one hundred yards clear of the camp when grall came charging through the darkness. Pushing Marlen behind me I stood with sword in hand prepared to defend her against the charging grall. As I prepared to meet the initial charge of the beasts head on they came sliding to a halt just short of trampling me into the ground and instantly I recognized Sodan seated on the back of the lead animal.

"Hurry," he yelled. "We don't have much time before the Tagus come to the realization that the stampede was a ruse for you and Marlen to escape. We need to get as far away as we can before the sun comes up."

"Sodan my friend you have impeccable timing," I praised as I helped Marlen into the saddle of one of the grall. Quickly gaining my seat on the third we spurred our mounts into a full sprint directly to the south. It was only a matter of time before the Tagus found the tracks of our animals but I expected that they would look first to the north and east towards Valcot. The delay should be enough to allow us to put enough distance between us and the camp that they wouldn't be able to make up the ground to catch us. Riding into the night we clung tenaciously to the backs of the grall as they moved at break neck speed out across the prairie.

Continuing to ride throughout the night we grew ever more confident that we had safely put enough distance between us and the Tagus. I was pretty sure that our troubles with Tallis were not over with. I expected that he would not give up on possessing Marlen or getting revenge on me for humiliating him so soundly back in the camp. I had no doubt that I would cross swords with Tallis one day and I intended to be ready.

The sun began to rise and looking over our back trail there was no sign of pursuit. Taking an opportunity to rest our mounts, stretch our legs and get a few minutes of rest we reigned in the grall and dismounted. The tired animals did not stray far as they ate from the abundant grasses and rested.

Convincing Marlen to curl up on the ground and rest I spoke softly with Sodan.

"How long do you think we have before they will be in pursuit?" I asked.

"They will have restored the camp to order by now," he replied. "Now that day light is here they will be gathering their mounts. I would estimate that we have about two more hours before they will begin searching for our trail. It will probably take them another two hours to find the tracks of our grall and begin the pursuit. Since we already have about an eight hour start it will take about twelve hours to get here."

"That isn't much of a lead but it is better than being at a dead run trying to get away," I said. "Let's rest here for about four hours and then be on our way. Where do we go from here?"

"I have an idea," Sodan responded. "In my youth I spent many summers living with one of the plains tribes, the Hollo. Their territory is due south of where we are now. If they are in their traditional summer hunting grounds and we can reach their camp before the Tagus catch up, we will be safe."

"That sounds like a really good plan to me," I responded. "I will stand guard for a couple of hours while you sleep. I will wake you in a couple of hours." Sodan curled up into a large tuft of grass and was quickly asleep.

I envied the people that I had met on Phoria for their ability to fall into a deep sleep instantly. In a land where survival is predicated by the skills of an individual it is important to get sleep when you can because you never know for sure when the next opportunity will present itself.

Two hours of watching the horizon to the north revealed no sign of pursuit. Marlen was still sleeping soundly when I woke Sodan to take his two hour watch while I grabbed a quick power nap. Two hours wasn't enough to get completely rested but it would take the edge off the weariness. Wasting no time I curled up next to Marlen and joined her in sleep.

Time went by too quickly for Sodan woke me up after what seemed like mere minutes since I had closed my eyes. Forcing myself to full wakefulness I called gently to Marlen. As she awoke she looked around quickly as if trying to ascertain where she was. Seeing me she seemed satisfied that everything was okay and we quickly re-mounted our grall and were once again increasing the distance between us and the Tagus.

We no longer pushed our mounts to their maximum speed. Maintaining a steady lope we covered vast distances across the plains as we sought any sign of the Hollo.

Around noon we again stopped and dismounted for a break from riding. The time in the saddle was beginning to take its toll on our bodies and stretching our legs we endeavored to work the cramps out that had set in from the long hours of clinging to the saddle with our thighs. A warning from Sodan brought our attention to the north and far in the distance we could barely make out a large number of riders pushing their mounts hard. The distance was still too great to make out the numbers but we didn't wait to see how many pursued us. Quickly we jumped to our saddles and set out again to the south as fast as the grall could carry us.

We seemed to be maintaining the distance between us and the riders when without warning my mount stumbled and went to the ground hard. Throwing me forward over its shoulders I hit the ground and rolled to a stop. Jumping to my feet I ran back to my mount only to find it struggling to get to its feet. The animal had stumbled in a hole covered with prairie grass and was now lame and there was no way that this animal would be able to run and keep us ahead of the Tagus.

Leaping to the saddle behind Marlen we again pushed her mount to a run but carrying two riders it was unable to keep pace with Sodan's mount and he was forced to slow his pace in order for us to keep up. Due to our hindered pace our pursuers were slowly closing the gap between us and within the hour they would catch us and we would be forced to fight. Still we pushed our mounts to their limits.

Racing across the plains the Tagus slowly gained ground on us. Looking back over my shoulder they were now close enough that I could not only make out the number of warriors that chased us but I could also see that Tallis was in the lead. In desperation we spurred our mounts even harder but still the Tagus gained ground.

It was now clear that we were not going to be able to outrun the Tagus and yelling to Sodan I told him that we must find a place to make a stand. In the near distance was a small rise that didn't provide much cover from our pursuers but it would give us the high ground on a raised knoll that would be more easily defended than the flat grasslands. Pointing out the knoll to him we raced to reach it before we were overtaken from behind.

Gaining the knoll we halted our mounts and leaped to the ground. Placing Marlen between us we drew our swords and waited for the ensuing battle to begin. Standing with my long sword in one hand and a short sword in the other I prepared to do battle until either death overtook me or none of my enemies still stood to oppose me.

Slowing their mounts to a walk the Tagus began making their way up the rise gaining ever closer to the summit of the knoll. Halfway up the rise they halted and after looking at us with hatred in their eyes they turned their mounts and pushing them to a run headed towards the north.

Confused I didn't understand what had happened. Why had the Tagus turned tail and run after getting so close to gaining the object of their pursuit? With confusion clearly written across my face I turned to Sodan to ask what had happened and as I did so I saw lined up across the near hill behind us fully one hundred mounted warriors. Sitting stoically in their saddles they merely watched as the Tagus disappeared to the north.

The leader of the unknown warriors approached up the backside of the knoll and as he neared us he raised his hand in greeting. "Welcome Sodan my brother," he said. "It seems that you have changed little, still getting into trouble."

Leaping from his mount he approached on foot and greeted Sodan warmly with a heavy embrace. "It is good to see you Sodan," he said. "It has been a long time since you have walked among the Hollo."

"It is good to see you too Okar," Sodan replied. "This is Jack Wilde and Princess Marlen of Pendak. Yes it would seem that Tallis angers easily but as usual when I needed my brother you were there."

"Come join us in our camp," said Okar. "We have much to catch up on."

Climbing aboard our mounts we followed slowly behind Sodan and Okar as we made our way to the camp of the Hollo.

Chapter Seventeen

The Hollo

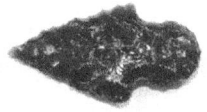

The encampment of the Hollo appeared to be more permanent in nature than the camp of the Tagus where we had been held captive. Asking Sodan about this fact he told me that this was the traditional summer camp of the Hollo and every summer the various bands that make up the Hollo tribe gathered at this location to trade and hunt. It is at this time also that the young men and women that are old enough to mate mingle and seek companionship. The intermarrying between the bands strengthened the genetic diversity of the tribe as a whole.

During the winter the tribe disperses into the individual bands or family groups and fades into the grasslands. Many of the bands head south towards warmer weather but it is only during the summer gathering or in a time of war that all the bands congregate in one place.

Riding into the camp following Okar the atmosphere was one of festivity and celebration in stark contrast to the dreariness that had permeated the camp of the Tagus. The camp of the Hollo was bustling with activity and children were running around everywhere playing a form of chase and tag or imitating the warriors hunting animals. Groups of women were gathered around large swaths of linen cloth that were covered with the seed heads of the grasses that scattered the plains. Rubbing the seed heads back and forth between the palms of their hands they separated the edible seeds from the chafe. Occasionally the women would gather around the circumference of the cloth and lifting it from all sides would throw the seeds into the air and as the seeds dropped back to the cloth the movement of air past them would blow the lighter chaff away. The remaining seeds could now be used for many culinary applications such as ground into flour for making breads, boiled in water for a thick gruel or even gently toasted, steeped in water and fermented to produce strong ale.

Other groups of women were cleaning and drying tubers that I would later learn were similar to dehydrated potatoes and when mixed with water and rehydrated were a wonderful addition to stews.

The tents of the Hollo were dyed bright colors and at the entrance to each tent was a rack of weapons containing pikes, spears and bows and arrows. Leaning against each rack was a shield that displayed the emblem of each individual band. While some of the shields were the same there were easily ten different patterns represented equating to ten different bands or family groups that made up the tribe of the Hollo.

On the edge of the camp young women were combing the loose hair from the tribes herd of grall. The hair was similar to wool and when spun into a durable yarn was used to make blankets and an assortment of clothing items. The young women giggled and laughed for nearby the young men of the tribe practiced with their weapons. Actually it was a combination of practice and showing off for the young women. The young men had placed a target consisting of an animal hide stuffed with grasses at twenty paces and they would take turns throwing spears at a red dab of paint that represented the sweet spot on the target. Very few hit the target and this only fueled the young women's laughter even more.

When we arrived at the camp the large band of riders that had come to our rescue dispersed and went about their own business. We continued to follow Sodan and Okar to a large tent in the middle of the camp and arriving at the entry to the tent we dismounted and unsaddled our mounts. Stacking our gear near the entrance we released the grall to make their way to the herd and entered the tent behind Okar. The trappings on the inside were relatively sparse for a chief's tent but comfortable. Linen hangings separated the tent into three large rooms. The main room in the center contained a large chair ornately decorated with pillows that served as the receiving area where Okar conducted the official business of his duties as the chief of the tribe

Pulling back a linen curtain Okar invited us to enter a second room within the tent. This room was more casually decorated with a low table and pillows for seating. Arrayed around the walls were baskets and chests containing Okar's personal belongings. Motioning for us to be seated he stepped to the back of the room and when he returned placed a wooden cask and four large tankards upon the table. Tapping a wooden spigot into the bung of the cask he filled the tankards with ale. It wasn't the ice cold ale that I preferred but it was wet and it would work to wash the dust from my parched throat. He passed the tankards around the table as he filled them and then began to speak.

"So my seafaring friend," he said speaking to Sodan. "What brings you once again onto the plains of Astor?"

"A rescue mission actually," replied Sodan. "Two days ago Tallis and his Tagus swine abducted Marlen from my father's palace in Valcot. After successfully avoiding an ambush we simply trailed the mounts of the dead Tagus to their encampment and affected a rescue."

"Old Tallis did not seem to be too happy with the results of your rescue," Okar said laughing.

"Old Tallis is never happy," replied Sodan encouraging more laughter.

Taking a deep draught of the ale I asked a question that had been puzzling me since we encountered the Hollo. "Forgive me Okar," I asked "but I don't understand how you happened to be on the hill directly in our path with such a large contingent of warriors. There were way too many for a hunting party and all seemed prepared for war."

"We were not there by chance Jack," he replied candidly. "Life on the plains requires that you know where your enemies are and what they are about. My warriors continuously track the Tagus and periodically report back to me. We were aware of Tallis leaving Valcot but we were not aware of the dire mission that he carried out. My scouts watched the attempted ambush on you from a distance as well as your daring escape from the chaos that you two created in the camp of the Tagus. As you escaped across the plains my scouts stayed just ahead of you beyond the horizon. Their arrival here gave us enough time to mount up and make our way to where you first encountered us."

"And your timing could not have been better," I replied with a chuckle.

"I would not have missed an opportunity to see Tallis turn tail and run like the coward that he is," Okar laughed. "Will you be staying for the games?" he asked turning to Sodan.

Sodan looked to me for my approval of the delay and with a nod of my head I signaled my acquiescence.

"Why yes, I believe that we will be staying for the games," he replied.

"Wonderful," Okar gushed. "I would like to invite both of you to compete. The scouts that observed your ambush spoke quite highly of the prowess that you both displayed in battle. It would be good for my men to see other fighters in action."

I began to get a little nervous. Not having any idea what constituted the games of which Okar spoke the mention of fighting caught my attention.

Sodan must have seen the concerned look on my face because he quickly interjected. "The games are a test of skills," he said. "Some events are performed from the back of a grall while others are on the ground. As a whole the games consist of the use of weapons on targets as well as physical endurance. They are quite fun actually and the atmosphere is one of competitive festivity."

Noticeably relieved I downed my ale and said, "I would love to compete." I have always been a little bit of a competitive person anyway from the time that I played little league baseball all the way through college. While competing for the sake of competing can be fun there is always that little extra drive that I liken to a little devil on my shoulder that pushes me to be the best. If you are going to put forth the effort to do something you might as well do what you can to be the best at it.

Marlen had been sitting quietly taking in the conversation. Taking this opportunity she chimed in her jab at me. "I think that it would be fun to see you compete in the games Jack," she said laughing. "It should be interesting to see how well you have adapted to the culture of Phoria in such a short time."

Looking a bit puzzled and confused Okar asked the next question, "You aren't from Phoria?"

"No I am not. I am from another world a long way away," I replied. His confusion seemed to grow ever deeper and I spent the next two hours and twice as many tankards of ale narrating the tale of my coming to Phoria and the events that had transpired since my arrival.

At the end of my tale Okar sat with his jaw agape trying to process the information that I had given. His world had no frame of technological reference by which to compare the feasibility of my story and after a few minutes of deep thought he responded.

"Let's just say you are from a land far way," he said.

At that we all broke into laughter and poured another ale.

It was now getting late into the evening and Okar had food brought to us. It was a thin stew of grall meat and vegetables that sat very well on the stomach after having drunk so much ale.

Marlen was growing noticeably tired and being the good host that he was Okar offered up the third room of the tent for her use. The three men would make do with the room in which we currently sat. After Marlen had retired for the night we continued to talk and share stories for another couple of hours before finally turning in to get some sleep. Throwing us linen blankets Okar motioned for us to pick a spot and get confortable. Curling up next to the table with the seating pillow beneath my head I lay there contemplating what the next few days would hold for me. I did not know for sure but I did know that I would sleep well tonight with a belly full of ale and stew and a large contingent of warriors protecting us. Slowly I drifted off to sleep.

The sun was beating down on the tent when I awoke the next morning. The temperature was already beginning to rise inside and stepping clear of the blankets that I had been wrapped in I could see that Sodan and Okar were already up and gone. Pulling back the curtain that divided the tent into separate rooms I walked through the main room and then out through the tent flap into the open air. A soothingly warm breeze pressed against the side of my face as I looked around the camp taking in the activities.

Not far from Okar's tent I saw Marlen conversing with a group of women that were working at a small spinning wheel. They were spinning the grall hair into a fine thread to be used for making cloth.

Sitting down on the ground next to the weapons rack in front of the tent I watched Marlen as she interacted with the Hollo women. She appeared to be very happy and in good spirits as she and the other women joked back and forth. I think that this was the happiest that I had seen her since we had first met and I loved to sit and look at the smile on her face and hear the pleasant ring of her laughter as she enjoyed the other women's company.

Lost in my revelry I didn't even notice as Sodan walked up and sat down next to me.

"Good morning sleepy head," he said with a smile.

"Good morning," I replied. "I guess the ale required a little longer to sleep off than I had expected."

"It happens," Sodan replied. "Today I will teach you some of the events for the games. After all I can't have you embarrassing us both," he said laughing.

Joining in I played along with his joke. "You are right," I said. "That would surely reflect poorly on your skills as a teacher."

Laughing loudly we both rose to our feet.

"You have the bite of a cornered banda Jack Wilde," he said. "I am glad that we are on the same side."

"As am I Sodan, as am I," I replied.

Moving through the camp we greeted people as we went. The sun of Phoria was darkening my tan so my light complexion did not draw as much attention as it had during my arrival in Valcot. The Hollo were a happy people and did not mind taking a few minutes of their time to share pleasantries with one another.

After many stops to say good morning and ask about one's health Sodan and I finally arrived at the spot adjacent to the camp where the young men practiced. Yesterday I had thought that they were merely showing off for the young women but now I realized they were also preparing for the upcoming games.

The young men were throwing spears at a target just as I had seen them doing the day before and taking a spear in hand Sodan stepped up to the line, brought his arm back and bringing it forward swiftly released the shaft. Watching in amazement my eyes tracked the path of the spear through the air and into the center of the red painted spot on the hide. The young men hooted with excitement and patted Sodan on the back. Now it was my turn.

The throwing of spears was a new thing for me. While I had thrown the javelin in high school that was based more upon distance rather than on accuracy but at least I had the basic fundamentals needed to get the spear to fly. Stepping to the line with my arm back I carefully took aim and bringing my arm forward swiftly I released the spear. While my throw had plenty of room for improvement I was pleased to see the tip of the shaft pierce deeply into the leather target. My effort garnered praise from the men as well as a chuckle or two from the young women that were gathered around. For the next hour Sodan and I took turns hurling spears at the target with the young men, all the time my accuracy getting better and better.

"That is a good start," Sodan said. "Now do you think that you can do as well from the back of a charging grall?"

I looked at him quizzically preparing to laugh and then I realized that he was serious.

"Are you serious?" I asked.

"Yes, that is the next event," he replied with a grin.

"Bring it on," I responded with confidence. "I will try anything once."

We made our way to the herd of grall that browsed nearby. Finding the two animals that we had ridden out of the camp of the Tagus we led them to Okar's tent and saddled them up. Climbing to our seats we each grabbed a spear from the rack in front of the tent and spurring the animals returned to the practice field.

With an outstretched arm Sodan pointed out another stuffed target about one hundred yards distant.

"The object is to charge the grall past the target and as you draw abreast of it release the spear," he said. "I will go first, follow my lead." Placing heels to the ribs of the grall Sodan let out a war cry as the animal charged like a bolt towards the target. Just before reaching it he pulled back his arm and prepared to throw and just as the head of the grall drew even with the target he brought his arm forward and released. Like a moth to a flame his spear sought out the center of the target and stuck fast.

Sodan made it a point of setting the bar high and forcing me to perform at my best. I wasn't going to let him down this time either.

With a savage yell I urged my mount into a heavy sprint. Preparing my throw I released as I came up beside the target. The throw was good but the release was a fraction of a second too soon and my spear dug deep into the earth just before reaching the target. Reigning in my mount I turned it quickly and trotted it back to the target. Sodan was already there when I arrived.

"You need to be patient and not push the release," he said.

"So it would seem," I replied. "Let's go again.

Pass after pass we assaulted the target. While my aim and release improved I continued to miss the sweet spot of the target. Continually missing would have discouraged a lesser man but for me it just drove me harder to get the timing right. Again and again I pushed the grall past the target. Sodan had given up the practice long ago and left me to stew in my own efforts for success. At one point I saw him and Marlen standing at the edge of the camp watching me. Finally I had had enough. I never did find the center of the target but it wasn't for lack of trying. Turning the grall back towards the camp I returned to Okar's tent arriving just in time for the evening meal.

Unsaddling the grall I turned it loose and Marlen met me at the entryway to the tent demanding that I clean up before coming in to eat. A small barrel of water was positioned at the corner of the tent. Immersing my head into the water I scrubbed the prairie dust from my face and neck. Turning my attention to my arms I scrubbed vigorously with calloused hands and water very nearly having to scrape the caked on dust and sweat from them. Once I felt that I was presentable I returned to the interior of the tent and joined Marlen, Sodan and Okar for a meal of roasted grall and warm ale.

"We must rest tonight," Okar said. "The opening events of the games are tomorrow."

With a little food and ale in my body I was finding it hard to stay awake from sheer exhaustion. Bidding us good night Marlen went to her room. Curling up in our blankets we were sound asleep within minutes.

Chapter Eighteen

The Games

At dawn the next morning I was feeling the anticipation of what the day held. Sitting outside the tent flap I watched as the sun rose slowly into the sky and the heart of the camp began to beat with life as people awoke and set about their morning routines. Sitting quietly and meditating I went over and over the riding event in my head trying to visualize the process from the beginning all the way to the point that the spear penetrated the center of the target. In my mind this allowed me a way to practice without physically performing the steps of the event.

I had not been sitting long when I felt the presence of Marlen standing next to me. Looking up at her I greeted her with a smile. Sitting down next to me she leaned her head on my shoulder watched the activities of the camp as they increased.

"You are up early this morning Jack," she stated. "Is everything okay?"

"It is now that you are here with me," I replied.

"Are you ready for the games today?" she asked.

"I am as ready as I will ever be I think. My only concern is ensuring that I make a good showing today. I don't have to win but I would prefer to not be the laughing stock of the camp if I can help it," I said.

"You will do just fine Jack," she said. "Sodan says that you have a natural skill with weapons like he has never seen before and that most warriors require years of practice just to get to the level that you are at now. Give it your best and I will be proud of you regardless of the outcome."

Blushing I tingled with excitement at her words. If nothing else I needed to perform well for her because I did not want her to be embarrassed as a result of my actions.

"Thank you Marlen," I replied. "Your support and belief in my abilities means a lot to me." I would not let her down.

We sat there for a little while longer just enjoying each other's company and watching the morning activities of the camp. Soon we were joined by both Sodan and Okar.

"The games will start when the sun is directly overhead," Okar said. "Relax and get something to eat, it is going to be a long day."

Marlen entered the tent and returned shortly with wooden bowls filled with cold meat and vegetables. She passed two bowls to Sodan and Okar who thanked her and then left to set about the preparations for the beginning of the games at noon.

The food was cold but it filled that empty spot deep in our stomachs. After we had finished eating Marlen pulled me to my feet.

"Walk with me Jack," she said.

Continuing to hold my hand we walked through the camp. The women were stoking the fires and beginning to cook the food that everyone would be eating throughout the day and the warriors were gathered on the practice field preparing for the expected events of the day. One group was pacing out distances for the spear throw and driving stakes into the ground while another group was pounding similar stakes topped with red linen flags into the ground to delineate the event area for the mounted competition. Okar was overseeing the preparations.

As we walked Marlen would stop occasionally to exchange greetings with many of the women that we passed and halfway through the camp she turned to speak to me.

"I really like it here Jack," she said. "The people are all so friendly and even though the nomadic life is hard work it is a simple life that I could really throw my heart into."

"I am really enjoying it here as well," I said.

"I would love to see my father again," she said. "But I would be perfectly content to live here among the Hollo with you."

Taken by surprise I wasn't sure how to respond and after a few seconds of thought to process her words I replied simply, "Maybe one day this will be an option for us Marlen, but first I need to make good on my promise to you. That promise was to get you safely home to Pendak and back in your father's arms. Once that promise has been fulfilled then we can determine what path suits us together."

With a smile she kissed me on the cheek and then walked off looking back at me over her shoulder. Joining in with a group of women that were cooking large pots of vegetables on a fire she assisted them with the preparations.

Left to my own devices I continued to wander through the camp back towards the field of the games. Stopping more than once I played tag with groups of overly active children and laughing loudly wrestled them to the ground and tickled them. The children were an interactive part of the camp and it was impossible to not be impacted with their infectious laughter and exuberant youthful energy.

Agreeing with Marlen, living among the Hollo would be a wonderful life that I would truly enjoy sharing with her and maybe one day we could.

My thoughts deep in my own mind were interrupted by the sound of Sodan calling my name loudly. Drifting back from my daydreams I located him and made my way to his side.

"Okar has requested that we ride for his band today," he said. "The band that successfully wins the most events today will garner bragging rights as the winning band until next year. Already there are personal wagers being taken among the warriors and you seem to be the focus of many of the bets."

"Me?" I asked questioningly. "How can that be, I'm not well known here."

"Easy my friend," he said laughing. "Many of the warriors witnessed your practice sessions yesterday and the bet is split. Half think that you will surprise everyone with a win and the other half thinks that you will fail miserably."

"That doesn't exactly inspire one with confidence," I said sarcastically. "So which side of that fence are you on?" I asked.

"Well of course I am your most ardent supporter," he laughed. "I must admit though that it has been pretty easy finding people to take my wagers."

"Wonderful," I laughed. "Just remember to give me my cut."

As we laughed Okar approached. "My young warriors are looking forward to your show of prowess today," he said straining to keep a straight face.

"Well I will do my best to not disappoint them," I replied.

"It is all in good fun Jack," he said with a snicker. "I remember the last unknown warrior that we had participating in the games. He cost me a fortune in grall and supplies," he said looking squarely at Sodan and laughing.

Somehow I felt a little relieved knowing that not long ago Sodan had been in my same position and yet he had survived to earn both the respect and admiration of these warriors. There was hope for me yet.

The playful ribbing came to an end as I was rescued by the arrival of a couple of warriors carrying a cask of ale and a sack full of tankards. Tapping the barrel they passed full mugs to everyone. Once everyone had a fresh draught in hand Okar began to speak.

"The games will begin within the hour," he said. "The first event will be the spear toss for accuracy, the second will be the mounted spear toss for accuracy, and the final event will be a surprise to all participants. When it is time, it will be revealed. Drink up."

Sensing that the games would soon begin, the rest of the members of the Hollo started to gather round. Okar called the leaders of the bands to the line for the first event. After speaking with them briefly each leader called two warriors forward. Sodan and I would team with Okar. The rules of the event were explained clearly to all. All three members of each band would throw at the first distance of twenty paces. Anyone that missed the target would be eliminated from the event. After each round the target would be stretched out another ten paces and the remaining participants would throw again. The event would continue in this fashion until all but one participant had been eliminated. The one participant left would be declared the winner of the event.

The first two rounds of throws at twenty and thirty paces were uneventful. The third round at forty paces began to stretch out the throwing capabilities of most of the participants and the field began to thin as a number of spears fell short of the target. The fourth round at fifty paces was the breaking point for most of the warriors. To my great surprise both Okar and Sodan were eliminated in this round. After all the throws had been completed only three bands remained in the competition, two others and I.

The warriors tending the target marched out another ten paces and propped the target up with bunches of grass so that it could be clearly seen from a distance. Drawing straws we determined the order in which we would throw. I drew the second toss.

The first warrior approached the line and then took two big steps backwards. At this distance a standing throw was impossible at best and a short run up to the release was required to gain the additional distance. Stepping forward on his approach the warrior released his spear as he hit the line. Watching the spear cut through the air I could see that his left to right alignment was on the money and I breathed an audible sigh of relief as the tip of his spear impacted the dirt a foot short of the target.

Beginning to feel the pressure of the situation I took two deep breathes before I started my approach to the line. Looking back on my track and field experience with the javelin I went through my mental checklist visualizing the approach and release. Achieving maximum distance required that every step in the process be performed flawlessly. Launching myself forward with my arm back I snapped it forward in one smooth motion synchronized with the momentum of my body. Releasing the shaft smoothly and ensuring that my follow-through was complete I watched as the shaft pierced the air and zeroed in on a single point sixty paces away. Holding my breath I focused my concentration on the flight of the shaft as if I could will it into the target. The flight lasted only seconds but seemed like an eternity with an audible thud my spear impacted the target inches below the center mark. With shaking knees I exhaled the breath that I had been holding. Sodan and Okar both stepped forward to congratulate me on the achievement. Accepting their praise we stepped away from the line to allow the last participant to throw.

The results of this last throw would determine if another round was needed or if I would be hailed as the winner of the event. Quickly approaching the line the warrior released his spear into the air. My heart skipped a beat as I could clearly see that he had the necessary distance to reach the target. Watching with anticipation I was filled with elation when the spear impacted the ground to the right of the target.

The whole group broke out in celebration and pounded me on the back in congratulations. Stepping forward to my competitor I shook his hand and embraced him congratulating him on his valiant effort. There was no mistake in my mind that it was by the merest of chance that his spear had veered at the last second missing the target. Chance and luck had both been with me on this event.

Traditionally the tribe took breaks in between the events to eat, drink and socialize. Moving to where the food had been prepared and laid out everyone mingled while partaking of the warm ale, roasted meats and vegetables.

Marlen jumped into my arms and gave me a big hug. "I knew you could do it Jack," she said.

"I wish that I had been as confident as you," I replied. "I'm glad to have that event over with."

"Come and eat before the next event begins," she urged.

Preparing a small meal for the both of us we found a spot on the edge of the group and shared the food and drink between us.

It was still early afternoon when Okar again called everyone to the game field for the next event. The same three competitors from each band would again compete in the mounted event. This competition would be similar to the first in the sense that after each round the target would be moved an additional ten paces from the approach line that the grall would run along. Elimination followed the same rules, miss and you are out.

This event really perplexed me. For some reason I was unable to get the timing right for the release and flight of the spear to coincide with the momentum of the grall. I had a feeling that I would need a lot more practice before I would be competitive at this event.

The first round began with the target at twenty paces from the line. The competitors began their runs at the target and everyone was easily finding the target at twenty paces. Then it was my turn. Jumping to the back of the grall I kicked it soundly in the ribs and started my run up the line. Nearing the target I prepared to launch my spear and at what I judged in my mind to be the appropriate moment I bought my arm forward and released cleanly. The throw felt good but watching as I passed on the grall I was disappointed to see the tip of the spear graze past the target and bury itself into the dirt beside it.

Returning to the starting line I was met with many a pat on the back and poke in the ribs. The warriors playfully joked at my misfortune and many offered excuses that I might use such as the wind caught it or the target moved. Laughing along with them I took it all in stride. I had already won one event and being the good sport that I was I was big enough to take a loss graciously.

The first round continued and at the end of it I was the only one that had been eliminated. The target tenders moved the target out to thirty paces and the competitors began the next pass one-by-one. After the second round had been completed eight bands still had warriors in the event. Okar and Sodan had both survived the target at thirty paces.

The target now at forty paces the third round began. One at a time the competitors completed their passes and one at a time they were eliminated as their attempts at the target fell short. The result of Sodan's run at the target had a completely different result. His pass was flawless and his spear impaled the target dead center. Okar did not fare as well, his spear impacting the dirt just before the target resulting in his elimination. At the completion of the round only Sodan had successfully hit the target at forty yards from the back of a grall.

Again the entire tribe gathered around to congratulate the winner and console the losers. The whole event was for fun and nobody took the results of the events personally so the playful ribbing and joking that went back and forth was done in the spirit of festivity and not through any malice.

When an opportunity presented itself I asked Sodan what the trick was to judging the momentum of the grall and when to release the spear. It was then that I found out the secret to his success and the foundation of the skill that allowed him to excel in this event.

When I asked him he simply replied, "Practice."

"Practice?" I asked.

"Lots of practice, but not from the back of a charging grall," he replied.

I wasn't following along with the meaning of his explanation and the confusion on my face must have been apparent for he began to elaborate on his cryptic answer.

"As a young man growing up in Valcot I got a lot of practice spearing fish from the deck of a pitching boat," he began, "Compensating for the movement of the vessel, the deflection of the water and the quickness of the fish required the development of a keen instinct that calculates the variables subconsciously. So basically there is no one trick to hitting the target. For me it is all done by instinct that was honed over years practice."

I now knew what I had been doing wrong on every attempt to hit the target from the back of the grall. I had been trying to guide the spear to the target rather than letting my instinct tell me when to release. It would still take lots of practice to polish that instinct but I had no doubt that I would do much better the next time I tried that event.

It was now late afternoon and Okar jumped to the top of an ale cask and motioned for the gathered bands to be quiet. He started his speech by congratulating Sodan and I for winning the first two events. Then he turned the focus of the speech to the third and unknown event.

"Only one event remains of the games and it will take place tomorrow morning," he started. "At this point only I and a select few others know what the final event entails. Since the competition between the bands has already been decided by the first two events the final event will be to determine the heartiest warrior here. The last event will test your individual fighting skills but make no mistake it won't be easy. So to prepare I want everyone to eat well, drink much and have fun. Let the festivities of the evening begin."

Tankards were filled to overflowing with warm ale and musical instruments had been produced. As the sun set the music peeled through the evening air and men and women danced, ate and drank. The merriment was contagious and downing my ale I lead Marlen among the revelers and taking her in my arms we joined in with the dancing.

Chapter Nineteen

The Mondor

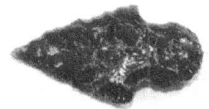

The revelry lasted late into the evening and the music and dancing fueled the festivities until the musicians could no longer play and only then did the crowd begin to thin. Marlen and I had turned in well before midnight while Sodan and Okar both fought to be the last one present.

With the sound of the music and laughter in the background I slept very well that night. My days of partying until the sun came up had passed me by long ago and now sleep was my elixir of choice to get through the nights.

It was early morning and I lay wrapped up tightly in the blankets listening to the snoring that was coming from Okar and Sodan and reflected upon the happenings of the first day of the games. Considering my abysmal performance in the mounted event, the results of the day were quite satisfying. I had won the spear tossing event and Sodan had won the mounted event. The third and main event was to take place today and I was a little bit nervous about it because nobody seemed to know what it would entail. Sodan and I had tried to ply Okar with enough ale the night before to get him to slip with some hint of what we could expect but he was as tight lipped as ever. He would only laugh at us and say, "don't worry about it." Either way we had already won the bragging rights for Okar's band of the Hollo.

The second day of the festivities would be starting with games of endurance for the children and events using small weapons for the women. Once those events were done the third event for the men would take place.

My body was feeling a little stiff from the activities of the night before and clambering out of bed I thought to take a walk and stretch out my sore muscles before the activities of the day began. Strapping on my swords I made my way to the entrance of the tent walking quietly to not wake anyone. Once outside the tent I could see that sunrise was still an hour or so away and I estimated that I had a good three hours to work with before people would wake up and be about the business of the morning. Making my way towards the edge of the camp I made it a point of passing directly by one of the perimeter guards so that they knew that I was out and about. I did not want to find myself in a position of being attacked upon my return because the guards mistook me for a stranger.

Walking steadily I cleared the protected edge of the camp and made my way out onto the prairie. Cresting the hill nearest to the camp I looked out upon flat rolling grasslands and as far as I could see there was nothing but gently waving thigh high grass.

Tightening my harness and checking the security of my weapons I broke into a gentle jog to loosen up my leg muscles and get my heart pumping. I had always been an occasional jogger back on Earth and while my running had not been frequent enough to develop an addiction to where I had to run every day I felt that running every now and then helped me to remain limber and maintain my flexibility. The stiffness and pain that I felt in all my muscles from the competition yesterday only reinforced my need to limber up.

Having covered about two hundred yards at a steady jog my body was feeling pretty good. Picking up the pace I was soon sprinting across the prairie as fast as my legs could carry me. Maintaining this pace for another two hundred yards I then reigned myself in and returned to the steady jog that I had started with. I maintained this pace for a good forty five minutes before I stopped to rest my aching lungs.

Continuing to walk with my hands behind my head I took slow steady breaths allowing my body to take in as much oxygen as it could distill from the air entering my lungs. When my body had quit struggling for air I turned back towards the camp. By the time I got back I expected that everyone would be up and about and the children's games should be well underway. Once again I began to jog retracing my steps back towards the camp.

Three quarters of the way back to camp I began to feel uneasy as if someone was watching me. The hair on the back of my neck stood up and I looked around me while I jogged. Looking back over my shoulder I caught sight of a trail of moving grass heading in my direction and I didn't need to see what it was that was making its way through the grass behind me. I had seen the grass move like that before just before the mondor had attacked the grall that Sodan and I had been tracking to the Tagus. A mondor had picked up my scent and was on my trail and closing fast. Breaking into a sprint I tried to increase the distance between us but the mondor only moved faster to keep pace.

Reaching the edge of the low hill overlooking the camp of the Hollo it was becoming clear that I would not escape from this toothy predator or that I would be able to make the safety of the camp. Although I could see the camp, the distance was too great for me to cover even at a full sprint. Looking around quickly I sought a location that I would be able to defend against the animal and twenty yards down the hill was a clear spot where the tall grasses had all been laid low by the heavy bodies of grall that had bedded there. Moving quickly to the center of the clear area I drew both of my swords and crouched low facing in the direction that the Mondor would come.

Sensing that I no longer fled the mondor crept slowly from the tall grass into the open. Knowing that this animal would strike quickly trying to bite into my flesh, I could not allow this to happen. The mondor began to slowly circle my position and I turned with it continually facing the threat.

Like a flash of lightning the mondor charged towards me. Meeting its gnashing teeth with solid steel I stepped to the side to prevent the animal from bowling me over. Hacking wildly at its back as it passed I inflicted numerous wounds that barely cut through the tough leathery hide. Turning quickly it again faced me looking for another opportunity to strike. The mondor hissed loudly at the pain that I had inflicted and the loud raspy noise had caught the attention of the camps perimeter guards and I could hear them sounding the alarm throughout the camp.

The mondor charged again into my bare steel, stepping quickly to the side at the last minute I swept my long sword low severing the animal's front leg from its body as I stabbed my short sword deep into its side. In pain the mondor lashed out with its teeth at my shoulder as I quickly rolled away. I wasn't quick enough as the sharp teeth of the mondor raked across my skin drawing blood. Springing to my feet I was beside the creature and clear of its claws and teeth. Taking advantage of my position I brought my long sword down across the back of the animal's neck slicing halfway through its thick body. Severing its spine the animal dropped to the ground on its stomach and hissed wildly as its life ebbed away.

Dropping to one knew from the exertion I braced myself with the long sword to keep from falling. Yelling could be heard coming from the direction of the camp and turning to look I saw Sodan and Okar leading a group of warriors at a dead sprint towards me. The hard work had already been done and the mondor lay in a growing pool of its own blood but I was beginning to feel a searing pain starting to shoot through the muscles of my shoulder where the mondor's teeth had ripped through my skin. Struggling to recall what Sodan had said about the bite of the mondor I finally remembered something about infection and bacteria but I could not clear my thoughts enough to put it all together. Sodan and Okar finally arrived with the other warriors close on their heels and as they ran up to me I looked squarely at both of them, then everything went black as I fell forward onto my face.

When I regained consciousness I slowly opened my eyes to see Marlen looking down at me. I was laid out on the blankets inside Okar's tent and disoriented I struggled to sit up and with Marlen's assistance I finally managed to get to a sitting position.

"How long have I been out?" I asked.

"Nearly three hours," Marlen responded.

"How did I get here?" I asked confused.

"After you killed the mondor you passed out from the rapid spread of bacteria from the bite in your shoulder," she said. "Sodan and Okar brought you here and we cleaned your wounds."

"My shoulder is killing me," I told her.

"Okar says that you will have some stiffness and pain for a while," she replied. "He said that it may take a week or more for the infection to clear your system but you should be fine. Fortunately for you the women of the Hollo have experience treating these types of wounds. They made a poultice of roots for you that will help to draw out the infection."

"My plan to get some exercise and stretch out my muscles seems to have backfired on me," I said with a slight laugh. "I feel worse now than I did before I went out to exercise this morning."

"For now you just need to rest," she said.

"I'm thirsty," I said. "Can you please get me some water?"

Moving to the stores along the wall of the tent she soon returned with a leather bag of water and a wooden cup. Filling the cup with water she handed it to me and I quickly downed the contents and asked for more. Twice more she passed me the cup full of water and my rehydration was complete.

Suddenly I remembered the games. "What of the games," I asked. "Has the last event happened yet?"

"Not yet," she replied. "Everything was delayed while we took care of you. It should be starting within the next hour though."

"I must be there," I said excitedly. "I can't miss the final event of the games."

"Slow down Jack," she said concerned. "There is no way that you will be able to compete in your condition."

I knew that she was right but I still had to know what the last event was and I intended to be there to support Sodan and Okar.

"I will help you to go watch the finale of the games," she said. "But you have to promise me that you will spend the day tomorrow resting and healing."

"Okay," I said with a tone of defeat.

Helping me to my feet Marlen held tight around my waist while I leaned my weight onto her shoulder. Walking slowly we made our way out of the tent and across to the game field.

A great cheer arose from the gathered Hollo at my arrival. Men, women and children all came forward to grasp my arm and congratulate me on my killing of the mondor. Sodan and Okar pushed their way through the crowd until they were near me.

"How is the shoulder," Sodan asked with concern.

"It hurts like hell," I said with a smile. "I hear that I owe you and your people for my survival," I said to Okar.

"You are lucky," he said. "Fortunately for you the wound wasn't deep. The deeper the wound the harder it is to stave off the infection."

"I am very grateful to you and the wonderful women of the Hollo for assisting me," I said sincerely. "So what is the story about the games? Did I make it in time to watch the last event?"

"You surely have Jack," Sodan said.

Okar joined in, "we are just now getting ready to start."

Stepping back onto the field Okar whistled loudly to get everyone's attention. Once everyone had gathered around he finally divulged what the finale entailed.

"The warriors from each band will gather in a great circle on the field," he said. "Two weeks ago I captured a wild grall bull and two warriors have kept him secure away from camp waiting for today. At a signal from me they will lead the bull into the center of the circle and release him. The goal of the game is for the warriors of each band to place as many marked bandanas as possible onto the horns of the grall. The event will last for only five hundred beats of a drum and at that time the band with the most bandanas on the grall will win the event and share the win with the winning band from the first two events." Another warrior stepped forward and pulled marked bandanas from a linen bag and distributed them to the appropriate bands with the corresponding markings. At Okar's direction the warriors circled up and prepared to compete. Waving his hand Okar signaled another warrior who raised a large red flag on a long pole and began waving it back and forth.

With excitement the crowd waited for the arrival of the wild grall and after a few minutes two riders could be seen herding a lone grall across the prairie in the distance. Once they had led the grall into the circle they turned and exited the way they had come. The circle of warriors closed behind them and at another wave of Okar's hand the beat of a drum began.

The circled warriors began to close in on the grall. The animal was clearly agitated and pawed at the ground and snorted wildly. Dropping his head he charged the warrior nearest him. Reacting quickly the warrior jumped to the side. As the grall was distracted by the one warrior another ran in close and slid a bandana which had been tied into a circle over the raging animal's horn. Then smacking the grall on the rump ran clear of the circle.

Again and again the animal charged at the warriors but the sheer numbers that surrounded him kept him confused and unable to focus on any one warrior. Fully half a dozen bandanas now hung from the horns of the grall.

Working together Sodan and Okar approached the animal from opposite sides. Once they were just behind the head on either side Sodan reached out and punched the grall in the neck. When the animal turned its head to try to gore him with its horn Okar slipped his bandana over the horn on the opposite side then quickly slapped the animal on the neck on his side. Quickly the animal turned its head towards him and like a flash Sodan slipped his bandana on the horn on the other side. Then sprinting clear of the circle they both joined me on the sidelines to watch the rest of the event.

Warrior after warrior attempted to slip his bandana onto the horns and while a few succeeded many more failed. Unannounced the rhythmic beating of the drum suddenly stopped. With a loud whistle Okar called an end to the event and the warriors scattered away from the grall as the two mounted warriors moved back in to herd the animal away from the crowd. Once back out onto the prairie the warriors quickly dispatched the animal with their pikes and removing the bandanas brought them to Okar.

Tallying the bandanas Okar announced that his band had placed two onto the horns of the grall, but another band had managed to place all three of their bandanas. Calling the leader of the other band forward Okar raised the leaders hand in victory. The entire crowd broke out in a loud cheer and milled about congratulating the victorious band.

The whole tribe began to make their way to where the wild grall had been dispatched. Asking where they were going my curiosity was answered by Okar.

"They are going to butcher the grall for tonight's feast," he said. "Not only was the animal part of the competition but now he will be the meal for the festivities."

Smacking Sodan on the back and waving him forward they both joined the crowd and made their way onto the prairie.

My shoulder was beginning to ache again and I was getting a little light headed.

"I think that I need to lie back down," I said to Marlen.

"Are you okay?" she asked with concern.

"I think so," I replied. "I'm just getting really light headed and nauseous."

"Let's get you back to the tent before you fall," she said.

Leaning heavily on her shoulder we slowly made our way back through the camp and to Okar's tent. While the distance that we needed to cover wasn't very far it took us a while to get there. I could only take about five steps before I needed to stop and rest and allow the nausea to clear but finally after a walk that seemed to take forever

Marlen lead me into the room where she had been sleeping.

"This is your room," I said.

"Yes it is," she replied. "But you are sleeping in here where I can keep an eye on you."

Too tired and weak to argue with her I conceded to her wishes and followed her to the bedding and with her assistance laid down. Wrapping the blankets around me she tucked me in and kissing me on the forehead sat there next to me holding my hand. The last thing that I remember before sliding into sleep was looking up into Marlen's eyes as she smiled down at me.

Chapter Twenty

Recovery

The infection took longer to clear my system than had been anticipated. For two weeks I drifted in and out of consciousness as my fever came and went. Other than to use the bathroom I had barely left the comfort of the linen blankets that Marlen had tucked me into. Every time that I would wake up in between the hallucinatory dreams induced by my fever I would see Marlen watching over me and tending to my immediate needs.

In my few moments of lucidity I remember Okar and Sodan speaking to me more than once but my mind could not grasp the subject of their visits. I assumed that they were checking on me and trying to determine my level of health.

When I finally awoke and came back to my senses I felt pretty good considering that I had spent two weeks in bed fighting off an infection. My body had been severely weakened by the illness and every movement was a struggle of mind over body. Throwing back the blankets I laid there for some time taking stock of my body. While I no longer felt any pain in my wounded shoulder every muscle in my body had been leeched of all energy.

Marlen came to sit next to me when I woke up. While I could still see the concern in her eyes for my condition I could also see the sense of relief that she felt at my recovery.

"Jack I am so glad you are finally awake. How do you feel?" she asked.

"I think that I will live but I am very weak," I replied. "How long have I been sleeping?" I asked.

"You have been in and out of consciousness for two weeks," she said.

"Two weeks?" I responded in surprise.

"Yes Jack," she said. "Right after the last event of the games I brought you here and you have been drifting in and out of consciousness ever since."

"I have got to get out of this bed," I said. "I need some fresh air, food and lots of water."

Helping me to my feet she braced me as we made our way out of the tent. Once outside I took up roost on the saddles that were piled just outside. She brought a blanket and wrapped it around my shoulders.

The people in the camp were busily attending to their daily duties and I just watched and soaked up the sun and fresh air.

"Would you like some food?" Marlen asked.

"I would love some food," I replied ravenously.

She left and made her way through the camp. Returning shortly she had a large piece of roasted meat and vegetables arrayed across a wooden platter and hanging over her shoulder was a leather water bag. Sitting down next to me she handed me the plate of food and poured me a large cup of water. My stomach felt like it was trying to eat my backbone and I tore into the meat and began eating. I had not eaten much before I began to feel nauseous and my stomach threatened to reject everything that I had already eaten. Taking a short break from the food I let it settle in my stomach before I attempted to eat any more. Although I had not eaten anything solid in two weeks I needed to pace my intake to avoid shocking my body.

Once I had eaten my fill I stiffly made my way to my feet. I needed to walk. Too much time of inactivity had caused my muscles to atrophy and I needed to stretch them out to get my energy back. Marlen and I took a short walk around the camp and my movements were extremely slow and I had to rely heavily on her to keep myself upright. Concentrating on the effort of putting one foot in front of the other I barely noticed when we had made our way back to the tent. Helping me back inside the tent she led me again to the bed and bending slowly I fell face forward onto the blankets. Exhausted from the efforts of trying to walk I was very quickly asleep again.

It took another week of the cycle of waking, eating and walking before I was once again feeling like myself. Towards the end of that week I started working with Sodan to get some exercise with my swords to ensure that not only had my strength returned but the agility and stamina that I had before my battle with the mondor was returning.

To my surprise when I woke up from my two week nap the Hollo had declared me the champion of the games as a result of my heroic efforts to kill the mondor and prevent it from getting into camp. To me the battle with the mondor had seemed to be no more spectacular than any one battle that I had fought with banda since my arrival on this planet and I was astonished when Okar had told me that on average it takes three warriors working in unison to bring one down. While I had never seen myself as an overly strong or accomplished warrior I did feel that a large measure of luck had been with me that day and I considered myself to be very fortunate to still be alive.

Marlen and I joined Sodan and Okar for the evening meal. The urge to be on with our mission had been weighing heavily on my mind as of late and even though we were enjoying every second of our stay among the Hallo I still had a promise to keep.

Picking at my food I addressed Sodan. "I think that I am ready to continue on with our journey to return Marlen to Pendak," I said.

"Are you sure Jack?" he replied. "Pendak is still a long way off and there are many potential dangers along the way."

"My sword arm is once again strong," I said. "And if our practice can be any measure then my endurance has once again returned to me. I think that I am ready for whatever dangers we may encounter."

"Very well," he said. "I will follow your lead. When do we leave?"

"We will get on our way at sunrise," I replied. "By what route would you recommend we travel?"

"We have two options. We can travel to the southwest and through the foothills of the southern range," he said. "Or we can ride to the southeast to Marduk and seek passage on a vessel to Pendak. Both routes will take about the same time to travel."

"What do you think Marlen?" I asked. "Would you prefer to travel overland or by sea?"

"My preference would be to travel by sea," she replied. "But I will go by whatever route you think is the safest."

Pondering the options for a few minutes I finally came to a decision. "I think that we shall go by way of Marduk," I said. "I long to have the feel of a pitching deck once again beneath my feet and I would like to become familiar with another city of Astor."

"Very well then," Sodan interjected. "We leave at sunrise for Marduk. We can travel by grall to the city and then seek passage to Pendak from there."

"I will ride with you as far as the city," Okar chimed in. "It won't hurt to have another sword at hand and I can't let the champion of our games travel unprotected."

Everyone around the table laughed at his jibe on my new found fame. I did not take it personally though having grown fond of Okar, his style of leadership and his sense of humor. The members of his tribe respected him and would follow him anywhere and that alone spoke volumes to his character.

While it would feel good to be traveling once again I could not help but feel a tinge of regret at leaving. A morose feeling began to permeate the air that left a sense of sadness where it went. In an effort to break the mood I interrupted the silence that had set in.

"We are travelling not dying," I exclaimed. "We have ale at hand and good friends close by. This should be a time of celebration not of mourning."

Raising my glass I proposed a toast. "To the good friends that we have met, to the adventures that we have had and to whatever the future holds," I said. Tapping our tankards over the table we raised them to our lips and downed the warm ale.

Pouring another round Sodan joined in to raise the spirits of the group. "I too would like to propose a toast," he said. "To my friend Jack and praise be to the luck that guided the speed of his sword so that he may be here with us today."

Again we downed the ale. Merriment began to push out the depressing feeling that had festered in our group and we continued throughout the night joking and drinking.

We rode out of camp early the next morning as the sun was beginning to creep over the plains. It felt good to be in the saddle and moving towards our destination. My mind was still foggy from the drink of the night before but the fresh air blowing in my face as we raced across the plains was quickly clearing it away. Four abreast we rode through the thigh high grass towards Marduk in the southeast. I was grateful to Okar for his decision to accompany us on this leg of the trip. While I was confident that Sodan and I could handle any dangers that may present themselves, having a third sword along was reassuring.

Pushing our mounts throughout the morning we had decided upon a plan to run them hard to cover as much distance as possible and then when they began to tire we would stop and allow them to rest. As the noonday sun shone brightly overhead Okar called a halt and we dismounted and removed their saddles.

"We have about three hours to rest before the grall will again be ready to travel," he said. "We should rest as well and stretch out our legs."

Sodan had already pulled from his saddle bags a number of lengths of wood and a sheet of linen cloth. After only a few minutes he had constructed a small lean-to shelter under which we could get some protection from the sun. Travelling during the hottest time of the day was not advisable if we wanted to keep our mounts alive and neither was resting under the full heat of the sun. The meager shade provided by the linen sheet was sufficient to keep us from roasting in the sun and being even more tired after we had rested.

Side-by-side we four lined up under the shelter of the lean-to and catnapped while the grall grazed nearby. We had packed sufficient supplies of food and water to get us through the trip and Sodan had estimated that we would be on the trail for three days and that we would reach Marduk on the afternoon of the third day.

Over the next three hours we took turns dozing, eating and standing guard. The plains were no place to let your guard down and more than once we had spotted Mondor in the distance. Occasionally we would see wild grall grazing across the grasslands. Giving them a wide berth we did not want to approach too near to them for fear that our mounts would succumb to their herd instinct and want to join them.

After everyone had taken a short nap and rehydrated, Okar and I gathered our mounts while Sodan disassembled the lean-to and stowed it into his saddle bags. Once we had the grall saddled we leaped to their backs and with a kick to the ribs sent them racing forward once again.

My thoughts drifted often as we rode. The tendency of the mind to wander while riding can lead to complacency that equates to inattention in keeping a watchful eye on your surroundings. Shaking my head I regained my focus on the trail ahead and glanced around me into the distance. I could see nothing moving for as far as I could see.

Midafternoon we slowed our mounts to a walk and allowed them to graze a little as we went. Taking this opportunity I engaged Marlen into conversation to see if I could learn a little bit more about the city that we were heading to.

"I haven't heard anything about Marduk," I said. "Obviously it is a coastal city since we plan to seek passage on a ship from there but is there anything else that I should know about what we are riding into?" I asked.

"Marduk is a rough city with danger everywhere," she said. "The waterfront areas are populated with all manner of brigands and cutthroats. While it is a major sea port for trading many of the vessels that berth there are slavers and pirates."

I was beginning to think that I should have chosen the overland route to Pendak rather than risk Marlen's safety among such unseemly sounding characters as she described. We were nearly a full day of travel in the opposite direction of Pendak and second guessing my decision now was too late. Now I just had to rely on the abilities of Sodan and myself to protect Marlen and get her onto a ship headed to Pendak.

"Is there any safety to be found among the leaders of Marduk?" I asked.

"The royal family of Marduk is quite honorable," she said. "But due to the fact that a large portion of the city's economy relies on the goods and money brought in by the pirate types the king has entered into a tenuous alliance with the cutthroats. Basically the alliance is that the king and his army will overlook the illegal activities as long as it profits the city."

"It sounds to me like a measure of lawlessness reigns in Marduk," I replied.

"That would be a fair estimation," she said. "It would behoove us to stay on guard and keep our wits about us until we are safely underway for Pendak."

Riding along in silence for a while I digested the information that Marlen had shared. I hoped that I had made the right decision in travelling to Marduk but only time would tell.

We made camp a short while later and the evening passed without incident.   The entire trip to Marduk was quite uneventful. We changed our path as needed to avoid any altercations with hunting mondor but kept a generally southeast heading.

On the afternoon of the third day I could begin to smell the salt in the air that was being blown inland from the coast. Late in the afternoon we could just start to see the silhouette of the city in the distance. Steadily pushing our mounts we set a pace that would put us into the city before sunset.

Racing across the last stretch of grassland that butted up against the city walls of Marduk we encountered no challenge until we reached the main city gate. Approaching the gate a guard came forth to ask our business and he seemed to be satisfied with our answer of seeking passage to Pendak and returned to his post at the gate.

Dismounting we removed what few personal affects that we had from our saddle bags. It was now time to say good bye to Okar.

Grasping his forearm I thanked him deeply for the assistance that he had provided to us during our stay with his tribe. Expressing my gratitude I made it clear that if it had not been for him and his people I might even now be lying dead out on the plains.

Embracing Okar in a hug Sodan thanked him and wished him good health. Marlen hugged him and kissed him on the cheek and expressed her thankfulness for everything that he and his people had done for us.

He remounted and looking down at us wished us all well and admonished us to not be strangers in the land of the Hollo. Once he had received our promises to someday again spend time with his tribe he turned his mount and trotted off back towards the northwest with our three mounts trailing along behind.

It is always sad saying good bye to a friend but moving on to the next part of our journey was important if I was ever going to get Marlen home.

Side-by-side the three of us turned and walked through the gate of Marduk and entered onto a busy thoroughfare of activity. The main avenue ran slightly downhill and straight through the city ending at the waterfront in the distance. Lining both sides of the street were two story wooden buildings that I was able to determine as we walked down the street housed everything from butcher shops to bakeries and every other type of shop in between. Street vendors were prevalent everywhere.

One particular street vendor caught my attention right away. He was selling thin strips of barbecued meat that had been skewered on a stick, marinated and slow grilled over a brazier. The odor of the cooking meat triggered my hunger responses and my mouth watered profusely and taking a few minutes to stop I purchased a fistful of the meat sticks and distributed them to Marlen and Sodan.

We first needed to find an inn near the waterfront where we could secure lodging for however long it would take to find passage to Pendak. Second we would need to work the taverns along the docks to find a captain willing to take on passengers that was sailing the right direction. Lastly and most importantly we needed to remain safe and alive until we set sail. With our destination being the waterfront we set out down the avenue making our way to the water that could be seen in the distance.

Chapter Twenty-One

Marduk

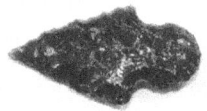

Nobody paid attention to us as we moved down the street. Marduk was obviously a place where the sight of people from different cultures was not a unique occurrence. In my mind this anonymity could work in our favor. Drawing as little attention as possible we were able to pass through Marduk quietly and without incident. My goal was to remain as incognito as we could and hopefully that would last.

Nearing the waterfront the number of people moving about on the street increased and jostling between people we struggled to remain together.   After nearly losing Marlen in the crowd once I took her hand in mine and used my great bulk to muscle my way among the throng. Sodan was easier to keep track of because of his height and towering over most of the people he and I were still able to see each other although ten people or more may be between us.

Traveling west along the waterfront numerous piers jutted out into the bay and in the distance was a natural sand breakwater deposited by the tidal flow over unknown centuries. The breakwater provided a barrier from the forces of the surf on the seaward side and the waters of the bay were relatively calm with the only wave action being created by passing vessels. Lining either side of each pier were ships of every type imaginable including some that sported lines even I wasn't familiar with. Rugged men of the sea worked diligently either loading cargo for shipment or unloading cargo for delivery to local merchants.

Opposite the piers were housed a seemingly never ending line of taverns and inns. Sailors could be seen staggering in and out of the establishments in various stages of inebriation and groups of men weaved their way down the street singing what I took to be a very poor rendition of a local sea shanty. Keeping Marlen tucked in close by my side I used my presence to protect her from being accosted by drunken men.

We had already passed a number of inns on our way down the street but each one that we thought to enter was fronted by a number of rough looking salty dogs that appeared to be seeking trouble. Trying to keep our profile low we opted to keep moving along the waterfront. About a quarter of a mile from the intersection of the main avenue through Marduk and the waterfront we came upon an inn called "The Hook and Ale." This inn seemed to be quieter than the others that we had passed and very few people could be seen loitering out front. Shooting Sodan a quick look as if to ask him what he thought he shrugged his shoulders and moved towards the entryway of the inn with us following close behind.

The door to the inn was propped open with a small wooden keg. Stepping through the door we stood for a few minutes allowing our eyes to grow accustomed to the half-light of the room that was coming from the fading sunlight filtering its way through partially shuttered windows. A large cooking fire blazed on a hearth located on the wall to the right of the entry and along the back wall of the room was a long wooden bar with a couple of patrons occupying seats along its length. In the middle of the room were arrayed a half dozen wooden tables and chairs with customers dotting them. A sailor was passed out face down onto a table against the wall on the right.

Finding an empty table along the wall to the left we sat down and signaled for service from the proprietor. He was a short dumpy fellow with a large balding forehead and wore a grease covered apron around his waist.

"What can I get for you today masters?" he asked as he approached our table.

"Bring us three of whatever you have on the fire," I replied.

Scurrying away he returned shortly with three wooden bowls of a thick stew and a large loaf of bread.

"We will also take three ales to wash it down," Sodan added.

After another trip to the bar the proprietor returned with tankards overflowing with ale. The foaming head on the ale splashed over the table as he set them heavily before us. Nodding our thanks he left us to our meal.

Removing my dagger I sliced thick chunks of the bread. Taking one myself I dipped it into the steaming stew. Tasting of the saturated bread I was impressed with the amount of flavor that the stew contained. The base of the stew appeared to be roasted chunks of grall meat with a heavy helping of vegetables and it was thick from a long day of slow cooking over the fire. I found my appetite appeased very quickly as I continued to sop up the stew with the bread and scoop meat and vegetables out of the bowl with a spoon.

Finishing the meal I sat back in the chair and sipped at the warm ale while Sodan and Marlen finished eating. Looking around the room I measured up the other customers of the establishment. Everyone in the place looked to be content to mind their own business dwelling upon their own thoughts.

Again I waved the proprietor over. "Do you have any rooms available?" I asked.

"I only have one available master," he said.

"That will be fine, we will take it," I replied.

He pointed to a narrow stairway in the corner of the room. "It is the second door on the left at the top of the stairs," he directed.

"Thank you," I replied sincerely. "We will pay for both the room and the meal when we are done eating."

"Very well master," he said. "I will be at the bar should you need anything else." He departed and returned to his roost at the bar.

My companions had completed their meals by this time and we sat enjoying the ale. It felt good to be relaxing and I looked forward to getting some sleep as well.

"I think that I am headed for an early night tonight," I said. "Traveling on the grall and sleeping on the ground has taken it out of me."

"I agree," Sodan replied. "Tomorrow morning I will ask around to see which ships are heading to Pendak and we can determine after that what the next step in our plan is."

"That sounds like a good plan," I said.

"I could use a hot bath," Marlen added as she wiped the foam of the ale from her lip.

"From the smell and look of the people that I have seen in Marduk so far I don't think that a bath will be available," I said laughing.

"That is okay," she replied. "Soon I will be bathing in my own room in my father's palace. I can wait."

A loud crash behind us brought Sodan and I to our feet. Looking towards the door with our hands on the hilts of our swords we saw three men entering the inn past the front door that lay in splinters as a result of being kicked open hard. Watching the men as they entered we were ready for whatever this intrusion on our peace and quiet would hold. Paying us little attention they passed by us and drew their swords as they approached a man sitting quietly at the bar nursing his ale.

The leader of the group spoke loudly to the man at the bar. "You owe us money Rawin," he said.

"I would say that we are even," the one called Rawin replied quietly without turning.

"There are only two ways that we will be even," said the leader. "You give us our money or you are dead. It is your choice."

With his back still turned to the three men Rawin laughed quietly. "This is how I measure even, I will keep your money and you will continue to live," he said.

In a fit of rage the three men charged towards the lone warrior. The next few moments were a blur of activity as Rawin spun off his seat and cold steel flashed through the air. His sword cleared its scabbard so quickly that the leader of the three didn't have a chance to strike before his sword was knocked to the side and a dagger was buried into his heart. The leader's body stiffened and his arms dropped to his side as he stared directly ahead into Rawin's eyes. Slowly his sword fell from his hand hitting the ground with a clang. Dropping to the ground as his knees buckled he fell onto his side dead.

The other two henchmen had not even had a chance to wet their swords. The flash of steel that I had seen flying through the air was daggers that had been buried to the hilt in the throats of the two men and they were both already dead before Rawin had struck the final blow to the leader.

Never had I seen a warrior move as quickly as Rawin had in the few seconds that it took to dispatch the three that harassed him. Sodan and I both looked at each other in amazement at the brief engagement that we had seen.

Turning back around Rawin climbed back onto his stool at the bar and spoke quietly to the proprietor as he signaled for a fresh tankard of ale. "I apologize for the mess," he said. "I will pay for the clean-up."

Sliding a fresh tankard of ale down the bar in Rawin's direction the proprietor replied quickly and respectfully. "That is okay master. I apologize for the interruption. Please don't give it another thought the clean-up is on me," he said.

Running to the front door of the inn the proprietor stepped out and a few minutes later returned with three men who proceeded to drag the dead bodies out. Once the floor had been cleared of bodies the innkeeper bent to scrubbing the fresh blood from the wooden planks.

We sat nursing our drinks until the proprietor had finished with the floor and returned to the bar. Rising from our seats we walked to the bar to pay for our meals, drinks and room before heading up the stairs.

Standing at the bar I glanced over at Rawin but I did not catch his eyes for he sat staring blankly ahead at the wall while he sipped at his ale. Respecting his privacy I said nothing and left him to whatever vision it was that haunted his mind.

At the top of the stairs we found the second door on the left that opened into the room that we had rented and unlatching it I swung it open and stepped in. On Earth I would have held the door for Marlen to enter first but here on Phoria my protective senses had been heightened and I wanted to ensure the room was clear of danger before Marlen came in.

The room was sparsely furnished with a wash basin on a low counter at the far end of the room and two sleeping platforms positioned at the base of the walls to the right and left. The sleeping platforms held thick linen mattresses stuffed with grass and at the foot of each bed were piled linen blankets and sheets. A small window above the wash basin looked out onto the roof of the building next door.

Once I had ensured that it was safe I waved them forward into the room. Marlen went to the bed on the left and pushed down on the mattress with her hands. It appeared to give very little under her weight and maintained its stiffness.

"Since there are only two beds Jack and I will take this one, Sodan the other is all yours," she said.

"That is good," he replied laughing. "Jack likes to fight banda in his sleep and I would like to get some rest tonight."

"One must get practice where one can," I said laughing along.

We set about getting the beds made and ready for the night. It was now fully dark outside the window and crossing to the door I ensured that it was closed and bolted tightly. The door wasn't very thick and if somebody really wanted in they could kick right through it but I wasn't going to make their entry easy. The more noise they made upon entering the more warning I would have to mount a defense.

Sodan was already wrapped tightly in his blankets and well on his way to sleep. Placing my weapons on the floor next to the bed where they would be easily found in the dark I crawled in next to Marlen. Snuggling close to her I could already hear the rhythmic breathing that comes with sleep and I lay there for some time reflecting back on the events that had transpired in the inn below. I was amazed at the speed with which Rawin had dispatched the three hoodlums. Speed like that only comes from years of practice and an uncanny natural ability. Drifting into sleep my last thoughts were that if I had the chance I wanted to talk to this man called Rawin.

Sodan was already gone when I awoke the next morning. Marlen had been awake for a while but continued to lie in bed beside me so as to not wake me. The funny thing is that I think it was her staring at me while I slept that woke me up but either way I now felt completely rested and ready for whatever the day may hold.

Crawling out of bed and strapping on my weapons I was feeling the pangs of hunger gnawing at my ribs. Marlen rolled out right behind me and standing up stretched her arms towards the ceiling. The sunlight shining through the small window glinted off her lithe body as she worked out the kinks from the night before. She was beautiful and aching to take her in my arms I reached out to put them around her as the door swung open and in walked Sodan. Sometimes his timing was not very good at all I thought with humor.

"Good morning my lazy friends," he greeted with a smile. "I was beginning to wonder if you would both sleep the whole day away."

"Actually we just got up," I responded. "Have you had any luck finding a vessel that is heading our way?"

"There are a couple of leads that I am working on but nothing definite at this point," he said. "The majority of the vessels that are in port now are either destined for other locations or are of the pirate type pulling out for a couple of days to ply their trade and then returning to Marduk. There still are a couple of merchant vessels whose captains I am trying to make contact with and hopefully one of those will be heading our way."

"Well while we are waiting for that I am going to go get something to eat," I said.

"Wait for me," Marlen said. "I could eat a full grown grall myself right now."

We made our way down the stairs into the dining area of the inn. Taking up roost at the same table as the night before, we waved over the innkeeper to order some food. While we waited for him I surveyed the room. Rawin still sat at the bar looking as if he had not moved from his position all night. There were only a couple of other people eating at the inn and they both seemed to be deeply occupied in their meals.

When the proprietor arrived we ordered our meals and with a limited selection on the menu he brought us the standard fare of grall stew and bread. The local fare was becoming quite redundant but it did meet the need of filling the stomach but for the afternoon meal I would have to find an establishment that served fish or poultry of some sort just to change it up a little.

After we had finished our meal Sodan took his leave to seek out the captains of the merchant vessels. Marlen returned to the room stating that she wanted to straighten up the beds before the evening. Left to my own thoughts I moved from the large table to a seat at the bar near where Rawin sat.

After ordering a tankard of ale from the proprietor I attempted to strike up a conversation with Rawin. "Good day friend," I said. "That was quite a performance yesterday."

"I am neither your friend nor is my business any of yours," he said dryly.

"Please forgive me," I said. "I have no intention of meddling in your business I was just impressed with the speed at which you were able to defend yourself yesterday."

"Again, my business not yours," he said.

"Okay, anyway my name is Jack. I heard the leader of the men call you Rawin yesterday," I said. "I am sorry for the intrusion but if at all possible I would like to talk to you and learn more about your fighting style."

Getting up from the bar I walked towards the stairs. Looking back over my shoulder I left him with one last thought as I walked away. "My friends and I will be here at the inn for the next couple of days," I said. "If you change your mind about talking just let me know."

He never looked up from his ale the whole time I had been trying to speak with him. He just sat staring blankly neither talking nor moving. I could only guess at what it could be that haunted this individual so bad that his life had become one not worth living. Feeling both confusion and pity for him I made my way up the stairs to the room that I shared with Marlen and Sodan.

Chapter Twenty-Two

Rawin

When I entered the room Marlen had just completed making the beds. I couldn't bring myself to hang out in the room all day or sit in the dining area waiting for Sodan to return and I wanted to see more of the city than what we had seen yesterday.

"Let's go for a walk," I told Marlen. "I would like to see more of the people and ships of Marduk."

"Okay," she said. "I would like to find the market and purchase some fresh clothing as well. I should be dressed as befits the Princess of Pendak when we arrive."

Following Marlen we walked down the stairs and out through the newly repaired front door to the inn. Letting our eyes adjust to the bright sunlight we made our way back up the street on the waterfront to the main avenue that lead back to the gate of the city. Making our way to the waterfront the previous day we had passed a number of shops that specialized in women's clothing and halfway up the avenue we entered into one of these shops.

Shopping with women on Phoria was eerily reminiscent of shopping with women on Earth. The adventure was filled with questions. How does this look? Do you like this one? Is this too short? After what seemed like an eternity to my male mind Marlen finally settled on an elaborate linen dress. It was entirely too fancy for the trip that we were on but would be perfect for her to look her part as a princess when we arrived in Pendak. The shopkeeper wrapped the dress in a covering of leather and we went back out onto the street.

Now was my chance to get something to eat other than grall stew. Examining the fare of the street vendors closely I found one that was serving roasted poultry. I wasn't really sure what kind of bird had donated itself to this meal but the golden brown crust of the roasted skin made my mouth water. The birds were little bigger than the guinea fowl of my home planet so I ordered two whole birds, one for each of us. Standing on the shaded side of the street we consumed our meal enjoying every last bit of the fowl as we picked the bones clean then licking our fingers. After finishing the meal we found another vendor that was selling fruit juice and quenched our thirst.

Having completed all that we had set out to we began to meander our way back down the street slowly working in the direction of the inn. As we reached the intersection of the main avenue and the waterfront street the hair on the back of my neck stood up and I couldn't escape the feeling that we were being followed. More than once I looked quickly back over my shoulder but there were too many people on the street for me to determine if any had been following and I began to get a very uneasy feeling in my stomach.

"We need to get back to the safety of the inn," I said quickly to Marlen. "I cannot clearly say what at this time but something is not right."

"We better hurry then," she said.

Increasing our pace down the street the inn finally came into sight. Quickly ducking through the door Marlen took a seat at our regular table while I stood in the shadows of the door watching for anything suspicious. A few small groups of men passed by the inn walking and talking but exhibited no signs that they had been following us and after a few minutes of watching people pass back and forth I gave up and sat down next to Marlen and ordered two tankards of ale. It must have been my over-protective imagination that had caused me to believe that we were being followed.

Rawin still sat in his regular position at the bar and a half a dozen other patrons took advantage of the food and drink that were being served. All seemed to be consumed by their own business and paid no attention to us.

We were sitting and talking quietly when a group of five men entered the inn. Watching them out of the corner of my eye I was surprised when they stopped next to our table rather than moving on to an empty one.

Looking up at them I gave them my best "what the hell do you want?" look. The one standing nearest our table stared back at me.

"We want the girl," he said.

"I'm afraid that will not be possible," I said forcefully. "She is with me and I intend to keep it that way."

"I wasn't asking for your permission stranger," he sneered. "The girl is coming with us."

Marlen sat quietly not getting into the conversation. She knew what was coming next and I had no doubt that she would find a safe place to be when it did.

Standing up very slowly my hand rested on the hilt of my long sword. "I will say this only once more, the girl is with me and will not be going anywhere," I said as my anger started to mount.

With a flash of steel all five men drew their swords as did I. Drawing my long sword with my right hand I upended the table towards the men with my left. The man that had been speaking slashed viciously downward towards my head. Blocking his strike I countered with a slashing blow towards his midsection as I pulled my short sword with my left hand.

The other four men were confined by the tables of the inn and unable to bring their swords to bear in assistance to their leader. Slashing low with my short sword I followed with a high cut in the opposite direction with my long sword. The man jumped backwards to avoid my steal only to trip over the others. As he struggled back to his feet two of the other men stepped forward and covered him by keeping my blades occupied.

The skill of my opponents was nothing spectacular. With a feigned blow at the man on the left I spun quickly and decapitated the man on the right. Before the man on the left could recover from dodging my ruse I skewered him through the ribs with a not so feigned blow.

The leader had regained his footing and with the help of the other two men kicked the tables out of the way they attempting to make some room in the dining area that would allow them to enclose me in a half-circle of steel. The additional room did not improve their skill with the sword one bit.

Charging forward I pressed my advantage by taking the offensive. Not wanting to get caught back on my heels I preferred to be pushing forward. A blur of shiny metal encircled me as I blocked blow after blow from the remaining three. A slight smile crossed my face as I felt the swords in my hands move as if possessed of a life all of their own.

Slowly and deliberately I was cutting the men to ribbons. The leader of the five was bleeding profusely from a number of wounds to his arms and face. The two men on either side of him were not faring any better. Blocking slashing blows with the sword in my left hand I pierced the shoulder of the man on my right. Glancing down at the wound he took his eyes off mine just long enough to miss the next stab with my sword that caught him full in the chest. My long sword caught between his ribs as he fell wrenching it from my grasp. Shifting my short sword from my left hand to the right there were only two men now opposing me.

The man on my left was a poor swordsman but he was quick and managed to avoid being run through more than once. The leader of the group was a fair hand with the sword and blocked my every effort to finish him. "Grab the girl," he yelled to his one remaining henchman.

The leader increased the pressure of his attack while the other jumped clear of the fight and stepped toward Marlen. He only got one step beyond the first when a dagger pierced his neck at the base of the skull killing him in his tracks. Surprised I looked quickly to see where the dagger had come from. Rawin, still sitting at the bar, had turned in his seat and was watching the fight. In his hand I saw a matching dagger to the one that had dispatched my opponent.

The leader of the group was losing confidence now that he faced me alone. Continuing to block the blows of my sword he backed his way towards the door. Following him I increased the intensity of my attack attempting to finish him before he could escape. Nearly to the door I could see the life bleed out of his face as he moved to jump through it and it was slammed closed from the outside effectively removing his only avenue of escape. A big smile crossed my face as I realized that he was now completely at my mercy. The speed of my sword increased with blow after blow against his steel and I could see that he was tiring and his arms began to sag low as the weight of his sword began to tell on him. A high blow aimed at his head proved to be his undoing. The effort to lift his sword and block my blow drained the last bit of endurance from him. His sword arm dropped like a stone and he was unable to raise it again quickly enough to block the second blow that I sent his way. His skill had failed him completely as my unblocked blow ripped through his chest and pinned him to the door. Shock showed in his eyes as mine looked into his mere inches away. "The girl stays with me," I said through gritted teeth. His head slumped forward onto his chest as his dead limp body hung from the door.

With the sound of battle no longer coming from inside the inn the door was pushed open slowly and I saw Sodan peek around the side of it.

"I see you have new friends Jack," he said smiling. "Or should I say had? Please tell me this isn't because they tried to serve you grall stew again."

The adrenaline coursing through my veins was starting to fade as Marlen rushed to my side. "No Sodan," I said returning his smile. "They mistakenly thought that Marlen belonged with them but I don't believe that they will make that mistake again."

The proprietor ran past us and through the door. My assumption was that he was seeking out his clean-up crew to get rid of the bodies that were strewn throughout the dining area.

Moving to the bar I walked up to Rawin. "Thank you for your assistance friend," I said.

"You were doing fine on your own," he replied. "The young lady on the other hand was unarmed and I couldn't allow him to assault her."

"You are very quick with those daggers," I commented. "Is that a skill that takes long to learn?"

"It has taken me my whole life to hone that skill," he said. "But the basics are easy and from there it just takes lots of practice."

"Will you join us for a drink?" I asked. "I would like to repay you for the help?"

Pondering my request for a minute he finally looked me squarely in the face and replied. "Yes, I believe that I will. There is something about you that intrigues me. I would talk with you for a while."

With his assistance we righted the table that we had been occupying and sat down. The proprietor returned and the men that he brought with him commenced to drag the lifeless corpses out through the front door. In response to my order for four tankards of ale the proprietor filled them and brought them to the table. Sloshing foam over the side in his haste to serve then he turned his attention to scrubbing the fresh blood from the floor before it began to dry.

Taking a big draught of my ale I contemplated how to start a conversation with Rawin. I didn't need to though because he spoke first.

"I can tell from your skin tone that you are not from here," he began. "Your mannerisms are not of Astor and your fighting style, while effective, borders on barbaric. Before I tell you about myself I would ask that you tell me a little bit about you."

Not entirely sure where to start or how much of my story I should tell I finally relented and starting with my arrival on Phoria narrated my entire tale to this point.

Rawin seemed to be neither shocked nor awed by my narration. He only looked at me digesting the information that I had told him.

Taking a big swallow of his ale he placed the tankard onto the table and began to speak. "You have taken a great risk in telling me all this," He said. "Something about you is telling me that you are a man to be trusted and for that reason only am I going to share my tale with you."

Pausing for a second he took another drink then began to tell us more of his story.

"By trade I have been a hired assassin for the majority of my adult life," he began. "As a sword for hire I have done many things of which I am not proud and in the end it has cost me everything."

"How so," I asked sympathetically?

"Not too long ago I was hired to kill a prominent merchant here in Marduk," he said. "I accepted partial payment for the hit and made my preparations to carry it out. On the night of the assassination I snuck into the merchant's house and hid behind a curtain in the living area waiting for my target to arrive. When he finally did he was surrounded by his wife and five young children. Morally I struggled with my paid duty to kill him and my sense of family. In the end I could not do it and when they had all gone to bed I slipped out of the house quietly."

"It would seem to me that you chose the more honorable path," I said supportively.

"Sometimes honor has its own price," he added sadly. "My employer was not happy with my decision and had my own wife and children murdered for my failure to follow through with our agreement. In my rage and sorrow I killed not only my employer but his entire family, women and children. I killed his guards, his servants, and his animals. I exterminated every living thing in his house but still my pain did not go away. To this day the consequences of my decision continue to haunt me."

"I am truly sorry to hear of your tale my friend," I said holding back the sadness that I felt in my own heart. "I have no doubt that your family would be proud of your honorable decision. Join with us, our travels may not always be full of adventure but like you we are following the honorable path. Maybe by assisting us we can assist you."

"My pain is my restitution for the life that I have led," he said. "I will think on your offer." Standing up he moved back to the bar and resumed his vigil over his ale.

A general feeling of melancholy remained after Rawin had left the table. We all three remained silent thinking on his story and nursing our drinks and after a short time Sodan broke the silence.

"I have found a vessel that is heading in our direction," he said. "I met with the captain this morning and he will allow us passage for the price of our sword arms."

"I'm not sure what you mean by that," I said.

"These waters are hazardous to any vessel carrying cargo," he said. "Any run in or out of Marduk is fraught with risk from pirates. Having additional fighting men along with the cargo increases the chances of successfully repelling an attack by privateers. If we are willing to fight to defend his vessel should the need arise the captain will allow us berth onboard until we safely reach Pendak."

"That seems fair enough to me," I said. "When does the vessel depart?" I asked.

"She sails on the afternoon tide tomorrow," he replied.

"Wonderful," Marlen exclaimed. "I am sure that I am not just speaking for myself when I say that I have had my fill of Marduk and can't wait to leave this place."

"Here, here," I cheered raising my glass in salute to her well spoken words. With a clink of metal both their tankards met mine over the table then raising them to our lips we quickly emptied them. Calling to the proprietor I requested three more drinks and food.

Rushing to do my bidding the innkeeper delivered three full tankards to the table and carted away the empties on his way to fetch our food. He returned shortly with three large bowls and bread. The meal had not changed any nor had I expected it to but I was determined to stomach through another bowl of grall stew rather than to venture out onto the street seeking alternatives.

Halfway through choking down my bowl of grall stew I felt a presence near my shoulder. Turning quickly I saw Rawin standing near the table.

"I have thought on your offer Jack Wilde," he said. "I will join you on two conditions."

"Very well Rawin," I said. "And what may those two conditions be?"

"The first condition is that no pity be taken on me for the decisions in my life," he said. "For I neither expect it nor do I deserve it."

"Okay," I said. "What is the second condition?"

"The second condition is that you allow me to teach you the art of fighting with finesse and speed rather than lumbering forward like a bull grall in heat," he said.

Sodan chuckled at this condition and I too felt a measure of mirth at the visual that passed through my mind.

"Agreed my friend," I said. "We sail on the afternoon tide tomorrow."

"Agreed," he replied back. "I will meet you here in the morning."

Taking his leave he departed the inn. Sodan and I looked at one another and cracking a smile he began to laugh at me.

"A bull grall in heat," he laughed. "I can see that."

Not to be left out Marlen made a grunting sound meant to imitate the sound of a bull grall. I couldn't be mad at them though. If you can't laugh at yourself then you are taking life way too seriously. Joking and laughing we enjoyed each other's company late into the evening then calling it a night we retired to our room and went to sleep. All three of us were excited to nearly be on our way again.

Chapter Twenty-Three

The "Winds of Astor"

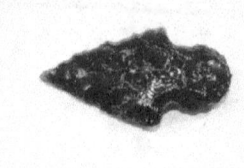

We had very little problem waking up early the next morning. All three of us were looking forward to getting out to sea and beginning the final leg or our journey. Personally I was looking forward to seeing Marduk disappearing into the distance as we sailed away for while I enjoyed the activity of the city I did not enjoy spending every second of the day looking over my shoulder to see where the next attack would be coming from.

Still too early to report to the ship we went down to the dining area of the inn to grab something to eat. At the bottom of the stairs I saw Rawin already sitting at our table waiting for us.

"Good morning Rawin," I greeted. "You are the early bird this morning."

"Good morning to you all," he replied. "I was beginning to wonder if you had already left without me."

"Not possible my friend," I said. "We were just taking advantage of the halfway comfortable beds while they were available. I expect the deck of the ship will be much less accommodating in comfort."

"So very true," he said smiling.

Joining him at the table we ordered meals and drinks from the proprietor. I would wager that the innkeeper would be just as happy for us to be underway as we would. Since our arrival he has had to clean up the mess of eight corpses in his establishment and while he would miss our money I don't think that he would miss us.

Placing our food and drink onto the table he quickly shuffled his way back to the bar and wasting no time we dug into the food with relish. It was the same fare that we had been eating since our arrival, grall stew, but knowing that it might be the last solid meal we would have until we reached Pendak it seemed to taste much better.

"What vessel shall we be sailing on today," Rawin asked.

"I have booked us passage on the "Winds of Astor"," Sodan replied.

"She is a good vessel," Rawin stated. "Her size and the large number of fighting men that the captain employs make her a hard target for pirates."

"That was my thoughts exactly," replied Sodan.

"Make no mistake though my friends the pirates will try anyway," Rawin replied. "The "Winds of Astor" is too large of a prize for them not to."

"That is okay," I replied. "That will allow us the opportunity to pay for our passage."

"Let's hope that we don't pay too dearly," Sodan said.

After completing our meal we paid the proprietor what we owed him and headed down the waterfront back in the direction of the intersection with the main avenue. Stopping only once we purchased linen blankets from a shop along the waterfront street because Sodan suggested that by bringing our own blankets we would be assured of comfort from the chilly night sea air. After making our purchases we continued on past the intersection for about a quarter of a mile before we arrived at an area of the wharf that was fronted by large warehouses. Fewer people were present on the street and those we did see were carting loads of goods between the warehouses and ships.

Following Sodan we turned and walked down a long pier being careful to stay out of the way of the carts moving back and forth. Towards the end of the pier we approached a large wooden sailing ship that was surrounded by a bustle of activity as goods were being hoisted from the pier to the cargo holds of the vessel. Directing us to wait on the pier Sodan mounted the gangplank and made his way to the deck of the ship and after only a couple of minutes of waiting he waved us aboard. At the top of the gangplank we stepped down onto the deck and saw Sodan talking with a gruff looking older gentleman wearing a long coat over his linen tunic and a high browed black hat.

Calling us forward Sodan introduced us to the captain of the vessel. "Jack, Marlen, Rawin please meet Captain Faron," he said. Shaking the captain's hand we thanked him for the passage that he was providing us.

"Welcome aboard," Faron said. "We won't be setting sail for a while yet. The crew is finishing the loading of the cargo but you are welcome to remain aboard until we get underway. For your own safety please stay clear of the loading process."

The safest place on the deck seemed to be forward in the bow of the ship so carefully picking our way through the various loading processes we soon found ourselves milling about as far forward as we could get. The railing of the ship provided a little shade from the sun as it climbed towards noon and sitting down with our backs against the rail we relaxed and watched as the crew took on the cargo and stores.

For two hours we sat watching the back-breaking work as the cargo was hoisted aboard using pulleys, nets and brute force and finally it appeared that the loading was done and the crew set about preparing the vessel to get underway. Walking around the area of the bow and stretching out our legs we continued to remain clear of the activities that were happening on deck.

The ship itself was a much larger version of the vessels that I had become acquainted with in Valcot. The two main differences between the "Winds of Astor" and the vessels of Sodan's home city were that the larger vessel was outfitted with two large masts for rigging sails and the conspicuous absence of oars and oarlocks. The larger vessel relied solely on the wind for propulsion and the space normally occupied by rowing benches and oar storage was used to lash cargo to the deck. Once the cargo hold had been filled the remaining items were tied down on the deck leaving a clear passage down the middle and along the rails.

The gangplank was hauled in and groups of men on the pier with long poles pushed the ship clear of the dock. With a loud whistle the master of the vessel called the ship underway and barked out orders to hoist the forward sail and the crew jumped to carry out his orders and quickly had a sheet of linen stretched below the forward yardarm. The softly blowing wind gathered in the sail and began to slowly push the ship forward. Clearing the end of the pier the captain ordered a starboard tack turning the ship towards the opening in the seawall that allowed passage to the open ocean and as the ship neared the opening in the seawall the captain again barked orders directing a port tack that put us into the center of the channel leaving the port. Once clear of the protective seawall the captain ordered the second sail raised into the brisk sea air and the ship shot forward with a lurch as the wind caught in the aft sail. Both sails were now fully engulfed with the salty air and bulged forward towards the bow as the wind sought to rip them from the yardarms. The masts flexed in their sockets but held fast transferring the energy of the wind to forward momentum as the hull of the vessel climbed up on plane and headed directly out to sea.

One thing that had caught my attention as we sat in the bow observing the loading process was the minimal amount of weapons that the crew wore. Now that the ship was under full sail that curiosity was being answered. From a storage compartment accessed through a door in the aft part of the ship's deck a crew member could be seen handing out swords and pikes to the rest of the crew and it didn't take long before the ship was veritably bristling with armed men. The crew of sailors had been transformed into a floating army and I began to understand how the "Winds of Astor" had maintained her success in light of being home ported in the midst of the pirates den.

Just before we crested the horizon two vessels could be seen leaving the port of Marduk behind us but we saw them only for a few minutes before the curvature of the planet obscured them from our view.

We continued to sail due south of Marduk with the prevailing wind assisting us to increase the distance between us and the two vessels that we could only assume pursued us. The sun began to set in the west and Faron ordered a forty-five degree tack to starboard. His tactics were now becoming clear to me. He aimed to travel in a large arc to the southwest and approach Pendak from the south rather than sail due west along the coast and he was banking on the speed of his vessel to keep us out of reach of the pursuing ships while we completed the arcing path of travel. I was beginning to admire the tactical mind of Faron.

Darkness began to settle around the ship and Faron ordered that no lights be lit. We would sail in darkness throughout the night in hopes that the cover of darkness would help us to elude our followers.

The crew of the ship began to spread out their sleeping linens and furs across the deck and following their lead we did the same forward in the bow. While Marlen, Rawin and I prepared our beds for the night Sodan went aft to speak with Faron.

Sleeping on the deck of a ship near the bow tends to be a rocky experience for at the most forward section of decking along the centerline a person can feel every side to side roll of the ship, as well as every up and down movement as the hull climbs a wave and then descends the other side. Two things were in our favor this evening though. First, the seas were relatively calm so the movement of the ship was minimal. Second, our evening meal had consisted of dried grall meat and stale water. This combination of food stuck well to the ribs and helped to avoid seasickness but if the sea had been any rougher my stomach would have been turned inside out.

When Sodan returned he narrated to us his conversation with Faron. The captain's plan was verbatim with what I had already surmised. We would make a long arcing loop from Marduk to Pendak. He did not anticipate any problems as we ran silent and dark throughout the night but the rising sun would tell how successful we were at avoiding pursuit.

"The captain has said that all hands not on watch should get as much rest tonight as possible," Sodan said. "He expects that if we are to see action it will be shortly after sunrise once the large white sails are illuminated by the sunlight. If we can pass the morning without being sighted we should have enough of a lead to stay ahead of our pursuers all the way to Pendak."

"Did he believe that the two vessels we saw leaving port intend to pursue us?" I asked.

"From what I could tell he doesn't care," Sodan said. "He isn't going to take a chance either way."

"I have to respect his decision in that regard," I replied. "With Marlen onboard I would prefer that he not take any more chances than are necessary to get us to Pendak."

Captain Faron is one of the most respected captains in the entire fleet of Marduk," Rawin interjected. "His skill at avoiding pirates has become legendary and the "Winds of Astor" has become somewhat of a mythical prize to the privateers that ply these waters."

"If his skill at evasion is so legendary then why does he man his vessel with a small army?" I asked.

"Very few pirates ever get close enough to board his ship," Rawin said. "Faron being the tactical genius that he is does not gamble with the cargo that constitutes his livelihood. The first obstacle is finding the "Winds of Astor", the second is catching her. For those pirates lucky enough to accomplish the first two feats the real challenge comes in boarding her. Very few pirate ships have a crew large enough to overcome the floating army that Faron has amassed."

"I guess we shall see what the morning light holds for us," Marlen said.

"I guess we shall," I agreed.

All four of us were rolled up tight into our linen blankets but each of us was lost in our own thoughts about what the morning light would reveal.

Lying on the slowly pitching deck I watched the multitude of stars in the sky slowly moving back and forth with the rocking of the ship. Other than the stars the sky was as black as tar and I assumed that the moons were both in their fully waned cycle for the month. I couldn't help but wonder if that too had been part of Faron's plan, to sail under the moonless sky to make it harder for pursuing vessels to track us in the dark. My admiration for the captain of the "Winds of Astor" was rapidly growing in leaps and bounds.

Sleep had barely overtaken me when I heard a muffled yell denoting that a light was visible on the horizon to the north. Curious I jumped out of my blankets and rushed to the starboard rail to see. Far in the distance at the edge of the horizon a light could be seen faintly glowing and it appeared to be the bow light of a vessel of some sort.

A lone figure approached the rail next to me. Turning in the direction of the new arrival I saw Faron standing next to me. "They are much closer than usual," he commented.

Quietly he passed the word to the steersman to change his heading another thirty degrees to port. At this angle the "Winds of Astor" slowly widened the gap between us and the other vessel and after a period of time the light dropped below the horizon and was gone. Faron directed that the steersman maintain the current heading for another hour then to tack thirty degrees back to the starboard to resume our original course.

Faron returned to his bedding in the aft of the ship and I crawled back into my blankets in the bow. It took some time before my adrenaline subsided and I was again able to go back to sleep.

The steady breeze continued throughout the night continually pushing the ship closer to our destination of Pendak and more than once throughout the night I woke up with a start and quickly looking around realized that all was as it should be and returned to sleep. The anticipation of sunrise was clearly playing on my subconscious mind and working its way into my dreams it ensured that while I rested well I did not sleep too soundly.

Well before dawn the next morning a clear call rang through the air instantly awakening every member of the crew. "Sail ho, dead ahead."

Scrambling to the bow we looked forward and directly in our path lay one of the small pirate ships similar to the ones that I had seen moored in Marduk. It would seem that the tactical skills of the captain had finally run their course. As the result of many a failed chase trying to run down the "Winds of Astor" it would seem that the pirates had figured out that rather than chase her it would be better to place a vessel in her path and await her arrival.

There is no telling how many days this vessel had lain in wait for us but the light on the vessel of last night was now clear. Last night's vessel was herding us towards the ship that lay ahead.

Clearly Faron did not intend to give up easily barking directions to the steersman he ordered a forty five degree tack to port. The approaching vessel was on our starboard bow and closing quickly.

Again the lookout cried, "Sail ho, to the stern."

Looking back over the aft portion of the ship another vessel could be seen approaching rapidly from behind us. So the tactic would be to drive us to the waiting vessel and then pounce on us from behind. The situation began to look fairly grim and it appeared that a fight was soon to be at hand.

The vessel off the starboard bow had now closed to within a quarter mile of us when Faron barked out to the steersman to change course ninety degrees to the starboard. The new angle would take us directly past the vessel ahead of our bow. I could now see the tactical advantage that Faron intended to exploit. The ship off the stern was still far back on the horizon and had about fifteen miles to cover to catch us. He intended to attack the vessel off the bow in a bid to eliminate it from the foray before the second vessel arrived.

"Bring us alongside," he yelled. "Prepare to drop the sails and ready the grappling hooks."

The crew of the "Winds of Astor" raced around the deck rapidly following the orders that had been given and as the two ships came together a small portion of the crew dropped the sheets to the deck and gathered them in while the rest of the crew prepared to board the attacking vessel. Grappling hooks were thrown from both ships across the intervening gap of water and digging deeply into the railing the ships were quickly pulled together. Faron's crew met that of the pirate vessel at the rails and quickly pushed them back onto the deck of the pirate ship.

Sodan and Rawin had already joined in the melee on the deck of the other ship. Hiding Marlen in the bow underneath our accumulated blankets I stood my ground between her and the threat from the other vessel. The swords of Rawin mowed down the pirates leaving a pile of bloody corpses stacked around him. His sword cut in and out so fast that I could barely follow them with my eyes. Sodan was amassing his own pile of lifeless flesh not more than two sword lengths away. Faron had chosen his crew wisely for in a matter of minutes they had decimated the crew of the privateer and with a yell from Faron the crew jumped back to the deck of the "Winds of Astor" and guarding the rail to prevent any of the pirates from following cut the lines to the grapples that held the two ships together.

Instantly the crew manning the sails again raised the sheets and with a snap they caught the wind and the ship began to gain speed as once more we were free to run. The pirate vessel had been left with too few of their crew alive to be able to mount a pursuit and now the race was on to outdistance the vessel coming up from the stern.

In the time that it had taken to attack the lead pirate ship the second had halved the distance towards us. Moving at speed under full sail she continued to close the gap as the "Winds of Astor" struggled to gain speed. The second ship was moving too fast and it became clear that outdistancing them would not be possible but still Faron and his crew pushed the vessel to its limits and the two ships raced across the ocean of Phoria with the gap between the two growing ever smaller.

Chapter Twenty-Four

Pirates

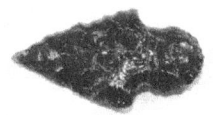

The two vessels sped across the waves, one fleeing and one pursuing. The "Winds of Astor" was a fast ship but heavily laden with cargo as she was it took time for her to reach her maximum potential speed under the wind conditions and with every minute that passed it was becoming clearer that we would not be able to outdistance our pursuers.

The pirate vessel was drawing near our stern and I could clearly see the intricately carved dragon head that graced her bow.

An idea came to me that might work in our favor to reduce the numbers that assailed us before they had the opportunity to attack. Gathering Sodan and Rawin together we quickly met with Faron as I outlined my plan.

In order for the plan to be successful it required perfect timing and flawless execution. Fraught with risk the plan was not without its measure of danger but if it were executed perfectly it would allow us to take the fight to the pirates and reduce their numbers before the "Winds of Astor" was at risk.

Faron directed the details of the scheme himself to ensure that it was successfully carried out and at direction from him the crew manning the forward sail trimmed the sheet slightly creating a barely perceptible reduction in forward speed. The pirate vessel closed the remaining gap quickly and as their bow came abreast of the stern of the "Winds of Astor" we prepared for our part in the plan.

With a running leap from the aft starboard rail Rawin, Sodan and I vaulted ourselves toward the bow of the pirate ship. The other two landed cleanly on the deck of the pursuing vessel and drawing their swords set about defending themselves as they were attacked. My leap did not end as successfully for as I leaped from the rail my footing slipped on the salt water saturated railing. Losing most of my momentum I failed to clear the railing of the pirate ship and slammed hard into it with my stomach. Gasping for air I struggled to get over the rail and with an extreme amount of effort I finally gained my footing on the deck just a few seconds behind them.

A split second after our leap from the deck Faron ordered a hard to port turn. His evasive maneuver pulled the deck of the "Winds of Astor" farther away from the pirates and eliminated their opportunity to throw grappling hooks and reel her in. She continued around to her left scribing a tight circle in the sea effectively coming about and approaching the pirate ship from the stern.

We three were pinned in the bow as the pirates crowded towards us. Standing side by side we weaved a web of steel destruction around us. The front of the pirates attack was five across which was all that the width of the deck would allow and fending off blow after blow we simply waited for an overzealous fighter to step in too close or be just a split second too slow on his defense and then seizing the opportunity we would run him through leaving his body where it fell. The lifeless corpses of the pirate's unfortunate enough to be in the front of the crowd began to pile up on the deck hindering the approach of those behind. Their lifeblood saturated the deck planks making them slick and it became a chore just to retain my footing.

The "Winds of Astor" had completed her circle and was coming alongside the stern of the pirate vessel. Grappling hooks flew through the air and biting deeply into the railing served as the shackles that allowed Faron's crew to pull her in.

Looking over the top of the pirates that confronted us I could see the crew of the "Winds of Astor" swarming over the rails of the pirate ship and as they set upon the horde from behind the rearmost pirates turned to defend themselves. We now had them pinched between us with no option but to fight.

The clanging sound of steel on steel rang out across the sea as men fought and died on the deck. The overwhelming number of men in Faron's sailing army quickly subdued the remaining pirates. While most of the men dropped their weapons to the deck others chose to jump over the side and into the sea rather than be taken prisoner. The captain of the vessel had gone down in the first wave as Faron's men swarmed the deck.

Faron addressed those of the pirate crew that remained. " My vessel is not a ship of war, she is merely a cargo vessel and we do not take prisoners," he said. "On your word to give up the chase of my vessel I will leave your ship afloat and those of you that remain will live. If you continue the chase I will burn your ship to the waterline and leave you adrift at sea."

Many of the captured sailors quickly nodded their ascent to his terms and Faron ordered his crew back to the ship.

Rawin, Sodan and I returned with the crew and Faron being the last to leave the pirate vessel shot the defeated pirates a parting comment, "Tell your shipmates back in Marduk that the price they would pay to possess my ship and its cargo is high and any that assault us will go down in defeat." With that he leaped over the rail and ordered the grapples cut loose. Hoisting the sails into the wind the "Winds of Astor" again began to gain speed in the direction of Pendak.

Making my way to the stern I found Marlen wrapped tightly among our sleeping blankets. The last part of my assault plan on the pirate ship was for Faron to hide her among the items stowed near the stern.

Looking out from the blankets she saw me approaching and jumping up ran into my arms. "Jack I thought I had lost you," she said. "When I saw you go down on the rail of the pirate ship I thought for sure that you had fallen into the sea."

"I'm fine Marlen," I reassured her. "It was simply a small case of clumsiness. I didn't want to make that jump seem too easy."

I winced in pain as she hugged me tightly and my movement had not gone without notice.

"Are you hurt?" she asked.

"Just a little bruising in the ribs from hitting the rail," I responded. "Please don't worry, I will be fine."

The pain shooting through my ribs made me wonder if I was being completely truthful or not. It was entirely possible that I may have cracked a rib or two when I impacted the rail but for Marlen's sake I would carry on as if nothing was wrong.

With Sodan and Rawin in tow Faron approached me and slapped me on the shoulder. "That was a wonderfully strategic plan," he said. "They absolutely did not expect that a heavily laden cargo ship such as this would turn and attack them in the open ocean. The element of surprise was ours and was the key to our winning the day."

"Thank you," I replied. "I learned a long time ago that sometimes the best defense is a strong offense. I'm just glad that the ship and its crew are safe."

"All are definitely safe," he commented. "In fact we lost not a single man in the battle while the pirates lost half their crew."

"I thought that we lost you in the water," Sodan commented with a snicker. "We were convinced that you had set up the plan and then decided to take a bath before the battle." He elbowed Rawin as they both chuckled at my mishap.

"I knew that you two had matters well in hand," I replied brushing off their harassment as playful camaraderie. "It all worked out in the end and I was there to share in the assault with you," I said. "Now Captain Faron how much farther until we reach Pendak?" I asked trying to change the subject.

He led us to a large wooden chest that was lashed to the aft decking among the cargo that had been secured there. Reaching inside the chest he produced a large bundle of charts on rolled linen parchment and thumbing through them he found the one that he was looking for. Laying the chart across the top of a wooden cargo crate we each grabbed a corner to hold it flat.

Spread out before me was a much larger picture of the world in which I found myself. I was surprised to see that Astor was only one of four continents that were pictured on the map. Two others were located to the northwest of Astor and if they were drawn to scale appeared to be much larger than the continent that I had become familiar with. The fourth was southwest of Astor and was small enough to be classified as a large island rather than a small continent.

"Faron, have you been to all these places?" I asked pointing at the other continents on the map.

"Many times have I travelled between these lands," he replied.

Intrigued by the unknowns of these other places my explorers mindset was piqued. If given the opportunity I would have to visit these lands for myself and see what wonders they held. My mind had wandered from the purpose of looking at the map. Regaining my focus I asked Faron where he believed us to be on the map.

Performing the mental calculations of time and distance since we left port and estimating speed of travel Faron pointed at a location on the map south of Astor and midway between Marduk and Pendak. "By my estimation we are here," he said. "Once the sun goes down and I can get a bearing from the stars I can be more accurate."

"Providing the winds stay strong then we should reach Pendak in two more days," I said.

"That is correct." he replied.

"Do you expect any more encounters with pirates?" I inquired.

"There is still one vessel unaccounted for," he said. "Two ships left port behind us but only one of the vessels that we encountered was one of those. The second was already at sea waiting for us. My expectation is that if the second vessel that left port were to be after us we would have already encountered them. All we can do is maintain a vigilant watch and stay on course for Pendak."

"Agreed," I said.

Marlen and I spent the remainder of the day together in the bow. The nearer that we got to Pendak the more anxious I became. Since I knew very little about her home city I did not know what to expect when we arrived and her reassurances that everything would be okay helped me to feel better but the unknown still concerned me.

Visibility began to decline late into the afternoon as a thick fog progressed across the ocean and entering into the leading edge of the mist Faron ordered the aft sail lowered and the forward sail trimmed. I was disappointed at the greatly reduced speed with which we picked our way through the fog but at the same time somewhat relieved by the delay in our arrival to Pendak.

Continuing to creep slowly across the ocean the darkness of night set in as everyone onboard found their sleeping blankets and located a comfortable place to curl up for the night. A minimum crew remained awake in shifts to keep the ship functioning properly and maintain a watch for unfriendly vessels or seagoing hazards.

Wrapped tightly in my blankets I lay on the deck near Marlen and as we continued to talk quietly I finally hit upon the source of my trepidation of arriving in Pendak, I was afraid of losing her. My concern was that once we reached Pendak and she was safe she would return to her normal life and I would no longer be needed as her protector so I decided to share my concerns with her.

"So what do you foresee happening when we get to Pendak," I asked.

"I expect that my father and the people of Pendak will be happy to see me alive," she said.

"I understand that but that is not quite what I meant," I told her. Not sure of the cultural expectations or taboos of this world I wasn't sure how to tell Marlen what I was trying to ask. Realizing that I had nothing to lose by just coming out and telling her I blurted out what I was really trying to say. "What I meant was what will happen to us? In the time that I have known you I have fallen deeply in love with you and I don't think that I could bear not having you in my life," I said.

Reaching out she grabbed my hand. "I never thought that it would be possible to feel that I could not live without someone until I met you," she said softly. "I love you too Jack and never want to experience life without you in it ever again. If you stay in Pendak I will be there with you. If you leave then I will leave with you but wherever you go I shall follow and be right by your side."

Pulling her closer to me I kissed her gently on the lips and held her in my arms. "What do you think that your father will think of this?" I asked,

"My father is a wonderful man," she said. "He is also very wise and perceptive. He will see how happy you make me and I know that he will accept you."

"I hope you are right," I replied. "I don't know how I would deal with it if he thought that I wasn't good enough for you or disapproved of us being together."

"Do not despair Jack," she said. "I know that he will accept you but also know that even if he doesn't, I do and that is all that matters."

Kissing her again I continued to hold her tight while she drifted off to sleep. Feeling happy and content with our conversation I soon joined her in slumber.

The thick fog still had not lifted as the sun rose the next morning. The visibility was slim and a noticeable lightening of the mist was the only sign of dawn. Getting up I placed my blanket over Marlen as she continued to sleep and walking the deck I attempted to stretch out my stiff muscles. Faron was already awake and stood in conversation with the steersman. When he saw me threading my way through the cargo on deck he greeted me heartily.

"Good morning Jack," he said. "Did you sleep well?"

"Wonderfully," I said sarcastically while I rubbed my lower back.

"The hard deck does take some getting used to," he replied.

"Will this fog delay our entry into port today?" I asked.

"It would be foolhardy to try to approach shore under these conditions," he responded. "We turned back to the northwest in the middle of the night and with any luck we should sail out of this damnable fog as we get closer to land."

"I hope so," I said. "While I have enjoyed the journey onboard your vessel I am ready to complete this quest."

"I expect to be moored by late afternoon," he said. "However, if we cannot sail out of this fog we will have to drop anchor and wait for it to clear."

The sea was glass smooth and rolled gently. The light winds were barely sufficient to keep the ship moving forward and the entire crew had awakened by this time and scurried around the deck attending to the duties of the ship. Marlen, Rawin and Sodan sat together in the bow eating dried fish and drinking stale water. I found myself missing the grall stew from the inn on the waterfront in Marduk and my mouth watered at the thought. If this damn fog would just lift, we would all be eating a solid meal tonight and enjoying large quantities of ale.

As if in answer to my desires I felt the breeze blowing against my cheek start to increase. The mast began to creak as the main sail stretched taut under the additional wind. We were still under half-sail and the speed of the ship increased only slightly. The increasing wind was causing the mist around the ship to swirl and move. In less than an hour the mist started to thin as the wind carried it away. Two hours later we finally sailed clear of the fog and out into full sunlight.

The land could be seen on the horizon to the north. Along with the sun served to improve the spirits of the entire crew. Following Faron's orders the crew soon had us sailing under full sail with both sheets snapping in the wind. Paralleling the coast we continued sailing due west in our quest to reach Pendak before nightfall.

By mid-afternoon we could see land directly ahead as well as to the north.

"The Noral peninsula," Sodan said quietly as he stood near Marlen and I in the bow. "Pendak is located on the southernmost tip of the peninsula. It won't be long now."

Drawing near the coast the steersman adjusted the course of the ship as necessary to follow the contours of the land to the south. Nearing the southern end of the peninsula a large city came into view. The seaward side of the city was protected by a thick rock abutment wall with multiple gates that were secured against entry from the sea. The steersman pointed the bow directly at one of the gates and continued to sail directly at it. Armed soldiers could be seen atop the wall watching out to sea for any vessels that would approach.

Nearing the gated entry to the protected harbor of the city the large wooden gates began to slowly open wide and had barely opened fully as the carved prow of the "Winds of Astor" slipped past them. The crew moved quickly to take in the sails leaving just enough of the heavy linen material in place to allow slow movement and maneuvering of the ship as it sought out an open berth.

Inside the protective seawall hundreds of ships were at anchor or moored securely to long wooden docks. Identifying an empty moorage the steersman expertly guided the ship to a position parallel to the pier and dock workers were standing by to receive the mooring lines and haul the ship up tight against large grass bumpers that kept the ships from grinding against the dock. When the ship was in position crewmembers threw lines to the pier while others furled the sail and lashed it to the yardarm.

Once the ship was secured to the pier Faron directed that the gangplank be lowered. No sooner had it touched the dock and the dock supervisor scrambled aboard to talk with the captain regarding the unloading of the vessel. While they spoke I could see the dock supervisor looking in our direction and once Faron had identified that Marlen was onboard the supervisor rushed to her side and bowing deeply paid her the respect that she warranted as the daughter of his king.

"Princess Marlen it is so wonderful to see you," he said. "The whole city thought you were lost in the great swamp."

"I thank you for your concern," she replied. "You can see though with your own eyes that I am alive and safe. Please dispatch a runner to the palace to let my father know of my arrival."

The dock supervisor hurried back to the pier where the dockworkers congregated awaiting his orders. He could be seen speaking with them and then one of the workers took off at a sprint up the pier headed towards the castle of the king.

Chapter Twenty-Five

Homecoming to Pendak

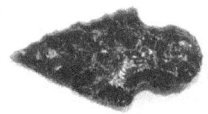

The crew began offloading the cargo from the ship while the dockworkers carted it away to warehouses in the distance. Marlen, Sodan, Rawin and I stayed forward in the bow so as to not get in the way of the crews activities. My desire was to get off the ship and make our way through the city to return Marlen to her father's castle but she advised against that and when I had asked her why she told me to just be patient and that I would find out later. Removing the dress that she had bought in Marduk she slipped it over the top of her leather harness and attempted to straighten her disheveled hair.

We did not have long to wait onboard the ship though before a long procession of warriors could be seen making its way two abreast down the length of the pier. As they grew closer I could see that they were escorting an ornately decorated litter.

The litter was stopped adjacent to the gangplank and lowered to the wooden decking of the pier and as the curtains on the litter were swept aside a tall regal looking figure stepped out. I took this to be Marlen's father.

All other activities both on the pier and the ship had come to a complete halt as the king made his way up the gangplank. Faron greeted him as he stepped down onto the deck of the ship. We stood back while the captain completed all the required formalities of receiving a person with the king's status onboard and at the conclusion of the formalities Marlen ran forward into her father's arms and embraced him tightly. He held her for some time as if letting her go would cause her to disappear.

When he finally released the embrace he began to assail her with a barrage of questions to which she simply answered I am okay.

"I owe my safety to these men," she said waving us forward. After introducing the three of us she gave him a quick rundown of the adventures that had led to her return to Pendak. Taking my hand in hers she smiled up at her father and expressed how grateful she was to me in particular for keeping her safe. With a knowing look he slapped me heavily on the shoulder.

"My gratitude and the hospitality of my kingdom are yours for bringing my jewel of Pendak home safely," he said. "Tonight we will feast in your honor."

The king thanked Sodan and Rawin as well then as a group we all turned to leave the ship. Faron was waiting at the head of the gangplank and the king thanked him as well then departed the ship. In turn we each embraced Faron and thanked him for having provided us safe passage.

"Thank you my friend," I said.

"It has been my pleasure Jack Wilde," he replied. "My ship, my crew and I will always welcome you aboard and will sail with you anywhere. The legends that will be told of this voyage will echo through time."

"I look forward to the day when again I can sail with you and your crew aboard such a wonderful vessel," I replied with conviction as I stepped to the gangplank and holding Marlen's hand made my way to the pier.

The curtains of the litter had been lashed open as Marlen and her father climbed aboard. She waved to Faron and his crew as the litter bearers hoisted their burden and the soldiers escorted us off the pier. We walked beside the litter as we moved from the waterfront and through the city towards the palace.

It became clear why Marlen had me wait for her father's arrival. Word had quickly spread to all quarters of the city announcing her return and the avenues to the palace were lined with the subjects of Pendak craning their necks to see for themselves that the princess they had thought lost had truly been brought home. Without the royal escort we would have been swarmed with people if we had opted to walk to the palace. Marlen waved to everyone graciously and I followed along once again with that feeling of inadequacy beginning to creep over me but this was not about me it was about being happy for Marlen and the city of Pendak. It was a time of rejoicing and festivity then why did I have such an overwhelming feeling of impending doom.